Julia Quinn started writing her first book one month after finishing university and has been tapping away at her keyboard ever since. The No. 1 *New York Times* bestselling author of more than two dozen novels, she is a graduate of Harvard and Radcliffe Colleges and is one of only sixteen authors ever to be inducted in the Romance Writers of America Hall of Fame. She lives in the Pacific Northwest with her family.

Please visit Julia Quinn online:

www.juliaquinn.com
www.facebook.com/AuthorJuliaQuinn
@JQAuthor

By Julia Quinn

Ten Things I Love About You

Julia Quinn

PIATKUS

PIATKUS

First published in the US in 2010 by Avon Books,
An imprint of HarperCollins, New York
First published in Great Britain as a paperback original in 2010 by Piatkus
by arrangement with Avon
This paperback edition published in 2021 by Piatkus

3 5 7 9 10 8 6 4

A CIP catalogue record for this book
is available from the British Library

ISBN 978-0-3494-3052-2

Printed and bound by Clays Ltd, Elcograf S.p.A.

Papers used by Piatkus are from well-managed forests
and other responsible sources.

Piatkus
An imprint of
Little, Brown Book Group
Carmelite House
50 Victoria Embankment
London EC4Y 0DZ

An Hachette UK Company
www.hachette.co.uk

www.littlebrown.co.uk

For my readers.
Without you, I couldn't have
the coolest job in the world.

And also <u>from</u> Paul,
for precisely the same reason.

Families are complicated.

Annabel Winslow has a grandfather who refers to her mother as "that fool who married that damned fool" and a grandmother who prefers to view personal propriety as an option.

Sebastian Grey has cousins who want to see him married and an uncle who'd like to see him dead.

Luckily for the two of them, they'll soon have each other . . .

Prologue

A few years ago

He couldn't sleep.

This was nothing new. One would think he'd be used to it by now.

But no, each night Sebastian Grey closed his eyes with every expectation of falling asleep. Because why shouldn't he? He was a perfectly healthy fellow, perfectly happy, perfectly sane. There was no reason why he shouldn't be able to sleep.

But he couldn't.

It didn't happen all the time. Sometimes—and he had no idea why it happened or why it didn't—he laid his head on his pillow and fell almost instantly into blissful slumber. The rest of the time, he tossed, turned, got up to read, drank tea, tossed, turned some more, sat up and looked out the window, tossed, turned, played darts, tossed, turned, and then finally gave up and watched the sunrise.

He'd seen a lot of sunrises. In fact, Sebastian now considered himself something of an expert on the sunrises of the British Isles.

Inevitably, exhaustion would set in, and sometime after dawn he would fall asleep, on his bed or in his chair or a few unpleasant times with his face pressed up against the glass. This didn't happen every day, but often enough so that he'd gained a reputation as a slugabed, which frankly amused him. There was nothing he liked so much as a crisp and energetic morning, and certainly no meal could ever be as fulfilling as a robust English breakfast.

And so he trained himself to live with his affliction as best he could. He'd got into the habit of taking breakfast at the home of his cousin Harry, in part because Harry's housekeeper laid a damned fine meal, but also because it meant that Harry now expected him to show up. Which meant that nine times out of ten, Sebastian *had* to show up. Which meant that he could not allow himself to pass out at half seven every morning. Which meant that he was more tired than usual the following night. Which meant that when he crawled into bed and closed his eyes, he would fall asleep more easily.

In theory.

No, that wasn't fair, he thought. No need to turn his sarcasm inward. His grand plan didn't work perfectly, but it worked some. He was sleeping a little better. Just not tonight.

Sebastian got up and walked to the window, resting his forehead against the pane. It was cold outside, and the icy chill pressed up against him through the glass. He liked the sensation. It was big. Grand. The sort of vivid moment that reminded him of his humanity. He was cold, therefore he must be alive. He was cold, therefore he must not be invincible. He was cold, therefore—

He stood back and let out a disgusted snort. He was cold, therefore he was cold. There wasn't really much more to it.

He was surprised it wasn't raining. When he'd arrived home that night it had looked like rain. He'd grown uncommonly good at predicting the weather while on the Continent.

It would probably start raining soon.

He wandered back to the center of his room and yawned. Maybe he should read. That sometimes made him sleepy. Of course, being sleepy wasn't the issue. He could be dead sleepy and still not sleep. He'd close his eyes, tuck his pillow just the right way, and yet—

Nothing.

He'd just lie there, waiting, waiting, waiting. He'd try to empty his mind, because surely that was what was needed. A blank canvas. A clean slate. If he could embrace absolute nothingness, then he would fall asleep. He was sure of it.

But it didn't work. Because every time Sebastian Grey tried to embrace nothingness, the war came back and embraced *him*.

He saw it. Felt it. Again. All those things for which frankly, once had been more than enough.

And so he opened his eyes. Because then all he saw was his rather ordinary bedchamber, with its rather ordinary bed. The quilt was green, the curtains gold. His desk was wood.

It was quiet, too. During the day there were the regular sounds of the city, but at night this part of town almost always fell silent. It was amazing, really, to actually enjoy silence. To listen to the wind and maybe the song of birds without always keeping one ear perked for footfall, or gunshot. Or worse.

One would think he'd be able to sleep in such a happy quiet.

He yawned again. Maybe he'd read. He'd picked a few books from Harry's collection this afternoon. There hadn't been much to choose from; Harry liked to read in French or Russian, and while Sebastian knew both of those languages as well (their shared maternal grandmother had insisted upon it), they did not come as naturally to him as they did to Harry. Reading in anything but English was *work*, and Seb just wanted to be entertained.

Was that too much to expect from a book?

If *he* were to write a book, there would be excitement. Lives would be lost, but not too many. And never any of the main characters. That would be much too depressing.

There ought to be a romance, too. And danger. Danger was good.

Maybe a little of the exotic, but not too much. Sebastian suspected that most authors did not do their research properly. He'd read a novel recently that took place in an Arabian harem. And while Seb definitely found the idea of a harem interesting—

Very interesting.

—he couldn't imagine that the author had got any of the details right. He liked an adventure as best as the next man, but even he found it difficult to believe that the plucky English heroine managed to escape by hanging a snake out the window and sliding down to safety.

To add insult to injury, the author had not even indicated what sort of snake she'd used.

Really, he could do better.

If he wrote a book, he would set it in England. There would be no snakes.

And the hero would not be some pissy little dandy, concerned only with the cut of his waistcoat. If he wrote a book, the hero would damn well be heroic.

But with a mysterious past. Just to keep things interesting.

There would have to be a heroine, too. He liked women. He could write about one. What would he name her? Something ordinary. Joan, maybe. No, that sounded too fierce. Mary? Anne?

Yes, Anne. He liked Anne. It had a nice definite sound to it. But no one would call her Anne. If he were to write a book, his heroine would be adrift, without family. There would be no one to use her Christian name. He needed a good surname. Something easy to pronounce. Something pleasant.

Sainsbury.

He paused, testing it out in his mind. Sainsbury. For some reason it reminded him of cheese.

That was good. He liked cheese.

Anne Sainsbury. It was a good name. Anne Sainsbury. Miss Sainsbury. Miss Sainsbury and . . .

And what?

What about that hero? Ought he to have a career? Certainly Sebastian knew enough about the ways of nobility to paint an accurate portrait of an indolent lord.

But that was boring. If he were to write a book, it would have to be a cracking good story.

He could make the hero a military man. He certainly knew about that. A major, perhaps? Miss Sainsbury and the Mysterious Major?

Gad no. Enough with the alliteration. Even he found it a bit too precious.

A general? No, generals were too busy. And there really weren't that many of them running around. If he were going to get that rarefied he might as well throw in a duke or two.

What about a colonel? High in the ranks, so he would have authority and power. He could be from a good family, someone with money, but not too much of it. A younger son. Younger sons had to make their way in the world.

Miss Sainsbury and the Mysterious Colonel. Yes, if he were to write a book, that's what he would call it.

But he wasn't going to write a book. He yawned. When would he find the time? He looked at his small desk, utterly empty save for a cup of cold tea. Or the paper?

The sun was already starting to come up. He ought to crawl back into bed. He could probably get a few hours of sleep before he had to get up and head over to Harry's for breakfast.

He looked over at the window, where the slanted light of dawn was rippling through the glass.

He paused. He liked the sound of that.

> *The slanted light of dawn was rippling through the glass.*

No, that was unclear. For all anyone knew, he could be talking about a brandy snifter.

> *The slanted light of dawn was rippling through the windowpane.*

That was good. But it needed a little something more.

> *The slanted light of dawn was rippling through the windowpane, and Miss Anne Sainsbury was huddled beneath her thin blanket, wondering, as she often did, where she would find money for her next meal.*

That was really good. Even he wanted to know what happened to Miss Sainsbury, and he was making it up.

Sebastian chewed on his lower lip. Maybe he should write this down. And give her a dog.

He sat at his desk. Paper. He needed paper. And ink. There had to be some in his desk drawers.

The slanted light of dawn was rippling through the windowpane, and Miss Anne Sainsbury huddled beneath her threadbare blanket, wondering as she often did, how she would find money for her next meal. She looked down at her faithful collie, lying quietly on the rug by her bed, and she knew that the time had come for her to make a momentous decision. The lives of her brothers and sisters depended upon it.

Look at that. It was an entire paragraph. And it had taken him no time at all.

Sebastian looked up, back at the window. The slanted light of dawn was still rippling through the glass.

The slanted light of dawn was rippling through the glass, and Sebastian Grey was happy.

Chapter One

Mayfair, London
Spring 1822

"The key to a successful marriage," Lord Vickers pontificated, "is to stay out of the way of one's wife."

Such a statement would normally have little bearing on the life and fortunes of Miss Annabel Winslow, but there were ten things that made Lord Vickers's pronouncement hit painfully close to her heart.

One: Lord Vickers was her maternal grandfather, which pertained to **Two**: the wife in question was her grandmother, who **Three**: had recently decided to pluck Annabel from her quiet, happy life in Gloucestershire and, in her words, "clean her up and get her married."

Of equal importance was **Four**: Lord Vickers was speaking to Lord Newbury, who **Five**: had once been married himself, apparently successfully, but **Six**: his wife had died and now he was a widower, and **Seven**: his son had died the year prior, without a son of his own.

Which meant that **Seven**: Lord Newbury was looking for a new wife and **Eight**: he rather thought an alliance with Vickers was just the thing, and **Nine**: he had his eye on Annabel because **Ten**: she had big hips.

Oh, blast. Had that been two sevens?

Annabel sighed, since that was the closest she was permitted to slumping in her seat. It didn't really signify that there were eleven items instead of ten. Her hips were her hips, and Lord Newbury was presently determining if his next heir ought to spend nine months cradled between them.

"Oldest of eight, you say," Lord Newbury murmured, eyeing her thoughtfully.

Thoughtfully? That could not be the correct adjective. He appeared about ready to lick his lips.

Annabel looked over at her cousin, Lady Louisa McCann, with a queasy expression. Louisa had come by for an afternoon visit, and they had been quite enjoying themselves before Lord Newbury had made his unexpected entrance. Louisa's face was perfectly placid, as it always was in social settings, but Annabel saw her eyes widen with sympathy.

If Louisa, whose manner and bearing were consistently correct no matter the occasion, could not keep her horror off her face, then Annabel was in very big trouble indeed.

"And," Lord Vickers said with pride, "every one of them was born healthy and strong." He lifted his glass in a silent toast to his eldest daughter, the fecund Frances Vickers Winslow, who, Annabel could not help but recall, he usually referred to as That Fool who married That Damned Fool.

Lord Vickers had not been pleased when his daughter had married a country gentleman of limited means. As far as Annabel knew, he had never revised that opinion.

Louisa's mother, on the other hand, had wed the younger son of the Duke of Fenniwick a mere three months before the elder son of the Duke of Fenniwick had taken a stupid jump on an ill-trained stallion and broken his noble neck. It had been, in the words of Lord Vickers, "Damned good timing."

For Louisa's mother, that was; not for the dead heir. Or the horse.

It was not surprising that Annabel and Louisa had crossed paths only rarely before this spring. The Winslows, with their copious progeny squeezed into a too-small house, had little in common with the McCanns, who, when they weren't in residence at their palatial London mansion, made their home in an ancient castle just over the Scottish border.

"Annabel's father was one of ten," Lord Vickers said.

Annabel turned her head to look at him more

carefully. It was the closest her grandfather had ever come to an actual compliment toward her father, God rest his soul.

"Really?" Lord Newbury asked, looking at Annabel with glintier eyes than ever. Annabel sucked in her lips, clasped her hands together in her lap, and wondered what she might do to give off the air of being infertile.

"And of course we have seven," Lord Vickers said, waving his hand through the air in the modest way men do when they are really not being modest at all.

"Didn't stay out of Lady Vickers's way all the time, then," Lord Newbury chortled.

Annabel swallowed. When Newbury chortled, or really, when he moved in any way, his jowls seemed to flap and jiggle. It was an awful sight, reminiscent of that calf-foot jelly the housekeeper used to force on her when she was ill. Truly, enough to put a young lady off her food.

She tried to determine how long one would have to go without nutrients to significantly reduce the size of one's hips, preferably to a width deemed unacceptable for childbearing.

"Think about it," Lord Vickers said, giving his old friend a genial slap on the back.

"Oh, I'm thinking," Lord Newbury said. He turned toward Annabel, his pale blue eyes alight with interest. "I am definitely thinking."

"Thinking is overrated," announced Lady Vickers. She lifted a glass of sherry in salute to no one in particular and drank it.

"Forgot you were there, Margaret," Lord Newbury said.

"I never forget," grumbled Lord Vickers.

"I speak of gentlemen, of course," Lady Vickers said, holding out her glass to whichever gentleman might reach it first to refill. "A lady must always be thinking."

"That's where we disagree," said Newbury. "My own Margaret kept her thoughts to herself. We had a splendid union."

"Stayed out of your way, did she?" Lord Vickers said.

"As I said, it was a splendid union."

Annabel looked at Louisa, sitting so properly in the chair next to her. Her cousin was a wisp of a thing, with slender shoulders, light brown hair and eyes of the palest green. Annabel always thought she looked like a bit of a monster next to her. Her own hair was dark and wavy, her skin the sort that would tan if she allowed herself too much time in the sun, and her figure had been attracting unwanted attention since her twelfth summer.

But never—never—had attentions been any less wanted than they were right now, with Lord Newbury staring at her like a sugared treat.

Annabel sat quietly, trying to emulate Louisa and not allow any of her thoughts to show on her face. Her grandmother was forever scolding her for being too expressive. "For the love of God," was a familiar refrain. "Stop smiling as if you *know* something. Gentlemen don't want a lady who knows things. Not as a wife, anyway."

At this point Lady Vickers usually took a drink and added, "You can know lots of things after you're married. Preferably with a gentleman other than your husband."

If Annabel hadn't known things before, she certainly did now. Like the fact that at least three of the Vickers offspring were probably not Vickerses. Her grandmother, Annabel was coming to realize, had, in addition to a remarkably blasphemous vocabulary, a rather fluid view on morality.

Gloucestershire was beginning to seem like a dream. Everything in London was so . . . shiny. Not literally, of course. In truth, everything in London was rather gray, dusted over by a thin sheen of soot and dirt. Annabel wasn't really sure why "shiny" was the word that had come to mind. Perhaps it was because nothing seemed simple. Definitely not straightforward. And maybe even a little slippery.

She found herself longing for a tall glass of milk, as if something so fresh and wholesome might restore her sense of balance. She'd never thought herself particularly prim, and heaven knew that she was the Winslow most likely to fall asleep in church, but every day in the capital seemed to bring yet another shock, another moment that left her slack-jawed and confused.

A month she'd been here now. A month! And still she felt as if she were tiptoeing along, never quite sure if she was doing or saying the right thing.

She *hated* that.

At home she was certain. She wasn't always

right, but she was almost always certain. In London the rules were different. And worse, everyone knew everyone else. And if they didn't, they knew *about* them. It was as if all the *ton* shared some secret history that Annabel was not privy to. Every conversation held an undercurrent, a deeper, more subtle meaning. And Annabel, who in addition to being the Winslow most likely to fall asleep in church was the Winslow most likely to speak her mind, felt she could not say a thing, for fear of making offense.

Or embarrassing herself.

Or embarrassing someone else.

She could not bear the thought. She simply could not bear the thought that she might somehow prove to her grandfather that her mother had indeed been a fool and her father had been a damned fool and that she was the damnedest fool of them all.

There were a thousand ways to make an idiot of oneself, with new opportunities arising every day. It was exhausting trying to avoid them all.

Annabel stood and curtsied when the Earl of Newbury took his leave, trying not to notice when his eyes lingered on her bosom. Her grandfather exited the room along with him, leaving her alone with Louisa, their grandmother, and a decanter of sherry.

"Won't your mother be pleased," Lady Vickers announced.

"About what, ma'am?" Annabel asked.

Her grandmother gave her a rather jaded look, with a tinge of incredulity and a twist of ennui.

"The earl. When I agreed to take you in I never dreamed we might land anything above a baron. What good luck for you he's desperate."

Annabel smiled wryly. How lovely to be the object of desperation.

"Sherry?" her grandmother offered.

Annabel shook her head.

"Louisa?" Lady Vickers cocked her head toward her other granddaughter, who gave her head an immediate and negative shake.

"He's not much to look at, that's true," Lady Vickers said, "but he was handsome enough when he was young, so your children won't be ugly."

"That's nice," Annabel said weakly.

"Several of my friends set their caps for him, but he had his eye on Margaret Kitson."

"Your friends," Annabel murmured. Her grandmother's contemporaries had wanted to marry Lord Newbury. Her *grandmother's* contemporaries had wanted to marry the man who most likely wanted to marry *her*.

Dear God.

"And he'll die soon," her grandmother continued. "You couldn't hope for more."

"I think I will have that sherry," Annabel announced.

"Annabel," Louisa said with a gasp, giving her a what-are-you-*doing* glance.

Lady Vickers nodded approvingly and poured her a glass. "Don't tell your grandfather," she said, handing it over. "He doesn't approve of spirits for ladies under the age of thirty."

Annabel took a large swallow. It went down her throat in a hot rush, but somehow she didn't choke. She'd never been given sherry at home, at least not before supper. But here, *now*, she needed fortification.

"Lady Vickers," came the voice of the butler, "you had asked me to remind you when it was time to leave for Mrs. Marston's gathering."

"Oh, right," Lady Vickers said, groaning as she rose to her feet. "She's a tedious old windbag, but she does lay a nice table."

Annabel and Louisa stood as their grandmother left the room, and then, as soon as she was gone, they sank back down and Louisa said, "What *happened* while I was gone?"

Annabel sighed weakly. "I assume you refer to Lord Newbury?"

"I was in Brighton for only four days." Louisa cast a quick glance at the door, making sure that no one was about, and then resumed in an urgent whisper, "And now he wants to *marry* you?"

"He hasn't said as much," Annabel replied, more out of wishful thinking than anything else. Based upon Lord Newbury's attentions toward her these last four days, he'd be off to Canterbury to obtain a special license by the week's end.

"Do you know his history?" Louisa asked.

"I think so," Annabel replied. "Some of it." Certainly not as much as Louisa would. Louisa was already on her second London season, and more to the point, she had been born to this world. Annabel's pedigree might have included a grandfather who was a viscount, but she was a country gentleman's daughter, through and through. Louisa, on the other hand, had spent every spring and summer of her life in London. Her mother—Annabel's aunt Joan—had passed away several years earlier, but the Duke of Fenniwick had several sisters, all of whom held prominent positions in society. Louisa may have been shy, she may have been the last person anyone would expect to spread gossip and rumors, but she *knew* everything.

"He's desperate for a wife," Louisa said.

Annabel gave what she hoped was a self-deprecating shrug. "I'm rather desperate for a husband myself."

"Not *that* desperate."

Annabel did not contradict, but the truth was, if she didn't marry well and soon, heaven only knew what would become of her family. They had never had a lot, but when her father had been alive, they'd always managed to make do. She wasn't sure how they had afforded the tuition to send all four of her brothers to school, but they were all where they should be—at Eton, receiving a gentleman's education. Annabel would *not* be responsible for their having to leave.

"His wife died, oh, I'm not sure how many years ago," Louisa continued. "But that did not signify, as he had a perfectly healthy son. And his son had two daughters, so obviously his wife was not barren."

Annabel nodded, wondering why it was always the woman who was barren. Couldn't a man be incapable, too?

"But then his son died. It was a fever, I think."

Annabel had been made aware of this part already, but she was sure Louisa would know more, so she asked, "Has he no one else to inherit? Surely there must be a brother or cousin."

"His nephew," Louisa confirmed. "Sebastian Grey. But Lord Newbury *hates* him."

"Why?"

"I don't know," Louisa said with a shrug. "No one knows. Jealousy, maybe? Mr. Grey is terribly handsome. All the ladies fall at his feet."

"I should like to see that," Annabel mused, imagining the scene. She pictured a blond Adonis, muscles straining his waistcoat, wading through a sea of unconscious females. It would be best if a few of them were still somewhat sentient, perhaps tugging on his leg, setting him off balance—

"Annabel!"

Annabel snapped to attention. Louisa was addressing her with uncommon urgency, and she'd do well to listen.

"Annabel, this is important," Louisa said.

Annabel nodded, and an unfamiliar feeling washed over her—maybe of gratitude, certainly of love. She'd only just got to know her cousin, but already there was a deep bond of affection, and she knew that Louisa would do everything in her power to keep Annabel from making an unhappy alliance.

Unfortunately, Louisa's power was, in this capacity, limited. And she did not—no, she *could* not—understand the pressures of being the eldest daughter of an impoverished family.

"Listen to me," Louisa implored. "Lord Newbury's son died, oh, I think it must be a bit over a year ago. And he started looking for a wife before his son was cold in his grave."

"Shouldn't he have found one by now, then?"

Louisa shook her head. "He almost married Mariel Willingham."

"Who?" Annabel blinked, trying to place the name.

"Exactly. You've never heard of her. She died."

Annabel felt her eyebrows rise. It was really a rather emotionless delivery of such tragic news.

"Two days before the wedding she took a chill."

"She died in only two days?" Annabel asked. It was a morbid question, but, well, she had to know.

"No. Lord Newbury insisted upon delaying the ceremony. He said it was for her welfare, that she was too ill to stand up in church, but everyone knew that he really just wanted to make sure she was healthy enough to bear him a son."

"And then?"

"Well, and then she did die. She lingered for about a fortnight. It was really very sad. She was always very kind to me." Louisa gave her head a little shake, then continued. "It was a near miss for Lord Newbury. If he'd married her, he would have had to go into mourning. As it was, he had already tried to wed scandalously soon after his son's death. If Miss Willingham hadn't died before the wedding, he'd have had another year of black."

"How long did he wait before looking for someone else?" Annabel asked, dreading the answer.

"Not more than two weeks. Honestly, I don't think he would have waited that long if he thought he could have got away with it." Louisa looked about, her eyes falling on Annabel's sherry. "I need some tea," she said.

Annabel rose and rang for it, not wanting Louisa to break the narrative.

"After he returned to London," Louisa said, "he began to court Lady Frances Sefton."

"Sefton," Annabel murmured. She knew that name but couldn't quite place it.

"Yes," Louisa said animatedly. "Exactly. Her father is the Earl of Brompton." She leaned forward. "Lady Frances is the third of nine children."

"Oh my."

"Miss Willingham was the eldest of only four, but she . . ." Louisa trailed off, clearly unsure of how to phrase it politely.

"Was shaped like me?" Annabel offered.

Louisa nodded grimly.

Annabel gave a wry grimace. "I suppose he never looked twice in your direction."

Louisa looked down at herself, all seven and a half stone of her. "Never." And then, in a most uncharacteristic display of blasphemy, she added, "Thank *God*."

"What happened to Lady Frances?" Annabel asked.

"She eloped. With a *footman*."

"Good heavens. But she must have had a prior attachment, wouldn't you think? One wouldn't run off with a footman just to avoid marriage to an earl."

"You don't think so?"

"Well, no," Annabel said. "It's not at all practical."

"I don't think she was thinking about practicality. I think she was thinking about marriage to that . . . that . . ."

"I beseech you, do not finish that sentence."

Louisa kindly complied.

"If one were going to avoid marriage to Lord Newbury," Annabel continued, "I would think there must be better ways to do it than marrying a footman. Unless of course she was in love with the footman. That changes everything."

"Well, it's neither here nor there. She dashed off to Scotland and no one has heard from her. By then the season was over. I'm sure Lord Newbury has been looking for a bride ever since, but I would think it's much easier during the season, when everyone is gathered together. Plus," Louisa added, almost as an afterthought, "if he had been pursuing another lady, I'd hardly have heard about it. He lives in Hampshire."

Whereas Louisa would have spent the entire winter in Scotland, shivering in her castle.

"And now he's back," Annabel stated.

"Yes, and now that he's lost an entire year, he'll want to find someone quickly." Louisa looked over at her with a horrible expression—part pity, part resignation. "If he is interested in you, he's not going to waste any time with a courtship."

Annabel knew it was true, and she knew that if Lord Newbury did propose, she'd have a very difficult time refusing. Her grandparents had already indicated that they supported the match.

Her mother would have allowed her to refuse, but her mother was nearly a hundred miles away. And Annabel knew exactly the expression she'd see in her mother's eyes as she assured her she didn't have to marry the earl.

There would be love, but there would also be worry. There was always worry on her mother's face lately. The first year after her father's death there had been grief, but now there was only worry. Annabel thought that her mother was so worried about how to support her family that there was no longer any time for grief.

Lord Newbury would, if he did indeed wish to marry her, bring enough financial support to ease her mother's burdens. He could pay her brothers' tuitions. And provide dowries for her sisters.

Annabel would not consent to marry him unless he agreed to do so. In writing.

But she was getting ahead of herself. He had not asked to marry her. And she had not decided that she would say yes. Or had she?

Chapter Two

The following morning

"Newbury's got his eye on a new one."

Sebastian Grey opened one eye to look at his cousin Edward, who was sitting across from him, eating a pie-like substance that even from across the room smelled revolting. His head was pounding—too much champagne the night before—and he decided he liked the room better dark.

He closed his eye.

"I think he's serious this time," Edward said.

"He was serious the last three times," Sebastian replied, directing the comment to the insides of his eyelids.

"Hmm, yes," came Edward's voice. "Bad luck

for him. Death, elopement, and what happened with the third?"

"Showed up at the altar with child."

Edward chuckled. "Maybe he should have taken that one. At least he would have known she was fertile."

"I suspect," Sebastian replied, shifting his position to better accommodate his long legs on the sofa, "that even I am preferable to some other man's bastard." He gave up on trying to find a comfortable position and heaved both legs over the arm, letting his feet dangle over the side. "Difficult though it is to imagine."

He thought about his uncle for a few moments, then attempted to thrust him from his mind. The Earl of Newbury always put him in a bad mood, and his head hurt enough already as it was. They'd always been at odds, uncle and nephew, but it hadn't really mattered until a year and a half earlier, when Sebastian's cousin Geoffrey had died. As soon as it had become apparent that Geoffrey's widow was not increasing, and that Sebastian was the heir presumptive to the earldom, Newbury hurried himself off to London to search for a new bride, declaring that he would die before he allowed Sebastian to inherit.

The earl, apparently, had not noticed the logistical inconsistencies of such a statement.

Sebastian thus found himself in an odd and precarious position. If the earl could find a wife and sire another son—and, the Lord knew, he was trying—then Sebastian was nothing but another of London's fashionable yet untitled gentlemen.

If, on the other hand, Newbury did not manage
to reproduce, or worse, managed only daughters,
then Sebastian would inherit four houses, heaps
of money, and the eighth most ancient earldom
in the land.

All of this meant that no one knew quite what
to do with him. Was he the marriage mart's
grandest catch or just another fortune hunter? It
was impossible to know.

It was all just too amusing. To Sebastian's
mind, at least.

No one wanted to take a chance that he might
not become the earl, and so he was invited everywhere, always an excellent circumstance for a
man who liked good food, good music, and good
conversation. The debutantes flittered and flut-
tered around him, providing endless entertainment. And as for the more mature ladies—the
ones who were free to take their pleasure where
they chose . . .

Well, more often than not, they chose *him*. That
he was beautiful was a boon. That he was an excellent lover was delicious. That he might eventually become the Earl of Newbury . . .

That made him irresistible.

At present, however, with his aching head and
queasy stomach, Sebastian was feeling exceed-
ingly resistible. Or if not that, then resist*ant*.
Aphrodite herself could descend from the ceiling, floating on a bloody clamshell, naked but for
a few well-placed flowers, and he'd likely puke at
her feet.

No, no, she ought to be completely naked. If he

was going to prove the existence of a goddess, right here in this room, she was damned well going to be naked.

He'd still puke on her feet, though.

He yawned, shifting his weight a little more onto his left hip. He wondered if he might fall asleep. He had not slept well the night before (champagne) or the night before that (nothing in particular), and his cousin's sofa was as good a spot as any. The room wasn't so bright as long as he kept his eyes closed, and the only sound was Edward's chewing.

The chewing.

It was remarkable how loud it sounded, now that he'd stopped to think on it.

Not to mention the stench. Meat pie. Who ate meat pie in front of someone in his condition?

Sebastian let out a groan.

"Sorry?" Edward said.

"Your food," Seb grunted.

"Do you want some?"

"God no."

Sebastian kept his eyes closed, but he could practically hear his cousin give a shrug. There would be no tender mercies tossed in his direction this morning.

So Newbury was panting after another broodmare. Sebastian supposed he shouldn't be surprised. Hell, he *wasn't* surprised. It was just that—

It was just that—

Well, hell. He didn't know what it was. But it wasn't nothing.

"Who is it this time?" he asked, because it wasn't as if he was *completely* uninterested.

There was a pause, presumably so that Edward could swallow his food, and then: "Vickers's granddaughter."

Sebastian considered that. Lord Vickers had several granddaughters. Which made sense, as he and Lady Vickers had had something approaching fifteen children of their own. "Well, good for her," he grunted.

"Have you seen her?" Edward asked.

"Have you?" Seb countered. He'd arrived in town late for the season. If the girl was new this year, he wouldn't know her.

"Country-bred, I'm told, and so fertile that birds sing when she draws near."

Now *that* deserved an open eye. Two, as a matter of fact. "Birds," Sebastian repeated in a flat voice. "Really."

"I thought it was a clever turn of phrase," Edward said, a touch defensively.

With a small groan, Sebastian heaved himself up into a sitting position. Well, something closer to a sitting position than he'd been in before. "And how, if the young lady is the snow-white virgin I'm sure Newbury insists upon, might one gauge her fecundity?"

Edward shrugged. "You can just tell. Her hips . . ." His hands made some sort of odd motion in the air, and his eyes began to acquire a glazed expression. "And her *breasts* . . ." At this he practically shuddered, and Sebastian wouldn't have been surprised if the poor boy started to drool.

"Control yourself, Edward," Sebastian said. "You are reclining on Olivia's newly upholstered sofa, if you recall."

Edward shot him a peevish look and went back to the food on his plate. They were sitting in the drawing room of Sir Harry and Lady Olivia Valentine, where the two men could frequently be found. Edward was Harry's brother, and thus lived there. Sebastian had come over for breakfast. Harry's cook had recently changed her recipe for coddled eggs, with delicious results. (More butter, Sebastian suspected; everything tasted better with more butter.) He hadn't missed a breakfast at La Casa de Valentine for a week.

Besides, he liked the company.

Harry and Olivia—who, incidentally, were not Spanish; Sebastian simply enjoyed saying "La Casa de Valentine"—were off in the country for a fortnight, presumably in an attempt to escape Sebastian and Edward. The two men had immediately degenerated into their bachelor ways, sleeping past noon, bringing luncheon into the drawing room, and hanging a dartboard on the back of the door to the second guest bedroom.

Sebastian was currently ahead, fourteen games to three.

Sixteen games to one, actually. He'd felt sorry for Edward halfway through the tournament. And it *had* made things more interesting. It was harder to lose realistically than it was to win. But he'd managed. Edward hadn't suspected a thing.

Game eighteen was to be held that evening. Sebastian would be there, of course. Really, he'd all but moved in. He told himself it was because someone had to keep an eye on young Edward, but the truth was . . .

Seb gave his head a mental shake. That was truth enough.

He yawned. Lord, he was tired. He didn't know why he'd had so much to drink the night before. It had been ages since he'd done so. But he had gone to bed early, and then he couldn't sleep, and then he got up, but he couldn't write because—

No because. That had been damned irritating. He just couldn't write. The words hadn't been there even though he'd left his poor heroine hiding under a bed. With the hero *in* the bed. It was to be his most risqué scene yet. One would think it'd be easy, just from the novelty of it.

But no. Miss Spencer was still under the bed and her Scotsman was still on it, and Sebastian was no closer to the end of chapter twelve than he'd been last week.

After two hours of sitting at his desk staring at a blank sheet of paper, he'd finally given up. He couldn't sleep and he couldn't write, and so more out of spite than anything else he'd got back up, dressed, and headed out to his club.

There had been champagne. Someone had been celebrating something, and it would have been rude not to join in. There had been several very pretty girls, too, although why they had been at the club, Sebastian wasn't quite sure.

Or maybe they hadn't been at the club. Had he gone somewhere else afterward?

Good Lord, he was getting too old for this non-sense.

"Maybe she'll say no," Edward said. Seemingly out of nowhere.

"Eh?"

"The Vickers girl. Maybe she'll say no to New-bury."

Sebastian sat back, pressing his fingers into his temples. "She won't say no."

"I thought you didn't know her."

"I don't. But Vickers will want the match with Newbury. They're friends, and Newbury has money. Unless the girl has an extremely indul-gent father, she'll have to do what her grand-father says. Oh, wait." He arched his brows, the accompanying furrow in his forehead meant to jog his currently sluggish mind. "If she's the Fen-niwick girl she'll say no."

"How do you *know* all this?"

Seb shrugged. "I know things." Mostly, he ob-served. It was remarkable what one could tell about another human being simply by watching. And listening. And acting so bloody charming that people tended to forget he had a brain.

Sebastian was rarely taken seriously, and he rather liked it that way.

"No, wait again," he said, picturing a wispy little thing in his mind, so thin she disappeared when she turned sideways. "It can't be the Fen-niwick girl. She has no breasts."

Edward finished off the last of his meat pie. The smell, unfortunately, did not immediately dissipate. "I trust you do not speak from first-hand knowledge," he said.

"I am an excellent judge of the female form, even from afar." Sebastian glanced about the room, looking for something nonalcoholic to drink. Tea. Tea might help. His grandmother had always said it was the next best thing to vodka.

"Well," Edward said, watching as Sebastian heaved himself off the sofa and crossed the room to ring for the butler, "if she accepts him, you've all but lost the earldom."

Seb flopped back on the sofa. "It was never mine to begin with."

"But it could be," Edward said, leaning forward. "It could be yours. Me, I'm probably thirty-ninth in line for anything of note, but you . . . you could be Newbury."

Sebastian pushed back the sour taste rising in his throat. *Newbury* was his uncle, huge and loud, with bad breath and a worse temper. It was difficult to imagine ever answering to the name. "Honestly, Edward," he said, giving his cousin as frank a stare as he could muster, "I really don't care one way or the other."

"You can't mean that."

"And yet I do," Seb murmured.

Edward stared at him as if he'd gone mad. Sebastian decided to respond to that by resuming his lengthwise position on the sofa. He closed his eyes, determined to keep them that way until the tea arrived. "I'm not saying I wouldn't appreciate the accompanying conveniences," he said, "but

I've lived thirty years without it, and twenty-nine without even the prospect of it."

"Conveniences," Edward repeated, apparently latching onto the word. "*Conveniences*?"

Seb shrugged. "I would find the money extremely convenient."

"Convenient," Edward said with amazement. "Only you would call it convenient."

Sebastian shrugged again and attempted to nap. He seemed to find most of his sleep this way, in little fits and bits, stolen on sofas, in chairs, anywhere, really, except for his own bed. But his mind proved stubborn, refusing to let go of this most recent gossip about his uncle.

He really *didn't* care if he inherited the earldom. People tended to have difficulty believing this, but it was true. If his uncle married the Vickers girl and got a son off her . . . well, bully for him. So he wouldn't get the title. Sebastian couldn't be bothered to upset himself over the loss of something he'd never really had in the first place.

"Most people," Sebastian said aloud, since it was only Edward in the room and he could sound like a bloviating buffoon with no consequences, "*know* if they are going to inherit an earldom. One is the heir apparent. Apparently, the heir. Unless someone manages to kill you first, you inherit."

"I beg your pardon?"

"One could really rename the whole thing heir *obvious*," Seb muttered.

"Do you always give vocabulary lessons when you've had too much to drink?"

"Whelp." It was Seb's favorite name for Edward, and as long as he kept it within the family, Edward didn't seem to mind.

Edward chuckled.

"Monologue, interrupted," Sebastian said, then continued: "With the heir presumptive, all is merely presumed."

"Are you telling me something I don't know?" Edward asked, not sarcastically. It was more of a query as to whether or not he needed to pay attention.

Sebastian ignored him. "One is *presumed* to be the heir, unless and of course, et cetera, et cetera, in my case, Newbury manages to foist himself on some poor young lady with fertile hips and large breasts."

Edward sighed again.

"Shut *up*," Seb said.

"If you saw them, you'd know what I mean."

His tone was so full of lust that Sebastian had to open his eyes and look at him. "You need a woman."

Edward shrugged. "Send one my way. I don't mind your leavings."

He deserved better than that, but Sebastian didn't really feel like getting into it, not without sustenance. "I really need that tea."

"I suspect you need something more than that." Seb quirked a brow.

"You seem rather annoyed with the tenuousness of your position," Edward explained.

Sebastian considered that. "No, not annoyed. But I will go so far as mildly aggravated."

Edward picked up the newspaper, and they fell into a companionable silence. Sebastian stared across the room and out the window. His eyesight had always been excellent, and he could see the pretty ladies promenading on the other side of the street. He watched for a while, happily thinking about nothing of import. Azure blue seemed to be the fashionable color this season. A good choice; it looked well on most people. He wasn't so sure about the skirts; they seemed a bit stiffer and more conical. Attractive, yes, but much more difficult for the man with an eye toward raising them.

"Tea," Edward called out, breaking into Sebastian's thoughts. A maid deposited the tray on the table between them, and for a moment they just stared at it, two big men with big hands, staring at the dainty teapot.

"Where is our dear Olivia when we need her?" Sebastian said.

Edward grinned. "I shall be sure to tell her that you value her for her pouring skills."

"It is quite possibly the most logical reason to get oneself a wife." Sebastian leaned forward and examined the tray, looking for the small jug of milk. "Do you want some?"

Edward shook his head.

Sebastian splashed some milk into his cup and then decided he needed the tea far too much to wait for it to steep properly. He poured, inhaling the aroma as it steamed through the air. It was remarkable how far it went toward settling his stomach.

Maybe he should go to India. Land of promise. Land of tea.

He took a sip, the heat rolling down his throat to his belly. It was perfect, just perfect. "Have you ever thought about going to India?" he asked Edward.

Edward looked up with only slightly raised brows. It was an abrupt change of topic, but then again, he was far too used to Sebastian to be overly startled. "No," he said. "Too hot."

Seb considered that. "I expect you're right."

"And the malaria," Edward added. "I met a man with malaria once." He shuddered. "You wouldn't want it."

Sebastian had seen his share of malaria while fighting with the 18th Hussars in Portugal and Spain. *You wouldn't want it* seemed a spectacular understatement.

Besides, it would be difficult to continue his clandestine writing career from abroad. His first novel, *Miss Sainsbury and the Mysterious Colonel*, had been a smashing success. So much 🐟 that Sebastian had gone on to write *Miss Davenport and the Dark Marquis*, *Miss Truesdale and the Silent Gentleman*, and the biggest best seller of them all—*Miss Butterworth and the Mad Baron*.

All published pseudonymously, of course. If it got out that he was writing gothic novels . . .

He thought about this for a moment. What *would* happen if it got out? The starchier members of society would cut him, but that seemed more of a boon than anything else. The rest of the *ton* would find it delicious. He'd be fêted for weeks.

But there would be questions. And people asking him to write *their* stories. It would be so tedious.

He liked having a secret. Even his family didn't know. If anyone wondered where he got his funds, they'd never inquired about it. Harry probably assumed he got a stipend from his mother. And that he cadged his breakfast every day as a means of economization.

Besides, Harry didn't like his books. He was translating them into Russian (and was getting paid a fortune for it, possibly more than Sebastian got for writing the original in English), but he didn't like them. He thought they were silly. He said so quite frequently. Sebastian didn't have the heart to tell him that Sarah Gorely, author, was actually Sebastian Grey, cousin.

It would make Harry feel so uncomfortable.

Sebastian drank his tea and watched Edward read the newspaper. If he leaned forward, he might be able to read the page facing him. His eyesight had always been freakishly sharp.

But not, apparently, sharp enough. The *London Times* used ridiculously small print. Still, he tried. The headlines were legible, at least.

Edward set down the paper and gave him a look. "How bored *are* you?"

Seb drank the last of his tea. "Oh, terribly. And you?"

"Quite a lot, since I can't read the newspaper with you staring at me."

"I'm that distracting?" Seb smiled. "Excellent."

Edward shook his head and held out the paper. "Do you want it for yourself?"

"Gad no. I was trapped into a conversation with Lord Worth last night, all about the new excise tax. Reading about it would be only slightly more pleasant than plucking out my toenails."

Edward stared at him. "Your imagination borders on the macabre."

"Only borders?" Seb murmured.

"I was trying to be polite."

"Oh, you should never do that on my account."

"Clearly."

Seb paused for just long enough for Edward to think that he'd let go of the conversation, then said, "You're getting quite dull in your old age, whelp."

Edward quirked a brow. "Which makes you . . ."

"Ancient but interesting," Sebastian answered with a grin. Whether it was the tea or the fun of baiting his young cousin, he was starting to feel better. His head still hurt but at least he didn't think he was going to ruin the carpet. "Do you plan to attend Lady Trowbridge's affair tonight?"

"Up in Hampstead?" Edward asked.

Seb nodded, pouring himself another tea.

"I think so. I haven't anything better. And you?"

"I do believe I have an appointment with the lovely Lady Cellars on the heath."

"On the *heath*?"

"I've always enjoyed the wilderness," Sebastian murmured. "I just have to figure out a way to get a blanket into the party without anyone noticing."

"Apparently you don't enjoy the wilderness in all of its glory."

"Just the bits about the fresh air and adventure. The twigs and grass burns I can do without."

Edward stood. "Well, if anyone can manage it, it's you."

Seb looked up, surprised and perhaps a little bit disappointed. "Where are you going?"

"I have an appointment with Hoby."

"Ah." He couldn't keep him, then. One did not disappoint Mr. Hoby, and one most certainly did not get between a gentleman and his boots.

"Will you be here when I return?" Edward asked from the doorway. "Or do you plan to go home?"

"I'll probably still be here," Sebastian replied, taking one last sip of his tea before lying back down on the sofa. It was barely noon, and he wouldn't need to head home to get ready for the Ladies Trowbridge and Cellars for hours yet.

Edward gave a nod and departed. Sebastian closed his eyes and tried to sleep, but after ten minutes he gave up and grabbed the newspaper.

It was too damned hard to sleep when he was alone.

Chapter Three

Later that night

She couldn't marry him. Oh dear God, she couldn't.

Annabel dashed through the darkened corridor, not caring where she was going. She had tried to do her duty. She had tried to behave as she ought. But now she felt sick, her stomach churning, and above all she needed air.

Her grandmother had insisted they attend Lady Trowbridge's annual affair, and after Louisa had explained that it was a bit out of town, all the way in Hampstead, Annabel had been looking forward to it. Lady Trowbridge kept a splendid garden, opening right up onto Hampstead's famous heath, and if the weather was fine, she'd likely put out torches and decorations, allowing the party to move out of doors.

But before Annabel could explore beyond the ballroom, Lord Newbury had found her. She had curtsied and smiled, acting for all the world as if she were honored by his attentions. She had danced with him—twice—making no comment when he stepped on her foot.

Nor when his hand had moved to her bottom.

She had drunk lemonade with him in the corner, trying to engage him in conversation, hoping and praying that something—anything—might prove to be of more interest than her breasts.

But then he had somehow maneuvered her into the corridor. Annabel didn't quite know how he had done so. Something about a friend, and a message that needed to be relayed, and then before she knew it, he had her in a darkened corner, pressed up against the wall.

"Good Lord," he groaned, grabbing one of her breasts with his beefy hand, "I can't even fit my fingers around it."

"Lord Newbury," Annabel cried, trying to twist out of his grasp. "Stop, please—"

"Wrap your legs around me," he ordered, slamming his lips against hers.

"*What*?" She tried to say it, tried to scream, but she could barely even move her mouth against the pressure.

He grunted and shoved against her, his arousal hard and angry against her belly. One of his hands grabbed at her bottom, trying to move her leg the way he wanted it to go. "Lift up your skirt if you have to. I want to see how wide you can go."

"No," she gasped. "Please. I can't."

"The morals of a lady and the body of a harlot." He chuckled and squeezed her nipple through the thin fabric of her dress. "The perfect combination."

Panic was rising in Annabel's chest. She'd dealt with unwelcome advances before, but never from a peer of the realm. And never from a man she was expected to marry.

Did that mean he expected liberties from her? Before he even asked for her hand?

No, he couldn't possibly. He might be an earl, used to having his every command obeyed, but surely that did not mean he thought he could compromise a respectable young lady.

"Lord Newbury," she said, trying to sound stern. "Release me. Immediately."

But he only smiled and tried to kiss her again.

He smelled like fish, and his hands were big flabby things, and she just could not bear it. This wasn't how it was supposed to be. She hadn't been expecting romance, or true love, or— Dear God, she didn't know what she had been expecting. But not this. Not this awful man up against a wall in a strange house.

This couldn't be her life. It simply could not be her life.

She didn't know where she got the strength; he must have weighed nearly twenty stone. But she managed to wedge both of her hands between them, and then she shoved, hard.

He staggered backward, cursing as he hit a table and nearly lost his balance completely. Annabel had just enough time to yank her skirts up over her ankles and run. She had no idea if Lord Newbury gave chase; she didn't pause to look behind her until she'd made it through a set of French doors and found herself in what had to be a side garden.

She leaned against the exterior stone wall and tried to catch her breath. Her heart was pounding, and her skin was now covered with a thin sheen of perspiration, which was making her shiver in the cooler air.

She felt dirty. Not inside. Lord Newbury could not make her doubt her own values and conscience. But on the outside, on her skin, where he'd touched her . . .

She wanted to bathe. She wanted to take a cloth and a fat bar of soap and erase every last memory of him. Even now, her right breast felt funny where he'd grabbed her. It wasn't pain. It just felt wrong. Her whole body felt like that. Nothing hurt. There was an indescribable sense of wrongness.

In the distance she could see the light from the torches in the back garden, but here it was nearly dark. Clearly this part of the property had not been meant for partygoers. She shouldn't be here, that much was obvious, but she could not bring herself to return to the party. Not yet.

There was a stone bench halfway across the lawn, so she walked over and plopped herself down, allowing herself an audible, "Ooof!" when she landed. It was the sort of unfeminine noise, accompanying the sort of inelegant motion, that she could not permit herself in London.

The sort of thing she did all the time when romping about with her brothers and sisters in Gloucestershire.

She missed home. She missed her bed, and her dog, and Cook's plum tarts.

She missed her mother, and she really missed her father, and most of all she missed the solid earth beneath her feet. She knew herself in Gloucestershire. She knew what was expected of her. She knew what to expect from other people.

Was it so much to want to feel like she knew what she was doing? Surely that wasn't an unreasonable wish.

She looked up, trying to make out the constellations. There was too much light coming from the party to find clarity in the night sky, but the stars were still twinkling here and there.

They had to fight through the pollution, Annabel thought, in order to shine. It was a pollution of light, of brightness.

Somehow that just seemed wrong.

"Five minutes," she said aloud. In five minutes she would return to the party. In five minutes she would have regained her equilibrium. In five minutes she would be able to affix her smile back to her face and curtsy to the man who had just mauled her.

In five minutes she would tell herself that she could marry him.

And with luck, in ten minutes she might actually believe it.

But in the meantime, she had four more minutes to herself.

Four minutes.

Or not.

Annabel's ears pricked at the sound of whispering, and with a frown, she twisted in her seat and looked back toward the house. She could see two people emerging through the French doors, a man and a woman, judging by their silhouettes. She groaned to herself. They must be sneaking outside for an assignation. There could be no other explanation. If they had sought out this side of the garden, and chosen that door, then they were trying to avoid detection.

Annabel did not want to be the one to ruin things for them.

She jumped to her feet, intending to find an alternate route back into the house, but the couple was advancing quickly, and there was no way she could go anywhere but deeper into the shadows if she wished to avoid them. She moved swiftly, not quite running but definitely doing something that was more than a walk, until she was at the hedge that clearly marked the edge of the property. She didn't particularly relish the thought of pressing herself into the bramble, so she scooted off to her left, where she could see an opening in the hedge, presumably leading out to the heath.

The heath. The huge, wonderful, glorious space that was everything that London was not.

This was definitely not where she was supposed to be. Definitely, definitely not. Louisa would be aghast. Her grandfather would be furious. And her grandmother . . .

Well, her grandmother would probably laugh, but Annabel had long since realized she ought not base any of her moral judgments on her grandmother's behavior.

She wondered if she might be able to find another way back from the heath onto the Trowbridge lawn. It was a huge property; surely there were multiple openings in the hedge. But in the meantime . . .

She looked out over the open expanse. How amazing to find such wilderness so close to town. It was fierce and dark, and the air held a crisp clarity she hadn't even realized she'd missed. It wasn't just that it was clean and fresh—that she'd *known* she'd missed, from the very first day she'd breathed in the slightly opaque gas that masqueraded as air in London. There was a bite to the air here, something cold, something tangy. Every breath made her lungs tingle.

It was heaven.

She looked up, wondering if the stars would be any more visible out here. They weren't, not much anyway, but she kept her face to the sky nonetheless, walking slowly backward as she gazed up at the thin sliver of moon hanging drunkenly above the treetops.

It was the sort of night that ought to be magical. And it would have been, if she hadn't been pawed at by a man old enough to be her grandfather. It would have been if she'd been allowed to wear red, which favored her complexion so much more than this pale peony of a pink.

It would have been magical if the wind blew in time to a waltz. If the rustle of the leaves were Spanish castanets, and there were a handsome prince waiting in the mist.

Of course there was no mist, but then again, there was no prince, either. Just a horrible old man who wanted to do horrible things to her. And eventually, she was going to have to let him.

Three times in her life she'd been kissed. The first was Johnny Metham, who now insisted upon being called John, but he'd been but eight when he'd smacked his lips on hers—definitely a Johnny.

The second had been Lawrence Fenstone, who had stolen a kiss on May Day, three years earlier. It had been dark, and someone had put rum in both bowls of punch, and the entire village had lost its sense. Annabel had been surprised, but not angry, and in fact when he'd tried to put his tongue in her mouth she'd laughed.

It had seemed *just* the most ridiculous thing.

Lawrence had not been amused, and he'd stalked off, his manly pride apparently too pricked to continue. He didn't speak to her again for an entire year, not until he'd come back from Bristol with a blushing bride—blond, petite, and brainless. Everything Annabel wasn't, and, she was relieved to note, quite a lot that she didn't care to be.

The third kiss had been tonight, when Lord Newbury had ground his body against hers, and then done the same with his mouth.

Suddenly that whole episode with Lawrence Fenstone's tongue no longer seemed so amusing.

Lord Newbury had done the same thing, trying

to jab his tongue between her lips, but she had clenched her teeth together so hard she'd thought her jaw might break. And then she had run. She'd always equated running with cowardice, but now, after having taken flight herself, she realized that sometimes it was the only prudent action, even if it meant that she now found herself alone on a heath, with an amorous couple blocking her way back to the ballroom. It was almost comical.

Almost.

She let her cheeks inflate with air, then blew it out, still walking slowly backward. What a night this had been. It wasn't magical at all. It wasn't—

"Oh!"

Her heel connected with something—dear God, was it a leg?—and she tumbled back. And all she could think—as macabre as her outlook had become—was that she'd tripped over a dead body.

Or at least she hoped it was dead. A dead body would certainly do less damage to her reputation than a live one.

Sebastian was a patient man, and he didn't mind waiting twenty minutes so that he and Elizabeth could make respectably separate reentrances to the ballroom. The lovely Lady Cellars had a reputation to uphold, even if he did not. Not that their liaison was anything approaching a secret. Elizabeth was young and beautiful, she'd already supplied her husband with two sons, and if Sebastian had it correctly, Lord Cellars was far more interested in his male secretary than he was in his wife.

No one expected Lady Cellars to remain faithful. No one.

But appearances had to be upheld, and so Sebastian happily remained on the blanket (smuggled in by an enterprising footman) and pondered the night sky.

It was uncommonly peaceful out here on the heath, even if he could hear the sounds of the party humming in on the wind. He'd not ventured too far past the border of the Trowbridge property; Elizabeth was not so adventurous as that. Still, he felt remarkably alone.

The strangest thing was, he liked it.

He didn't often enjoy solitude. In fact, he almost never did. But there was something charming about being out on the heath, out in the open. It reminded him of the war, of all those nights with nothing over his head save for the canopy of a tree.

He'd hated those nights.

It didn't make much sense that something that brought back memories of war would give him such contentment right now, but not much that went through his head made sense. There didn't seem to be much point in questioning it.

He closed his eyes. The insides of his eyelids were a brownish black, not at all the same as the thick purple of the night. Darkness had so many colors. It was strange, that, and perhaps a little disquieting. But—

"Oh!"

A foot slammed into his left calf, and he opened his eyes just in time to see a woman tumbling backward.

Right onto his blanket.

He smiled. The gods still loved him.

"Good evening," he said, scooching himself up onto his elbows. The woman didn't reply—no surprise there, as she was still busy trying to figure out how she'd ended up on her arse. He watched as she attempted to maneuver herself back onto her feet. She wasn't having an easy time of it. The ground was uneven under the blanket, and she had certainly been set off her equilibrium, if her rapid breathing was any indication.

He wondered if she, too, had an assignation. Perhaps there was another gentleman out here on the darkened heath, lurking in the background, waiting to pounce.

Sebastian tilted his head to the side, regarding the lady as she brushed off her dress, and then decided—probably not. She didn't have that furtive look about her. Plus, she was wearing white, or light pink, or some other virginal hue. Debutantes *could* be seduced—not that Sebastian had ever done so; he did subscribe to a certain moral code, not that anyone ever gave him credit for it. But from what he'd observed, virgins needed wooing *in situ*. You certainly weren't going to get one to walk herself across a lawn and into the heath for her own ruination. Even the stupidest of girls would come to her senses before she reached her destination.

Unless . . .

Now this could be interesting. Maybe his clumsy lady had *already* been deflowered. Maybe she was on her way to meet her lover. The enterprising gentleman would have had to have done a *very* good job of it the first time if he was getting a repeat engagement. Sebastian had it on the best authority that it was a rare girl who enjoyed her first time.

Then again, his scientific sample might be skewed. All of the women he'd slept with recently had had their first times with their husbands. Who were, almost by definition, bad in bed. Otherwise, why would their wives have sought out Sebastian's attentions?

At any rate, as delicious as his ponderings might be, it was extremely unlikely that this young lady was on her way to meet a lover. Virginity was just about the only commodity allowed to the young and unmarried of the female persuasion, and they generally did not squander it.

So what was she doing out here? All by herself? He smiled. He loved a good mystery. Almost as much as a good melodrama.

"May I be of assistance?" he asked, since she hadn't responded to his earlier greeting.

"No," she said, giving her head a quick shake. "I'm sorry. I'll be on my way. I really can't—" She looked over at him then, and swallowed.

Did she know him? She certainly looked as if she recognized him. Or maybe she just saw him for what he was, something of a libertine, no one with whom she ought to find herself alone.

He could not fault her for that reaction.

He did not know *her*, of that he was sure. He rarely forgot a face, and he certainly would not have forgot hers. She was lovely in a wild sort of way, almost as if she belonged out here on the heath. Her hair was dark and probably quite curly; the few tendrils that had escaped her coiffure formed loose coils that brushed against her neck. She looked as if she were easy to laugh, with an impish mouth—even now, when she was clearly flustered and embarrassed.

Most of all, she looked . . . *warm*.

He found himself curious at this choice of adjectives. He couldn't recall using it before, not about a complete stranger. But she looked warm, as if her personality was warm, and laugh would be warm, and her friendship, too.

And in bed . . . she'd be warm there, as well.

Not that he was considering it. For all her heat, she radiated virginity.

Which meant that she was very much off-limits.

Someone in whom he had no interest. None. He couldn't even be friends with the virgins, because someone would undoubtedly misunderstand or misconstrue, and then there would be recriminations or worse, expectations, and then he'd find himself off at some hunting lodge in Scotland, just to get away from it all.

Sebastian knew what he ought to do. He always knew what he ought to do. The difficulty—his difficulty, at least—was in the doing it.

He *could* rise to his feet like the gentleman he was, point her in the direction of the house, and send her on her way.

He could, but what would be the fun in that?

Chapter Four

When the dead body said, "Good evening," Annabel had to face the grim conclusion that it wasn't nearly as dead as she'd hoped.

She was happy for *him*, of course, not being dead and all that, but as for herself, well, his undeadedness was spectacularly inconvenient.

Dear Lord, she wanted to moan, *the night only needed this.*

She declined his offer of assistance, politely though it was made, and somehow managed to stagger to her feet without embarrassing herself any further.

"What brings you out on the heath?" the not-dead fellow asked conversationally, as if they were instead chatting in a churchyard, surrounded by all that was prim and proper.

She stared down at him. He was still reclining on the blanket—a blanket! He had a blanket?

This could not be good.

"Why do you want to know?" she heard herself ask. Which seemed to her to be proof that she'd lost complete sight of her sanity. Clearly she should have stepped around him and run back to the house. Or stepped over him. Or on him. But above all, she should not have engaged in conversation. Even if she ran right across the amorous couple in the garden, that *had* to be less dangerous to her reputation than being caught alone with a strange man on the heath.

If he was planning to attack and ravish, though, he gave no indication of being in a hurry to do so. He just shrugged and said, "I'm curious."

She looked at him for a moment. He did not look familiar, but it *was* dark. And he was speaking as if they had been introduced. "Do I know you?" she asked.

He smiled mysteriously. "I don't think so."

"Should I?"

At that he laughed, then said firmly, "Absolutely not. But that doesn't mean we can't have a perfectly delightful conversation."

From this Annabel deduced that he was a rake and well aware of it, certainly not appropriate company for an unmarried lady. She glanced in the direction of the house. She ought to go. She really ought.

"I don't bite," he assured her. "Or anything else you'd need to worry over." He sat up and patted the blanket beside him. "Have a seat."

"I'll stand," she said. Because she hadn't completely lost her sense. At least she hoped not.

"Are you certain?" He gave her a winning smile. "It's much more comfortable down here."

Said the spider to the fly. Annabel only barely managed to avoid letting out a squeak of nervous laughter.

"Are you avoiding someone?" he asked.

She'd been looking back toward the house again, but at this her head whipped around.

"It happens to the best of us," he said, almost apologetically.

"Are *you* avoiding someone, then?"

"Not precisely," he allowed, cocking his head in a way that was almost like a shrug. "It's more that I'm waiting my turn."

Annabel had *really* wanted to appear impassive, but she felt her eyebrows rise.

He looked at her, his lips curved into the tiniest smile. There was nothing wicked in his expression, and yet she felt it all the same, a shiver of anticipation, a hint of excitement pressing through her.

"I could give you the details," he murmured, "but I suspect it wouldn't be proper."

Nothing that evening had been proper. It could hardly get worse.

"I don't mean to make assumptions," he continued smoothly, "but based upon the hue of your gown, I can only deduce that you are unmarried."

She gave a quick nod.

"Which means that under no circumstances should I be telling you that I was out here with a woman who is not my wife."

Oh, she *should* be scandalized. She really should. But she couldn't quite manage it. He was just so *charming*. He oozed it. He was grinning at her now, like they were sharing a secret joke, and she couldn't help it—she wanted to be in on the joke. She wanted to be part of his club, his group, his anything. There was something about him—a charisma, a magnetism—and she knew, she just *knew* that if she could travel back in time, and in space, she supposed, to Eton or wherever he'd spent his formative years, he would have been the boy whom everyone wanted to be near.

Some people were just born with it.

"Who are you avoiding?" he wondered. "The most likely candidate would be an overly eager suitor, but that wouldn't explain your flight all the way out here. It's just as easy to lose oneself in a crowd, and far less dangerous to one's reputation."

"I shouldn't say," she murmured.

"No, of course not," he agreed. "That would be indiscreet. But it will be much more fun if you do."

She pressed her lips together, trying not to smile.

"Will anyone be missing you?" he asked.

"Eventually."

He nodded. "The person you're avoiding?"

Annabel thought of Lord Newbury, and his pricked pride. "I imagine I have a little bit of time before he starts searching."

"*He*?" the gentleman said. "The plot thickens."

"Plot?" she countered with a grimace. "That's a poor choice of words. It's not a book anyone would wish to read. Trust me."

He chuckled at this, then patted the blanket again. "Do sit. It's offending every one of my gentlemanly principles that you're up there while I'm reclining."

She gave him her best imitation of arch confidence. "Perhaps you should stand."

"Oh no, I couldn't possibly do that. It would make it all so formal, don't you think?"

"Considering that we have not been introduced, formality might be just the thing."

"Oh *no*," he objected. "You have it all backwards."

"Then I should introduce myself?"

"Don't do *that*," he said with the barest hint of drama. "Whatever you do, don't tell me your name. It's likely to awaken my conscience, and that's the last thing we want."

"You do have a conscience, then?"

"Sadly, yes."

That was a relief. He wasn't going to pull her off into the darkness, and he wasn't going to maul her as Lord Newbury had done. Regardless, she ought to return to the party. Conscience or no, he was not the sort of gentleman with whom a young unmarried lady ought to be alone. Of that she was absolutely certain.

Again, she thought of Lord Newbury, who *was* the sort of man she was supposed to be with.

She sat down beside him.

"Excellent choice," he applauded.

"It's just for a moment," she murmured.

"Of course."

"It's not you," she said, feeling a bit cheeky. But she didn't want him to think that she was staying because of him.

"It's not?"

"Over there." She pointed toward the side garden, flicking her wrist in a little wave. "There's a man and a woman, er . . ."

"Enjoying each other's company?"

"Exactly."

"And you can't get back to the party."

"I'd really rather not interrupt."

He gave her a commiserating nod. "Awkward."

"Very much so."

He frowned thoughtfully. "A man and a man would be more awkward, I think."

Annabel gasped, although she didn't really feel the indignation she ought. It was far too intoxicating to be near him, to feel included in his wit.

"Or a woman and a woman. I wouldn't mind watching *that*."

She turned away, instinctively wanting to hide her blush, then feeling silly because it was so dark, and he probably couldn't see it, anyway.

Or maybe he could. He seemed like the kind of man who could tell when a female was blushing based on the scent of the wind, or the alignment of the stars.

He was a man who knew women.

"I don't suppose you got a good look at them?" he asked, then added, "Our amorous friends."

Annabel shook her head. "I was really more preoccupied with getting away."

"Of course. Very sensible of you. It's too bad, though. If I knew who they were, I might have a better idea of how long they would take."

"Really?"

"Not all men are created equal, you know," he said modestly.

"I suspect I should not pursue that statement," she said daringly.

"Not if you truly are sensible." He smiled at her again, and good heavens, but it took her breath away.

Whoever this man was, he had been visited many times by the gods of dentistry. His teeth were white and even, and his grin was wide and infectious.

It was bloody unfair. Her own bottom teeth were a jumble, as were all of her siblings'. A surgeon had once said he could fix them, but when he'd come after her with a pair of pliers, Annabel had taken off running.

But this man—he had a smile that crept to his eyes, lighting his face, lighting the whole room. Which was a ridiculous statement, because they were outside. And it was dark. Still, Annabel would have sworn that the air around them had begun to shimmer and glow.

Either that or she'd drunk her punch from the wrong bowl. There had been one for young ladies and one for everyone else, and Annabel was quite sure that she . . . or at least fairly sure. It had been the one on the right. Louisa had said it was the right, hadn't she?

Well, she had a half-half chance, at the very least.

"Do you know everyone?" she asked, because, really, she *had* to. And he had been the one to introduce the subject.

His brows rose with incomprehension. "I beg your pardon."

"You asked for a description of the couple," she explained. "Do you know everyone, or only the ones who behave with impropriety?"

He laughed aloud. "No, I don't know everyone, but, sadly—even more sadly than the existence of my conscience—I know *almost* everyone."

Annabel considered some of the people she had met in the last few weeks and gave a wry smile. "I can see where that might be dispiriting."

"A lady of intelligence and discernment," he said. "My favorite kind."

He was *flirting* with her. Annabel fought back against the frisson of delight that seemed to roll across her skin. He really was quite beautiful, this man. His hair was dark, probably somewhere between walnut and chocolate, and it was dashing and unruly in the way that all the young gentlemen spent hours trying to achieve. His face was . . . Well, Annabel was no artist and never had learned how to describe a face, but his was somehow uneven and perfect at the same time.

"I'm very glad you have a conscience," she whispered.

He looked over at her and even leaned forward a touch, his eyes alight with amusement. "What did you say?"

She felt herself blush, and this time she *knew* he could see it. What was she supposed to say now? *I'm so glad you have a conscience because if you decided to kiss me, I do believe I'd let you?*

He was everything Lord Newbury was not. Young, handsome, witty. A little bit dashing, quite a lot dangerous. He was the sort of gentleman young ladies swore to avoid but secretly dreamed about. And for the next few moments, she had him all to herself.

Just a few more minutes. She would allow herself a few more minutes. That was all.

He must have realized that she was not going to tell him what she'd said, so instead he asked (again, as if this were an ordinary conversation), "Is this your first season?"

"It is."

"And are you enjoying yourself?"

"That would depend upon when you asked me that question."

He smiled wryly. "An indisputable truth, I am sure. Are you enjoying yourself right now?"

Annabel's heart flipped in her chest. "Very much so," she said, unable to believe how even her voice sounded. She must be getting better at the play-acting that passed for conversation in town.

"I am so pleased to hear it." He leaned toward her ever so slightly, his head dipping to the side in a gesture that was almost self-deprecating. "I do pride myself on being an excellent host."

Annabel glanced down at the blanket, then looked back up at him with dubious eyes.

He gazed at her warmly. "One must be a good host, no matter how humble the domicile."

"Surely you are not trying to tell me that you make your home on Hampstead Heath."

"Gad no. I'm much too fond of my creature

comforts for that. But it would be amusing, don't you think, for a day or two?"

"Somehow I suspect that the novelty of it all would fade with the morning light."

"No," he mused. His eyes took on a faraway expression, and he said, "Perhaps a bit after that, but not by the morning light."

She wanted to ask him what he meant, but she didn't know quite how to do it. He looked so lost in his own thoughts it almost seemed rude to interrupt. And so she waited, watching him with a curious expression, knowing that if he turned to her, he would see the question in her eyes.

He never did turn to her, but after a minute or so, he said, "It's different in the morning. The light is flatter. Redder. It catches the mist in the air, almost as if it creeps up from underneath. Everything is new," he said softly. "Everything."

Annabel's breath caught. He sounded so wistful. It made her want to remain right where she was, on the blanket beside him, until the sun started to rise on the eastern horizon. He made her want to see the heath in morning light. He made her want to see *him* in the morning light.

"I should like to take a bath in it," he murmured. "The morning light, and nothing else."

It should have been shocking, but Annabel sensed that he wasn't talking to her. Throughout the conversation he'd prodded and teased, testing how far he could go before she turned prude and ran away. But this . . . It was perhaps the most suggestive thing he'd said, and yet she knew . . .

It hadn't been for her.

"I think you're a poet," she said, and she was smiling, because for some reason, this brought her great joy.

He let out a short snort of laughter. "That would be lovely, were it true." He turned back in her direction, and she knew that the moment was gone. Whatever hidden part of himself he'd dipped into, he'd put it back, boxed it up tight, and once again he was the devil-may-care charmer, the man all the girls wanted to be with.

The man all the men wanted to be.

And she didn't even know his name.

It was best that way, though. She'd find out who he was eventually, and he'd do the same, and then he'd pity her, the poor girl forced to marry Lord Newbury. Or maybe he'd scorn her instead, thinking that she was doing it for the money, which of course she was.

She gathered her legs underneath her, not exactly kneeling but rather resting on her right hip. It was her favorite way to sit, utterly wrong for London but without a doubt the way her body liked to arrange itself. She gazed in front of her, realizing that she was looking away from the house. There was something fitting about that. She wasn't sure which way a compass would point, though; was she facing west, toward home? Or east, to the Continent, where she'd never been and likely never would go. Lord Newbury didn't seem the type to enjoy travel, and as his interest in her was limited to her childbearing talents, she rather doubted he would allow her to venture forth without him.

She'd always wanted to see Rome. She probably

would never have gone, even if there had been no Lord Newbury lusting over her wide, birthing hips, but there had always been the chance.

She closed her eyes for a moment, almost in mourning. She was already thinking as if the marriage was a *fait accompli*. She'd been telling herself that she might still refuse, but that was just the desperate corner of her brain trying to assert itself. The practical part of her had already accepted it.

So there it was. She really would marry Lord Newbury if he asked. As repulsive and horrifying as it was, she'd do it.

She sighed, feeling utterly defeated. There would be no Rome for her, no romance, no a hundred other things she couldn't even bring herself to think about. But her family would be provided for, and as her grandmother had said, perhaps Newbury would die soon. It was a wicked, immoral thought, but she didn't think she could enter the marriage without clutching onto it as her salvation.

"You seem rather pensive," came the warm voice from beside her.

Annabel nodded slowly.

"Penny for them."

She smiled wistfully. "Just thinking."

"Of all the things you need to do," he guessed. Except it didn't sound like a question.

"No." She was quiet for a moment, and then said, "All the things I'm never going to get to do."

"I see." He was quiet for a moment, and then he said, "I'm sorry."

She turned suddenly, shaking the fog from her eyes and settling on his face with a frank gaze. "Have you ever been to Rome? It's a mad question, I know, because I don't even know your name, and I don't *want* to know your name, at least not tonight, but have you ever been to Rome?"

He shook his head. "Have you?"

"No."

"I have been to Paris," he said. "And Madrid."

"You were a soldier," she stated. Because what else would he have been, seeing such cities at such a time?

He gave a little shrug. "It's not the most pleasant way to see the world, but it does get the job done."

"This is the farthest I have ever been from home," Annabel said.

"Here?" He looked at her, blinked, then pointed his finger straight down. "This heath?"

"This heath," she confirmed. "I think Hampstead is farther from home than London. Or maybe it's not."

"Does it matter?"

"It does, actually," she said, surprising herself with her answer, because obviously it *didn't* matter.

And yet it felt like it should.

"One can't argue with that kind of certainty," he said in a smile-tinged murmur.

She felt herself grin. "I very much enjoy being certain."

"Don't we all?"

"The best of us, perhaps," she said archly, getting into the spirit of their game.

"Some say it's foolhardy to be so eternally certain."

"Some?"

"Oh, not me," he assured her, "but some."

She laughed, deep and true, all the way from her belly. She was loud, and uncouth, and it felt *wonderful*.

He chuckled along with her, then asked, "Rome, I assume, is on your list of things you'll never get to do?"

"Yes," she said, her lungs still quivering from merriment. It no longer seemed so sad, that she would never see Rome. Not when she'd just laughed so hard and so well.

"I've heard it can be dusty."

They were both facing forward, so she turned, her profile lined up over her shoulder. "Really?"

He turned, too, so they were looking straight at one another. "When it doesn't rain."

"This is what you've heard," she stated.

He smiled, but just a little bit, and not even with his mouth. "This is what I've heard."

His eyes . . . oh, his eyes. They met hers with the most startling directness. And what she saw there . . . It wasn't passion, because why would it be passion? But it was still something amazing, something hot, and conspiratorial, and . . .

Heartbreaking. It was heartbreaking. Because as she stared at him, at this beautiful man who might as well have been a figment of her imagination, all she could see was Lord Newbury's face, florid and flaccid, and his voice rang in her ears, laughing, mocking, and Annabel was suddenly rocked by an overwhelming sorrow.

This moment . . . any moment like this . . .

They were not to be hers.

"I should be getting back," she said quietly.

"I am sure you should," he said with equal gravity.

She didn't move. She just could not seem to make herself do so.

And so he rose, because he was, as she'd suspected, a gentleman. Not just in name but in deed. He held his hand down to her, and she took it, and then—it was as if she floated to her feet—she rose, and she tilted her chin, and lifted her eyes to his, and then she saw it—her life, ahead of her.

All the things she would not have.

She whispered, "Would you kiss me?"

Chapter Five

There were a thousand reasons why Sebastian should not have done as the young lady requested, and only one—desire—why he should.

He went with desire.

He hadn't even realized he wanted her. Oh, he'd noticed that she was lovely, sensual even, in a rather delightfully unselfconscious manner. But he always noticed such things about women. It was as natural to him as noticing the weather. *Lydia Smithstone has an uncommonly attractive lower lip* was not terribly different from *That cloud over there is looking a bit like rain*.

At least not to his mind.

But when she'd taken his hand, and his skin touched hers, something flared within him. His heart leaped, and his breath seemed to skip, and when she rose, it was as if she were something magical and serene, moving along the wind into his arms.

Except when she reached her feet she wasn't in his arms. She was standing in front of him. Close, but not close enough.

He felt bereft.

"Kiss me," she whispered, and he could no more deny her than he could his own heartbeat. He lifted her fingers to his lips, then touched her cheek. Her eyes met his, deep and filled with longing.

And then he, too, was filled with longing. Whatever it was he saw in her eyes, it somehow moved within him, too, gentle and sweet. Wistful, even.

Wistful. He couldn't recall the last time he'd felt anything approaching wistful.

It made him want this kiss—want *her*—with the strangest intensity.

He didn't feel warm. He didn't feel hot. But something inside of him—maybe his conscience, maybe his soul—was burning.

He didn't know her name, didn't know anything about her except that she dreamed of Rome and smelled like violets.

And that she tasted like vanilla cream. This, he now knew. This, he thought as his tongue brushed against the soft inside of her upper lip, he would never forget.

How many women had he kissed? Far too many to count. He'd been kissing the girls long before he'd known there was anything else to be done with them, and he'd never really stopped. As a young lad in Hampshire, as a soldier in

Spain, as a London rogue . . . he had always found women intriguing. And he remembered them all. He truly did. He held the fairer sex in far too much esteem to allow them to melt into a hazy puddle in his mind.

But this was different. It wasn't just the woman he wasn't going to forget, it was the moment. It was the feel of her in his arms, and the scent of her skin, and the taste, and the touch, and the amazingly perfect sound she made when her breath twisted itself into a moan.

He would remember the temperature of the air, the direction of the wind, the precise shade of silver that the moonlight sprinkled upon the grass.

He dared not kiss her deeply. She was an innocent. She was wise, and she was reflective, but she was an innocent, and if she'd been kissed more than twice before this he'd have eaten his hat. And so he gave her the first kiss that young girls dreamed of. Soft. Gentle. A tiny brush of the lips, a tickle of friction, the barest, most wicked touch of the tongue.

And that had to be all. There were some things a gentleman simply could not do, no matter how magical the moment. And so with great reluctance, he pulled away.

But only so far that he could rest his nose against hers.

He smiled.

He felt happy.

And then she spoke. "Is that all?"

He went absolutely still. "I beg your pardon?"

"I thought there might be more," she said, not unkindly. In fact, more than anything else, she sounded perplexed.

He tried not to laugh. He knew he shouldn't. She looked so earnest; it would be beyond insulting to laugh at her. He pressed his lips together, trying to hold down the bubble of sheer amusement that was bouncing around within him.

"It was nice," she said, and it almost sounded as if she was trying to reassure him.

He had to bite his tongue. It was the only way.

"It's all right," she said, giving him the sort of sympathetic smile one gives to a child who is not good at games.

He opened his mouth to say her name, then remembered he didn't know it.

He held up a hand. A finger, to be more precise. A simple, concise directive. *Halt*, it said clearly. *Don't say another word.*

Her brows lifted in question.

"There's more," he said.

She started to say something.

He took his finger and pressed it right up against her mouth. "Oh, there's more."

And this time, he *really* kissed her. He took her lips with his, explored, nibbled, *devoured*. He wrapped his arms around her, pressing her against him, hard, until he could feel every one of her luscious curves against his body.

And she was luscious. No, she was *lush*. She had a woman's body, rounded and warm, with soft curves that begged to be stroked and squeezed. She was the kind of woman a man could lose himself in, happily surrendering all sense and reason.

She was the kind of woman a man did not leave in the middle of the night. She would be warm and soft, a languid pillow and blanket, all rolled into one.

She was a siren. A gorgeous exotic temptress who was somehow utterly innocent. She had no idea what she was doing. Hell, she probably had no idea what *he* was doing, either. And yet all it took was an untutored smile, a tiny sigh, and he was lost.

He wanted her. He wanted to *know* her. Every inch of her. His blood burned, his body sang, and if he hadn't suddenly heard a raucous shout from the direction of the house, heaven only knew what he would have done.

She stiffened as well, her head snapping a bit to the right, pointing her ear toward the commotion.

It was just enough for Sebastian to regain his senses, or at least a small piece of them. He pushed her away, more roughly than he'd intended, and planted his hands on his hips, breathing hard.

"That *was* more," she said, sounding dazed.

He looked over at her. Her hair wasn't quite undone, but it was certainly fashioned more loosely than it had been before. And her lips— he'd thought they were full and plump before, but now she looked positively bee stung.

Anyone who had ever been kissed would know that *she* had just been kissed. Thoroughly.

"You'll want to tidy up your hair," he said, and

he was quite certain it was the least appropriate post-kiss comment he had ever made. But he
couldn't seem to summon his usual flair. Style
and grace apparently required presence of mind.

Who would have imagined it?

"Oh," she said, her hand immediately patting
her hair, trying rather unsuccessfully to smooth
it down. "I'm sorry."

Not that she had anything to apologize for, but
Sebastian was too busy trying to locate his own
brain to say so.

"That shouldn't have happened," he finally
said. Because it was the truth. And he knew
better. He did not dally with innocents, and certainly not in (almost) full view of a filled-to-the-
brim ballroom.

He did not lose control. It simply wasn't his way.

He was furious with himself. Furious. It was an
unfamiliar, and wholly unpleasant emotion. He
did pity, and plenty of self-mockery, and he could
have written a book on mild annoyance. But fury?

It just wasn't something he cared to partake
of. Not toward others, and certainly not toward
himself.

If she hadn't asked him . . . If she hadn't looked
up with those huge, bottomless eyes and whispered, "Kiss me," he would never have done it. It
was a piss-poor excuse and he knew it, but there
was some consolation in the knowledge that he
had not initiated the encounter.

Some, but not much. For all his sins, he wasn't
that much of a liar.

"I'm sorry I asked," she said stiffly.

He felt like a heel. "I didn't have to comply," he responded, but not nearly as graciously as he ought.

"Clearly I'm irresistible," she muttered.

He shot her a sharp look. Because she was. She had the body of a goddess and the smile of a siren. Even now, it was taking every ounce of his will not to throw himself at her. Knock her to the ground. Kiss her again . . . and again . . .

He shuddered. This was *not* good.

"You should go," she said.

He managed to sweep his arm forward in a gentlemanly motion. "After you."

Her eyes widened. "I'm not going back there first."

"Do you really think I'm going to go in there and leave you alone on the heath?"

She planted her hands on her hips. "You *kissed* me without knowing my name."

"You did the same," he sniped back.

Her mouth opened into an indignant gasp, and Sebastian felt an alarming satisfaction at having bested her. Which was further unsettling. He adored a good verbal interplay, but it was a dance, for God's sake, not a bloody *competition*.

For an endless moment they stared each other down, and Sebastian wasn't sure whether he was waiting for her to blurt out her name or demand that he reveal his.

He rather suspected she was wondering the same thing.

But she said nothing, just glowered at him.

"Contrary to my recent behavior," he finally

said, because one of them had to act in a mature fashion, and he rather suspected it ought to be he, "I am a gentleman. And as such, I cannot in good conscience abandon you to the wilderness."

Her brows rose, and she glanced this way and that. "You call this the wilderness?"

He started to wonder just what it was about this girl that had made him so crazy. Because by God, she could be annoying when she set her mind to it.

"I beg your pardon," he said, with enough urbane sophistication to make him feel a bit more like himself. "Clearly I misspoke." He smiled at her, blandly.

"What if that couple is still   ." Her words trailed off as she waved her hand at the side lawn.

Sebastian let out an aggravated breath. If he were alone—which was what he should have been—he'd have toddled back onto the lawn with a cheerful, "Coming through! Anyone who is not with a person to whom they have a legal obligation, kindly make yourself scarce!"

It would have been delicious. And precisely what society expected of him.

But impossible with an unmarried lady in tow.

"They are almost certainly gone," he said, even as he approached the opening in the hedge and peered out. Turning back, he added, "And if not, they don't want to be seen any more than you do. Put your head down and barrel through."

"You seem to have a great deal of experience with such things," she stated.

"A great deal." Well, he did.

"I see." Her jaw went stiff, and he suspected that if he were closer he could hear her teeth grinding together. "How fortunate I must be," she said. "I'm being taught by a master."

"Lucky you."

"Are you always this horrid with women?"

"Almost never," he said without thinking.

Her lips parted, and he felt like kicking himself. She hid it well—clearly, she was a young woman of quick emotional reflexes—but before her surprise turned to indignation, he saw a flash of unadulterated hurt.

"What I meant," he began, not quite fighting the urge to groan, "is that when I . . . No. When *you* . . ."

She looked at him expectantly. He had no idea what to say. And he realized, as he stood there like an idiot, that there were at least ten reasons why this was a wholly unacceptable scenario.

One: He had no idea what to say. This might seem repetitive, except that **Two:** He always knew what to say, and **Three:** especially with women.

Which led rather conveniently to **Four:** A happy by-product of his glibness was **Five:** he'd never insulted a woman in his life, not unless she truly deserved it, which **Six:** this woman didn't. Which meant that **Seven:** He needed to apologize and **Eight:** He had no idea how to do so.

A facility with apologies would depend upon a propensity to behave in a manner requiring them. Which he did not. It was one of the few things in his life of which he was inordinately proud.

But this brought him back to **Nine:** He had no idea what to say, and **Ten:** Something about this girl had turned him absolutely stupid.

Stupid.

How did the rest of humanity endure it, this awkward silence in the face of a woman? Sebastian found it intolerable.

"You asked me to kiss you," he said. It wasn't the first thing that came to mind, but it was the second.

From her gasp—which he suspected was large enough to change the tides—he had a feeling he should have waited for the seventh, at least.

"Are you accusing me of—" She cut herself off, her lips clamping together in an angry, frustrated line. "Well, whatever it is . . . that . . . you're accusing me . . ." And then, just when he thought she'd given up, she finished with, "of."

"I'm not accusing you of anything," he said. "I'm merely pointing out that you wanted a kiss, and I obliged and . . ."

And what? What *was* he pointing out? And where had his mind gone? He couldn't think a complete sentence, much less speak one.

"I could have taken advantage of you," he said stiffly. Good God, he sounded like a stick.

"Are you saying you didn't?"

Could she *possibly* be that innocent? He leaned down, his eyes boring into hers. "You have no idea how many ways I *didn't* take advantage of you," he told her. "How many ways I could have done. How many—"

"What?" she snapped. "What?"

He held his tongue, or perhaps more accurately, bit the damned thing off. There was no way he was going to tell her how many ways he'd *wanted* to take advantage of her.

Her. Miss No Name.

It was better that way, certainly.

"Oh for the love of God," he heard himself say. "What the devil is your name?"

"I can see that you're most eager to know it," she snipped.

"Your *name*," he bit off.

"Before you tell me yours?"

He exhaled, a long frustrated whoosh of air, then raked his hand over his scalp. "Was it my imagination, or did we have a perfectly civil conversation not ten minutes earlier?"

She opened her mouth to speak, but he didn't let her. "No, no," he continued, perhaps a little too grandly, "it was quite more than civil. I might even dare to call it pleasant."

Her eyes softened, not to the point where he might have considered her malleable—oh very well, not even *close* to that, but they softened nonetheless.

"I shouldn't have asked you to kiss me," she said.

But he noticed that she did not apologize for it. And he noticed that he was very glad that she did not.

"Surely you understand," she continued quietly, "that it is much more important that I learn your identity than the other way around."

He looked down at her hands. They weren't balled, or fisted, or frozen into claws. Hands always

gave people away. They tensed, or they shook,
or they clutched at each other as if they might—
through some sort of impossible witchcraft—save
themselves from whatever dark fate awaited them.

This girl was holding the fabric of her skirt.
Tightly. She was nervous. Still, she was holding
herself with remarkable dignity. And Sebastian
knew that she spoke the truth. There was nothing she could do that would ruin him, while he,
through one loose or false word, could destroy
her forever. It was not the first time he'd been
inordinately glad not to have been born female,
but it was the first time he'd been presented with
such clear proof that men truly did have it easier.

"My name is Sebastian Grey," he said, dipping
his head toward her in a respectful bow. "I am
very pleased to make your acquaintance, Miss—"

But he couldn't possibly have gone on, because
she gasped, then blanched, then looked positively ill.

"I assure you," he said, not certain whether the
sharp note in his voice was amusement or irritation, "that my reputation is not as black as that."

"I shouldn't be here with you," she said frantically.

"That, we already knew."

"Sebastian Grey. Oh dear God, *Sebastian Grey.*"

He watched with some interest. Some annoyance, too, but that was to be expected. Really, he
wasn't as bad as all *that*. "I assure you," he said,
starting to feel a bit put out by the number of
times he was needing to begin his sentences in
such a fashion, "I have no intention of allowing

your reputation to be destroyed through your association with me."

"No, of course not," she said, then ruined the whole thing with a panicked burst of laughter. "You wouldn't want to do that. Sebastian Grey." She looked up at the sky, and he half expected her to shake her fist at the gods. "Sebastian Grey," she said. *Again.*

"Do I take this to mean you've been warned about me?"

"Oh yes," came her too-fast reply. And then she snapped back to attention, looking him directly in the eye. "I have to go. Now."

"As you might recall I've been telling you," he murmured.

She looked toward the side garden, grimacing at the thought of passing through a lovers' lawn. "Head down," she said to herself. "Barrel through."

"Some live their entire lives by that motto," he said cheerfully.

She looked at him sharply, clearly wondering if he'd gone mad in the last two seconds. He shrugged, unwilling to apologize. He was finally beginning to feel like himself again. He had every right to feel cheerful.

"Do you?" she asked.

"Absolutely not. I prefer life to have a bit more style. It's all about the subtleties, don't you think?"

She stared at him. Blinked a few times. Then said, "I should go."

And she went. She put her head down and barreled through.

Without telling him her name.

Chapter Six

The following afternoon

"You're terribly quiet today," Louisa said.

Annabel smiled weakly at her cousin. They were walking Louisa's dog in Hyde Park, accompanied—theoretically—by Louisa's aunt. But Lady Cosgrove had come across one of her many acquaintances, and while she was still in sight, she was no longer in earshot.

"I'm only tired," Annabel said. "I had difficulty sleeping after all the excitement of the party." It wasn't the whole truth, but neither was it a lie. She'd lain awake for hours the night before, making elaborate studies of the insides of her eyelids.

She refused to stare at the ceiling. On principle. She'd always felt that way. In the quest for sleep, open eyes were a clear admission of defeat.

Still, no matter where she looked, it was impossible to escape the magnitude of what she'd done.

Sebastian Grey.
Sebastian Grey.
The words rang like a miserable moan in her head. On the list of men she ought not to be kissing, he had to rank at the top, along with the King, Lord Liverpool, and the chimney sweep.

And frankly, she suspected he was higher up the list than the chimney sweep.

She hadn't known very much about Mr. Grey before the Trowbridge party, just that he was Lord Newbury's heir, and the two men did not tolerate each other's company. But once word had got out that Lord Newbury was pursuing her, everyone seemed to have something to tell her about the earl and his nephew.

Oh very well, not everyone, since most of society wasn't the least bit interested in her, but everyone *she* knew had an opinion.

He was handsome. (The nephew, not the earl.)
He was a rogue. (Again, the nephew.)
He was probably penniless and spent a great deal of time with his cousins on the other side of his family. (Definitely the nephew, and in fact, it had better be the nephew, because if Annabel married Lord Newbury and he turned out to be penniless, she was going to be *livid*.)

Annabel had left the ball straightaway after the disastrous interlude on the heath, but apparently Mr. Grey had not. He must have made quite an impression on Louisa, because this morning, good heavens, it was all she could talk about.

Mr. Grey this, and Mr. Grey that, and how was it possible that Annabel hadn't seen him at the party? Annabel had shrugged and made some sort of *I can't imagine* type of comment, but it didn't matter because Louisa was still nattering on about his smile and his eyes which were *gray* and oh wasn't it just the most marvelous coincidence and oh yes, everyone had noticed that he departed on the arm of a married woman!

This last bit did not surprise Annabel. He'd told her quite plainly that he'd been cavorting with a married woman before she'd tripped over him.

But Annabel had a feeling that this was a *different* married woman. The one on the blanket had been careful of her reputation, departing the scene well before Mr. Grey. No one who practiced such discretion would be so brazen as to leave on his arm. Which meant it had to be someone else, which meant he'd been with *two* married women. Good heavens, he was even worse than people said.

Annabel pressed her fingers to her temples. No wonder her head hurt. She was thinking too hard. Too hard, and about items too frivolous. If she had to develop an obsession, couldn't it be about something worthwhile? The new Cruel and Improper Treatment of Cattle Act would have done nicely. Or the plight of the poor. Her grandfather had been ranting about both this week, so Annabel had no excuse for not developing an interest.

"Is your head bothering you?" Louisa asked. But she wasn't paying much attention. Frederick, her ridiculously fat basset hound, had spotted a fellow canine in the distance and was yanking on the lead. "Frederick!" she yelped, tripping a step or two before she found her footing.

Frederick stopped, although it wasn't clear if it was due to Louisa's hold on the lead or outright exhaustion. He let out a huge sigh, and frankly, Annabel was surprised that he didn't collapse on the ground.

"I think someone has been sneaking him sausages again," Louisa grumbled.

Annabel looked elsewhere.

"Annabel!"

"He looked so *hungry*," Annabel insisted.

Louisa motioned toward her dog, whose belly slid along the grass. "*That* looks hungry?"

"His eyes looked hungry."

Louisa gave her a skeptical look.

"Your dog is a very good liar."

Louisa shook her head. She was probably rolling her eyes, too, but Annabel was watching Frederick, who was letting out a bored yawn.

"He'd be quite good at cards," Annabel said absently. "If he could speak. Or had thumbs."

Louisa gave her another one of those looks. She was very good at them, Annabel thought, even if she saved them for family.

"He'd win against *you*," Annabel said.

"That's hardly a compliment," Louisa answered.

It was true. Louisa was abysmal at cards. Annabel had tried everything—piquet, whist, *vingt-et-un*. For someone who was so good at keeping every emotion off her face in public, Louisa was dreadful when it came to games. Still, they played, mostly because Louisa was so bad it made it fun.

She was a good sport, Louisa.

Annabel looked down at Frederick, who had,

after about thirty seconds of standing in place, plopped his bottom down on the grass. "I miss my dog," she said.

Louisa looked over her shoulder toward her aunt, who was still engrossed in conversation. "What was his name again?"

"Mouse."

"That was very unkind of you."

"Naming him Mouse?"

"Isn't he a greyhound?"

"I could have named him Turtle."

"Frederick!" Louisa yelped, rushing forward to remove something—in all honesty, Annabel preferred not to know what—from his mouth.

"It's better than Frederick," Annabel said "Good heavens, that's my brother's name."

"Let go, Frederick," Louisa muttered. Then, still grabbing at whatever was in his mouth, she looked back over at Annabel. "He deserves a dignified name."

"Because he's such a dignified dog."

Louisa raised a brow, looking every inch a duke's daughter. "Dogs deserve proper names."

"Cats, too?"

Louisa let out a dismissive *pfft.* "Cats are entirely different. They catch *mice.*"

Annabel opened her mouth to ask how, exactly, that pertained to proper names, but before she made a sound, Louisa grabbed her forearm, hissing her name.

"Ow." Annabel reached down and tried to pry Louisa's fingers loose. "What is it?"

"Over there," Louisa whispered urgently. Her

head jerked toward the left, but in a way that said she was trying to be discreet. Except she wasn't. At all. *"Sebastian Grey,"* Louisa finally hissed.

Annabel had heard the hearts-dropping-to-the-stomach expression before, and she'd said it, too, but this was the first time she actually understood it. Her entire body felt wrong, as if her heart was in her stomach and her lungs were in her ears, and her brain was somewhere east of France.

"Let's go," she said. "Please."

Louisa looked surprised. "You don't want to meet him?"

"No." Annabel didn't care that she sounded desperate. She just wanted to be gone.

"You're joking, aren't you? You must be curious."

"I'm not. I assure you. I mean, yes, of course I am, but if I am going to meet this man, I don't want to do it like this."

Louisa blinked a few times. "Like what?"

"I'm just—I'm not prepared. I—"

"I suppose you're right," Louisa said thoughtfully.

Thank God.

"He will probably think you have loyalties toward his uncle and will prejudge you accordingly."

"Exactly," Annabel said, latching onto this like a lifesaver.

"Or he'll try to talk you out of it."

Annabel cast a nervous glance toward the spot where Louisa had seen Mr. Grey. Subtly, of course, and without actually turning around. If she could just escape before he saw her . . .

"Of course, I think you *should* be talked out of it," Louisa continued. "I don't care how much money Lord Newbury has, no young lady should be forced to—"

"I haven't agreed to anything yet," Annabel practically cried. "Please, may we just *go*?"

"We have to wait for my aunt," Louisa said, frowning. "Did you see where she went?"

"*Louisa.*"

"What is *wrong* with you?"

Annabel looked down. Her hands were shaking. She couldn't do this. Not yet. She couldn't face the man she'd kissed who happened to be the heir to the man she didn't want to kiss but whom she probably was going to marry. Oh yes, and she could not forget that if she did marry the man she didn't want to kiss, she was likely to provide him with a new heir, thus cutting off the man she did want to kiss.

Oh, he was *really* going to like her.

She was going to have to be introduced to Mr. Grey eventually, there was no avoiding it. But did it have to be now? Surely she deserved a little time to prepare.

She hadn't thought she was such a coward. No, she wasn't a coward. Any sane person would flee in such a situation, and probably half of the mad ones, as well.

"Annabel," Louisa said, her voice sounding exasperated. "Why is it so important that we leave?"

Annabel tried to think of a reason. She really did. But there was only the truth, which she was not prepared to share, so instead she stood there dumbly, wondering how on earth she was going to get out of this fix.

But alas, that particular moment of panic was brief. To be replaced by a far, far more horrific moment of panic. Because it soon became apparent that she *wasn't* going to get out of the fix. The lady on Mr. Grey's arm appeared to have recognized Louisa, and Louisa had already waved in greeting.

"Louisa," Annabel hissed.

"I can't ignore her," Louisa whispered back. "It's Lady Olivia Valentine. Her father is the Earl of Rudland. Mr. Grey's cousin married her last year."

Annabel groaned.

"I thought she was out of town," Louisa said with a frown. "She must have just got back." Then she turned to Annabel with an earnest expression. "Don't be fooled by her appearance. She's very kind."

Annabel didn't know whether to be horrified or confused. Don't be fooled by her appearance? What was that supposed to mean?

"She's quite beautiful," Louisa explained.

"What does—"

"No, I mean—" Louisa cut herself off, clearly dissatisfied with her ability to convey the extent of Lady Valentine's charms. "You'll have to see for yourself."

Thankfully, the staggeringly beautiful Lady Olivia didn't appear to be walking very quickly. Still Annabel judged that she had no more than fifteen seconds before the two parties intersected. She grabbed Louisa's arm. "Don't tell them about Lord Newbury," she hissed.

Louisa's eyes widened with astonishment. "Don't you think they'll already know?"

"I don't know. Maybe not. I don't think everybody knows yet."

"Of course not, but if anyone does, don't you think it would be Mr. Grey?"

"Maybe not by name. Everyone refers to me as 'that Vickers girl.' "

It was true. Annabel was being brought out by Lord and Lady Vickers, and no one had ever heard of her father's family, which, her grandfather was quick to point out, was how it should be. In his opinion, his daughter would have been far better off if she'd never become a Winslow.

Louisa frowned nervously. "I'm sure they know that I'm a Vickers grandchild as well."

Annabel grasped Louisa's hand in full panic. "Then don't tell them I'm your cousin."

"I can't do that!"

"Why not?"

Louisa blinked. "I don't know. But it can't possibly be proper."

"Hang proper. Just do this for me, please."

"Very well. But I still think you've gone a bit strange."

Annabel could not argue. She'd gone quite a few things in the last day, and really, *strange* was the least of it.

Chapter Seven

Five minutes earlier

"It's really too bad you married my cousin," Sebastian murmured, steering Olivia away from an enormous pile of horse dung that someone had failed to clean up. "I think you might be the perfect woman."

Olivia glanced over at him with a perfectly arched eyebrow. "Because I allow you to eat breakfast at my house every morning?"

"Ah, you couldn't have put an end to that," Seb replied, giving her a twist of a smile. "The habit was far too entrenched before you entered the scene."

"Because I didn't scold you for the three dozen dart holes on the back of the guest-bedroom door?"

"All Edward's fault. I have perfect aim."

"Still, Sebastian, it's a *leased* house."

"I know, I know. Odd that you kept it this year. Don't you want to be a bit farther from your parents?"

When Olivia had married Sebastian's cousin Harry, she had moved into his home, which was directly next door to her family's London house. They had conducted half of their courtship through their windows. Sebastian found the story rather charming.

"I like my parents," Olivia said.

Sebastian shook his head. "A concept so alien I think it must be unpatriotic."

Olivia turned to him with some surprise. "I know that Harry's parents were—" She gave her head a little shake. "Well, never mind. But I hadn't thought that yours were so dreadful."

"They're not. But I wouldn't *choose* to spend time with them." Sebastian considered this. "Especially my father. As he's dead."

Olivia rolled her eyes. "There must be something in that statement that will get you banned from church."

"It's too late for that," Seb murmured.

"I think you need a wife," Olivia said, turning to him with strategically narrowed eyes.

"You are in danger of losing your status as the perfect woman," he warned.

"You never did tell me what I had done to earn it."

"First and foremost was your heretofore restraint at nagging me about marrying."

"I shan't apologize."

He nodded in acknowledgment. "But there is also your sublime penchant for not being shocked at anything I say."

"Oh, I'm shocked," Olivia said. "I just hide it well."

"Just as good," Seb told her.

They walked for a few moments, and then she said it again. "You *should* marry, you know."

"Have I given any indication that I'm avoiding it?"

"Well," Olivia said slowly, "you haven't taken a wife . . ."

"Merely because I haven't found the perfect woman." He gave her a bland smile. "Alas, Harry got to you first."

"Not to mention that you'll do better if you marry before your uncle begets himself another heir."

Sebastian turned to her with perfectly feigned shock. "Why, Olivia Valentine, that is positively mercenary of you."

"It's true."

"I'm such a gamble," Sebastian said with a sigh.

"You are!" Olivia exclaimed, with enough excitement that he thought he might be frightened. "That is exactly what you are! You are a gamble. A risk. A—"

"You overwhelm me with compliments."

Olivia ignored him. "Trust me when I tell you that all of the young ladies would prefer you to your uncle."

"Again, the compliments."

"But if he gets an heir, you get nothing. So do they take a risk with you? The handsome rogue who might inherit or the portly earl who already has the title?"

"That is about as kind a description as I have ever heard applied to my uncle."

"Many would choose the bird in hand, but others would think, 'If I bide my time, I could have the handsome rogue *and* the title.'"

"You make your gender sound so appealing."

Olivia shrugged. "We can't all marry for love." And then, just when he'd decided this ought to depress him, she patted his arm and said, "But you should. You're far too lovely not to."

"And again, I am convinced," Seb murmured. "The perfect woman."

Olivia gave him a sickly smile.

"Do tell," Sebastian said, steering her away from another disgusting pile, this time of the canine variety, "where is the perfect woman's perfect husband? Or in other words, why did you require my services this fine morning? Other than to hone your matchmaking skills, of course."

"Harry is deep in his current project. He won't see the light of day for a week at least, and I"— she patted her belly, just rounded enough to indicate her pregnancy—"needed air."

"Still working on the Sarah Gorely novels?" he asked casually.

Olivia opened her mouth to speak, but before she could make a sound, the air was cracked by the sound of gunshot.

"What the hell was that?" Sebastian almost yelled. Good Lord, they were in the bloody *park*. He looked around him, aware that his head was jerking back and forth like some half-mad horizontal jack-in-the-box. But his heart was pounding, and the damned sound of the shot was still echoing in his head, and—

"Sebastian," Olivia said gently. And then: "*Sebastian*."

"What?"

"My arm," she said.

He saw her swallow, then looked down. He was clutching her forearm with a ferocious grip. He let go immediately. "Sorry," he mumbled. "I didn't realize."

She smiled weakly and rubbed the spot with her other hand. "It's nothing."

It wasn't nothing, but he didn't want to go into it. "Who is shooting in the park?" he asked irritably.

"I believe there is some sort of competition," Olivia said. "Edward mentioned it to me this morning."

Sebastian shook his head. A shooting competition in Hyde Park. Right during the busiest time of the day. The foolishness of his fellow man never ceased to amaze him.

"Are you all right?" Olivia asked.

He turned, wondering what she thought she was talking about.

"The noise," she clarified.

"It's nothing."

"It's not—"

"It's nothing," he said curtly. And then, because he felt like an ass for using such a tone of voice, he added, "I was taken by surprise."

It was true. He could sit and listen to guns exploding all day as long as he knew it was coming. Hell, he could probably sleep through the cacophony, assuming he was able to fall asleep in the first place. It was just when he wasn't expecting it. He *hated* being taken by surprise.

That, he thought dryly, had been *his* job. *Señor Sniper.* Death by surprise.

Señor Sniper. Hmmm. Maybe he should take up Spanish.

"Sebastian?"

He looked over at Olivia, who was still regarding him with some concern. He wondered if Harry had reactions like these, too; if his heart raced like a rabbit at unexpected noises. Harry hadn't said anything, but then again, Seb hadn't, either.

It was a stupid thing to talk about.

"I'm fine," he said to Olivia, this time in a considerably more typical tone of voice. "As I said, it was just the surprise of it."

Another gunshot cracked in the distance, and Seb didn't even flinch. "See?" he said. "Nothing to it. Now then, what were we talking about?"

"I have no idea," Olivia admitted.

Seb thought for a moment. He didn't remember, either.

"Oh, the Gorely books," Olivia exclaimed. "You had asked about Harry's work on them."

"Right." Funny that he'd forget that. "How is it coming along?"

"Quite well, I think." Olivia gave a little shrug.

"He complains all the time, but I think he secretly adores them."

Sebastian perked up. "Really?"

"Well, perhaps not *adores*. He still thinks they're dreadful. But he adores translating them. It's ever so much more fun than the War Office documents were."

Not the most ringing of endorsements, but Seb could not take offense. "Perhaps Harry ought to turn them into French when he's done."

Olivia frowned thoughtfully. "Perhaps he will. I don't know that he's ever taken something and translated it into two separate languages. I imagine he'd enjoy the challenge."

"He does have a ferociously mathematical brain," Sebastian murmured.

"I know." Olivia shook her head. "It's a wonder we have anything to talk about. I—Oh! Don't look now, but someone is pointing at you."

"Female, I hope?"

Olivia rolled her eyes. "They're always female, Sebastian. It's"—she squinted—"Lady Louisa McCann, I think."

"Who?"

"The Duke of Fenniwick's daughter. She's very sweet."

Sebastian thought for a moment. "The thin one who doesn't say much?"

"You have such a way with words."

Seb smiled slowly. "I do, don't I?"

"Don't scare her, Sebastian," Olivia admonished.

He turned to her with not entirely unfeigned indignation. "Scare her? Me?"

"Your charm can be terrifying."

"I suppose if you put it that way I cannot help but be complimented."

Olivia gave him a dry smile.

"May I look now?" he inquired. Because it was starting to grow tedious, this pretending not to know he was being pointed at.

"Hmm? Oh yes, I've already waved. I don't know the other one, though."

Sebastian hadn't had his back to the approaching pair, so he only needed to do a quarter turn to face them. Still, he was extremely glad that this movement turned him away from Olivia, because when he saw who was walking toward him—

He liked to consider himself a master at maintaining his unflappable façade, but even he had his limits.

"Do you know her?" Olivia asked.

Sebastian shook his head as he watched her, his curly-haired goddess with the gorgeous pink mouth. "Not at all," he murmured.

"She must be new," Olivia said with a slight shrug. She waited patiently for the two ladies to finish crossing the distance, then smiled. "Ah, Lady Louisa, it is so good to see you again."

Lady Louisa returned the greeting, but Sebastian wasn't paying attention. He was far more interested in watching the other one studiously trying to avoid eye contact with him.

He kept his own gaze on her face, just to make it all that more difficult.

"Have you met my dear cousin, Mr. Grey?" Olivia said to Lady Louisa.

"Er, I believe we have been introduced," Lady Louisa responded.

"It's silly of me to even ask," Olivia said. She turned to Sebastian with a hint of sly mischief in her eyes. "You've been introduced to everyone, haven't you, Sebastian?"

"Almost," he said dryly.

"Oh, do forgive me," Lady Louisa said. "May I present my, er—" She coughed. "Excuse me. Sorry. It must have been dust in my throat." She motioned to the woman at her side. "Lady Olivia, Mr. Grey, this is Miss Winslow."

"Miss Winslow," Olivia said. "How nice to meet you. Are you new to town?"

Miss Winslow bobbed a polite curtsy. "I am. Thank you for asking."

Sebastian smiled and murmured her name, and then, because he knew it would befuddle her, took her hand and kissed it. It was at times like these he was rather grateful for his reputation. Olivia wouldn't think twice about his flirtatiousness.

Miss Winslow, however, colored the most charming shade of pink. She was even more fetching by the light of day, he decided. Her eyes were a very nice shade of greenish gray. Combined with the rest of her coloring, it almost made her look a bit Spanish. And he rather liked the smattering of freckles across the bridge of her nose. She would have looked far too sultry without them.

He also approved of her emerald-green walking costume. It suited her far better than whatever pastel she'd been wearing the night before.

But he could not allow his perusal to last over-long. She might read too much into it, and besides, he mustn't ignore her friend. He turned away from Miss Winslow without even a pretense of lingering. "Lady Louisa," he said with a polite bow of his head. "How lovely to see you again. I am bereft that our paths have not crossed thus far this season."

"It does seem to be an uncommonly large crowd this year," Olivia said. "Did no one decide to skip?" She turned to Lady Louisa. "I've been away for several weeks, so I'm hopelessly out of date."

"Were you in the country?" Lady Louisa asked politely.

"Yes, in Hampshire. My husband had some important work, and he finds it difficult to concentrate in town."

"My fault," Sebastian chimed in.

"Note that I do not contradict," Olivia said lightly. She motioned toward him with a tilt of her head. "He's terribly distracting."

Sebastian could not let that pass. "It's one of my finest attributes."

"Pay attention to nothing he says," Olivia said with a shake of her head. She turned back to the young ladies and began to chatter on about something or another, and Sebastian was left with the most unfamiliar sense of irritation. He could not begin to count the number of times Olivia had made a comment like *Pay attention to nothing he says.*

This was, however, the first time that it bothered him.

"Are you enjoying your time in London, Miss Winslow?" Olivia asked.

Sebastian turned to Miss Winslow and regarded her with a bland smile. He was most interested in her answer.

"Er, yes," Miss Winslow stammered. "It is most diverting."

"Diverting," Sebastian murmured. "What an interesting word."

She looked up at him in alarm. He merely smiled.

"Will you remain in town for the rest of the season, Lady Olivia?" Lady Louisa asked.

"I think so. It depends upon whether my husband is able to concentrate with so many distractions."

"What *is* Sir Harry working on?" Sebastian asked, since Olivia had never got around to telling him which novel Harry was translating. "I tried to pester him this morning, but he waved me off." He looked over at Miss Winslow and Lady Louisa and said, "One would think he didn't like me."

Lady Louisa giggled. Miss Winslow maintained her stony expression.

"My husband is a translator," Olivia told the ladies, dismissing Sebastian with a roll of her eyes. "Right now he is translating a novel into Russian."

"Really?" Miss Winslow asked, and Sebastian had to admit, she sounded sincerely interested. "Which novel?"

"*Miss Truesdale and the Silent Gentleman*. The author is Sarah Gorely. Have you read it?"

Miss Winslow shook her head, but Lady Louisa

practically jumped forward, exclaiming, "No!"

Olivia blinked. "Er . . . yes?"

"No, I meant to say I haven't read it yet," Lady Louisa explained. "I have read all of her others, of course. How could I have missed it?"

"You are a fan, then?" Sebastian asked. He loved when this happened.

"Oh yes," she said. "I thought I had read them all. I cannot begin to tell you how excited I am to know there is one more."

"I must confess, I'm having a difficult time getting through it," Olivia said.

"Really?" Sebastian asked.

Olivia's lips curved into an indulgent smile. "Sebastian is also a huge fan," she said to the other young ladies.

"Of Mrs. Gorely?" Louisa asked. "She has the most fascinating plots."

"If you don't mind the occasionally implausible," Olivia put in.

"But that's what makes them so much fun," Louisa said.

"Why are you having difficulty with *Miss Truesdale*?" Sebastian asked Olivia. He knew he shouldn't press, but he couldn't stop himself. He'd been trying to get her to like his books ever since she'd said that he'd used the word *purview* incorrectly.

Not that she knew that it was he.

And furthermore, *purview* was a ridiculous word. He was planning to ban it from his vocabulary.

Olivia gave one of her uncommonly pretty

shrugs. "It's very slow," she said. "There seems to be an uncommon degree of description."

Sebastian nodded thoughtfully. "I don't think it's Mrs. Gorely's best myself." He'd never been fully satisfied with the final version, although he certainly didn't think it merited Olivia's criticism.

Difficult to get through. Bah.

Olivia wouldn't know a good book if it hit her on the head.

Chapter Eight

It took less than one second for Annabel to realize that Louisa had not been joking about Lady Olivia Valentine and the stunning beauty thereof. When she turned and smiled, Annabel actually had to blink at the brilliance of it. The young matron was breathtakingly gorgeous, all blond and milk-skinned, with high cheekbones and amazingly blue eyes.

It was all Annabel could do not to hate her on principle.

And then, as if the meeting could not get worse (and really, just the simple fact that she and Mr. Grey were meeting was bad enough), he had to go and kiss her hand.

Disaster.

Annabel had been utterly flustered, stammering something that might have passed for a greeting in a preverbal society. She did lift her eyes for a moment, because even she knew that one couldn't spend an entire introduction staring at the ground. But it was a mistake. A huge mistake. Mr. Grey, who had been quite good-looking in the moonlight, was even more heartstoppingly handsome by the light of day.

Good heavens, he ought not to be allowed to promenade with Lady Olivia. The two of them were likely to blind the good people of London with their combined beauty.

Either that or send the rest of humanity sobbing to their beds, because really, who could compete with that?

Annabel tried to follow the conversation, but she was far too distracted by her own panic. And by Mr. Grey's right hand, which was resting lightly against his leg. And by the sly curve of his mouth, which she was trying very hard not to look at, but somehow there it was, right in her peripheral vision. Not to mention the sound of his voice, when he said something about . . . well . . . something.

Books. They were talking about books.

Annabel held silent. She had not read the books in question, and besides, she thought it best to insert herself in the conversation as little as possible. Mr. Grey was still stealing the occasional glance in her direction and it seemed foolish to give him a reason to do so openly.

Of course that was when he turned right at her with those devilish gray eyes and asked, "And what of you, Miss Winslow? Have you read any of the Gorely books?"

"I am afraid not."

"Oh, you must, Annabel," Louisa said excitedly. "You will adore them. We shall go to the book-shop today. I would lend you mine, but they are all back at Fenniwick."

"Do you possess the entire set, Lady Louisa?" Mr. Grey asked.

"Oh, yes. Except for *Miss Truesdale and the Silent Gentleman*, of course. But that shall be rectified immediately." She turned back to Annabel. "What have we on the calendar for this evening? I do hope it is something we may skip. I want nothing more than a cup of tea and my new book."

"I believe we are to attend the opera," Annabel replied. Louisa's family had one of the finest boxes in the theater, and Annabel had been looking forward to attending a performance for weeks.

"Really?" Louisa said, with an utter lack of enthusiasm.

"You'd rather stay home and read?" Mr. Grey asked.

"Oh, definitely. Wouldn't you?"

Annabel regarded her cousin with something between surprise and disbelief. Louisa was normally so shy, and yet here she was, animatedly discussing novels with one of London's most notorious bachelors.

"I suppose it depends on the opera," Mr. Grey said thoughtfully. "And the book."

"*The Magic Flute*," Louisa informed him. "And *Miss Truesdale*."

"*The Magic Flute*?" Lady Olivia exclaimed. "I missed that last year. I shall have to make plans to attend."

"I would take *Miss Truesdale* over *The Marriage of Figaro*," Mr. Grey said, "but perhaps not *The Magic Flute*. There is something so cheering about hell boilething in one's heart."

"Heartwarming, even," Annabel muttered.

"What did you say, Miss Winslow?" he asked.

Annabel swallowed. He was smiling benignly, but she could hear the pointy little jab in his voice, and frankly, it terrified her. She could not enter into a battle with this man and win. Of that she was certain.

"I have never seen *The Magic Flute*," she announced.

"Never?" Lady Olivia said. "But how can that be?"

"Opera is rarely performed in Gloucestershire, I'm afraid."

"You must go see it," Lady Olivia said. "You simply must."

"I was planning to attend this evening," Annabel said. "Lady Louisa's family had invited me."

"But you can't go if she's home reading a book," Lady Olivia finished shrewdly. She turned to Louisa. "You will have to put off Miss Truesdale and her silent gentleman until tomorrow. You cannot allow Miss Winslow to miss the opera."

"Why don't you join us?" Louisa asked.

Annabel thought she might kill her.

"You said you missed it last year," Louisa continued. "We have a large box. It is never full."

Lady Olivia's face lit with delight. "That is most kind of you. I should love to attend."

"And of course you are invited as well, Mr. Grey," Louisa said.

Annabel was definitely going to kill her. By the most painful means imaginable.

"I would be delighted," he said. "But you must allow me to give you a copy of *Miss Truesdale and the Silent Gentleman* in exchange for the honor."

"Thank you," Louisa said, but Annabel could have sworn she sounded disappointed. "That would be—"

"I will have it delivered to your house this afternoon," he continued smoothly, "so that you may begin it right away."

"You are quite beyond thoughtful, Mr. Grey," Louisa murmured. And she blushed. She blushed!

Annabel was aghast.

And jealous, but she preferred not to dwell on that.

"Will there be room for my husband as well?" Lady Olivia asked. "He has turned into a bit of a hermit of late, but I think we may convince him to emerge for the opera. I know that the Queen of the Night's aria is a particular favorite of his."

"All that hell boilething," Mr. Grey said. "Who could resist it?"

"Of course," Louisa replied to Lady Olivia. "I would be honored to meet him. His work sounds fascinating."

"I myself am insanely jealous," Mr. Grey murmured.

"Of Harry?" Lady Olivia asked, turning to him with surprise.

"I can imagine no greater bliss than to lie about, reading novels all day."

"Very good novels at that," Louisa put in.

Lady Olivia chuckled, but she did say, "He does a bit more than read. There is the small matter of the translation."

"*Pfft.*" Mr. Grey dismissed this with a flick of his hand. "A mere trifle."

"To translate into Russian?" Annabel asked dubiously.

He turned to her with an expression that might have been condescending. "I was employing hyperbole."

He'd spoken softly, though, and Annabel did not think that either Louisa or Lady Olivia heard him. They were chatting about something or other and had moved off a bit to the right, leaving Annabel with Mr. Grey. Not alone—not even remotely alone—but it somehow felt like it, nonetheless.

"Have you a given name, Miss Winslow?" he asked softly.

"Annabel," she replied, her voice prim and curt and really rather unpleasant.

"Annabel," he repeated. "I would say that it suits you, except of course, how would I know?"

She clamped her lips together, but her toes were wiggling in her boots.

He smiled wolfishly. "Since we've never met."

Still she kept her mouth shut. She did not trust herself to speak.

This only seemed to amuse him more. He tilted his head in her direction, the very model of a polite English gentleman. "I shall be delighted to see you again this evening."

"Will you?"

He chuckled. "How tart! Positively lemonish of you."

"Lemonish," she said flatly. "Really."

He leaned in. "Why, I wonder, do you dislike me so much?"

Annabel shot a frantic glance at her cousin.

"She can't hear me," he said.

"You don't know that."

He looked over at Louisa and Lady Olivia, who were now kneeling next to Frederick. "They're much too busy with the dog. Although . . ." He frowned. "How Olivia is going to get back to standing in her state is beyond me."

"She'll be fine," Annabel said without thinking.

He turned to her with raised brows.

"She's not far enough along."

"Normally I would assume that such a statement comes from a voice of experience, but as I know that you have no experience, except me, I—"

"I am the oldest of eight," Annabel snapped. "My mother was with child throughout my entire childhood."

"An explanation I had not considered," he admitted. "I hate when that happens."

Annabel wanted to dislike him. She really did. But he was making it difficult, with his lopsided grin and self-effacing charm. "Why did you accept Louisa's invitation to the opera?" she asked.

He looked at her blankly, even though she knew his brain was whirring along at triple speed. "It's the Fenniwick box," he said, as if there could be no other explanation. "I'm not likely to get such a good seat again."

It was true. Louisa's aunt had raved about the location.

"And of course you looked so miserable," he added. "It was hard to resist."

She shot him a dirty look.

"Honesty in all things," he quipped. "It's my new credo."

"New?"

He shrugged. "As of this afternoon, at least."

"And until this evening?"

"Certainly until I reach the opera house," he said with a wicked smile. When she did not return the expression, he added, "Come now, Miss Winslow, surely you are in possession of a sense of humor."

Annabel nearly groaned. There were so many reasons this conversation was not funny she hardly knew where to start. There were so many reasons it was not funny it was almost funny.

"You needn't worry," he said quietly.

She looked up. His face had gone serious. Not dark, not grave, just . . . serious.

"I won't say anything," he said.

Somehow she knew that he was telling the truth. "Thank you."

He leaned over and kissed her hand again. "I do believe that today, Tuesday, is a lovely day to make the acquaintance of a young lady."

"It's Wednesday," she told him.

"Is it? I'm terrible with dates. It's my only flaw."

She really wanted to laugh. But she didn't dare draw attention. Louisa and Lady Olivia were

still chatting away, and the longer they were distracted the better.

"You're smiling," he said.

"No, I'm not."

"You want to. The corners of your mouth are
puckering."

"They are not!"

He gave her a sly grin. "They are now."

He was right, the fiend. He'd managed to make
her laugh—or at least make her smile in the
struggle not to laugh—in under a minute.

Was it any wonder she'd asked him to kiss her?

"Annabel!"

Annabel turned with relief at the sound of
Louisa's voice.

"My aunt is waving us over," Louisa said, and
sure enough, Lady Cosgrove was starting across
the grass at them, looking very stern.

"I expect she doesn't approve of your talking
to me," Mr. Grey said, "although I would think
that Olivia's presence would be enough to make
me palatable."

"I'm not *that* respectable," Lady Olivia said.

Annabel's lips parted in shock.

"She is completely respectable," Louisa hastily
whispered to Annabel. "She's just, oh, never mind."

Once again, everyone knew everything about
everyone else. Except Annabel.

Annabel just sighed. Or not really. She couldn't
sigh in such a close gathering; it would be hopelessly uncouth. But she wanted to sigh. Something inside of her felt like it sighed.

Lady Cosgrove arrived on the scene and immediately took Louisa's arm. "Lady Olivia," she said with a cordial nod. "Mr. Grey."

They returned the greeting, Mr. Grey with a smart bow and Lady Olivia with a curtsy so graceful it ought to be criminal.

"I have invited Lady Olivia and Mr. Grey to join us at the opera tonight," Louisa said.

"Of course," Lady Cosgrove said politely. "Lady Olivia, please do give my regards to your mother. I have not seen her in an age."

"She has had a bit of a cold," Lady Olivia replied, "but she is almost recovered. I am sure she would be delighted if you called upon her."

"Perhaps I shall do that."

Annabel watched the exchange with interest. Lady Cosgrove had not cut Mr. Grey, but she had managed not to speak a word in his direction after first greeting him. It was curious. She had not thought he was such a persona non grata. After all, he was heir to the earldom of Newbury, even if only the heir presumptive.

She would have to ask Louisa about this. When she was done killing her for inviting him to the opera.

Further pleasantries were exchanged, but it was apparent that Lady Cosgrove meant to remove her charges and depart. Not to mention Frederick, who looked as if he'd like to conduct some business in the shrubbery.

"Until this evening, Miss Winslow," Mr. Grey said, leaning over her hand once again.

Annabel tried not to react as the touch of his

lips on her hand sent a tingle up her arm. "Until this evening," she repeated.

And as she watched him stroll away, she could not remember when she had looked forward to anything more.

Chapter Nine

Sebastian was rather surprised by how much he was looking forward to the opera that evening. Not that he wasn't a fan; he was, even if he had now seen *The Magic Flute* enough times to recite both of the Queen of the Night's arias from memory.

Another item to add to his list of useless talents.

He wasn't quite sure why the theatrical companies of Great Britain kept insisting upon performing the same opera over and over again. He supposed it was for the benefit of the scores of Englishmen too stubborn to learn a foreign language. It was easier, in Seb's opinion, to follow along with a comedy than a tragedy. Or at the very least, know when to laugh.

But as much as he wanted to see the opera from the exalted position of the Fenniwick box, he wanted to see *her* more.

Miss Winslow.

Miss Annabel Winslow.

Annabel.

He liked that name. There was something bucolic about it, something that smelled clean, like grass.

He did not know many women who would find such a comparison complimentary, but somehow he suspected Miss Winslow would.

Other than that, he knew little about her, save for the fact that she'd befriended the daughter of a duke. It was a smart move for any young lady looking to elevate herself in the ranks of society, but Miss Winslow and Lady Louisa had seemed truly to enjoy each other's company.

Another point in Miss Winslow's favor. Sebastian never could abide those who faked friendship to advance their position.

He also knew that she had an unwanted suitor. This was nothing out of the ordinary; most young ladies of acceptable looks and/or fortune had an unwanted suitor or two. What *was* interesting was that she had actually fled the party to avoid the man. It could mean that he was particularly heinous.

Or that she was given to foolish behavior.

Or that said suitor had made an unwanted advance.

Or that she had overreacted.

Sebastian considered the options as he rode to the opera house. If he were writing the story (and he did not discount the possibility that someday he might; it *did* sound like something out of a Gorely novel), how would *he* do it?

The suitor would have to be dreadful. Very rich, perhaps with a title—someone who could exert pressure on her poor, penniless family. Not that he had the slightest clue if Miss Winslow's family was poor and penniless, but it did make for a better plot that way.

He would have attacked her in a darkened corner, away from the party. No, that wouldn't do. It would be too early in the novel for such drama, and probably too lurid for his audience. His readers did not actually want to see a woman fending off an unwanted advance; they only wanted to read about people gossiping about it after the fact.

Or at least that was what his publisher told him.

Very well, if she hadn't been attacked, then perhaps she had been blackmailed. Sebastian felt himself perk up. Blackmail was *always* a good story element. He used it almost every time.

"Guv!"

Sebastian blinked and looked up. He hadn't even realized that he'd arrived at the opera house. He'd taken a hired hack, unpleasant though it was. He did not keep a carriage of his own, and he'd told Olivia that she and Harry need not pick him up on their way. Better to give the not-quite-newlyweds some time alone.

Harry would thank him for it later, Seb was sure.

Sebastian hopped down, paid the driver, and made his way inside. He was a bit early, but there were already quite a few people milling about, seeing and being seen in their glittered finery.

He made his way slowly through the crowd, chatting with acquaintances, smiling, as he always did, at the young ladies who least expected it. The evening was promising all sorts of delight, and then, just when he'd almost made it across to the stairs—

His uncle.

Sebastian stiffened, barely suppressing his groan. He did not know why he was surprised; it made perfect sense that the Earl of Newbury would be attending the opera, especially if he was on the prowl for a new wife. Still, he had been in such a good mood. It seemed almost criminal that his uncle should be here to spoil it.

Normally, he'd have changed his course so as to avoid him. Seb was no coward, but really, why go out of one's way to encounter unpleasantness?

Unfortunately, there was no escaping him this time. Newbury had seen Sebastian, and Sebastian knew he knew that he'd seen him, too. More to the point, about four other gentlemen had seen them see each other, and while Seb did not consider himself a coward for staying out of Newbury's way, he was aware that others might.

He was not so deluded as to think that he did not care for the good opinion of others. He'd be damned if he was going to allow half of London to whisper that he was afraid of his uncle.

And so, since avoidance was not possible, he employed tactics of the opposite pole, and made sure his path led right to Newbury's side.

"Uncle," he said, pausing briefly to acknowledge him.

His uncle scowled, but he was clearly so surprised by the direct hit that he did not have time to plan a scathing retort. Instead he gave a curt nod accompanied by a grunt, since he was obviously unable to make his mouth form Sebastian's name.

"Delightful to see you as always," Sebastian said with a broad smile. "I had not realized you enjoyed music." And then, before Newbury could do anything more than grind his teeth, he gave a nod of farewell and walked away.

All in all, a successful encounter. Which would be made only better once the earl realized his nephew was sitting in the Fenniwick box. Newbury was a horrible snob and would certainly be furious that Sebastian was sitting in a better location.

Which hadn't been his intention in accepting Lady Louisa's invitation, but really, who was he to argue with an unexpected boon?

When Sebastian reached the box, he saw that Lady Louisa and Miss Winslow had already arrived, along with the Ladies Cosgrove and Wimbledon, who, if his memory served, were sisters to the Duke of Fenniwick. Who was not present, despite his name being the one attached to the box.

Sebastian noted that Lady Louisa was flanked by both aunts. Miss Winslow, on the other hand, had been left out to dry, seated in the front row by herself. Undoubtedly, Ladies C and W were acting to protect their charge from his insidious influence.

He smiled. All the better to influence Miss Winslow, who, he could not help but notice, looked positively delicious in her apple-green gown.

"Mr. Grey!" Lady Louisa cried out in greeting.

He bowed. "Lady Louisa, Lady Cosgrove, Lady Wimbledon." And then, turning slightly, and smiling differently: "Miss Winslow."

"Mr. Grey," she said. Her cheeks went a bit pink, barely noticeable in the evening candlelight. But it was enough to make him smile inside.

Sebastian surveyed the seat selection and was instantly glad that he had chosen to come early and alone. His options were up front with Miss Winslow, the final seat in the middle next to the frowning Lady Wimbledon, or in the back, awaiting whomever else might arrive.

"I cannot allow Miss Winslow to sit by herself," he announced, and promptly took a seat next to her.

"Mr. Grey," she said again. "I thought your cousins were planning to attend as well."

"They are. But it was not convenient for them to pick me up en route." He turned in his seat to include Lady Louisa in the conversation. "As I am not precisely en route."

"That was very kind of you not to insist upon it," Lady Louisa said.

"Kindness had nothing to do with it," he lied. "They would have insisted upon sending the carriage for me before they alighted, and I would have had to be ready a full hour earlier."

Lady Louisa chuckled, and then, as if the thought had burst quite suddenly into her mind, said, "Oh! I must thank you for the book."

"It was my pleasure," he murmured.

"What book?" one of the aunts asked.

"I would have sent one to you, too," he said to Miss Winslow while Lady Louisa conferred with her aunt, "but I did not know your address."

Miss Winslow swallowed uncomfortably and said, "Er, that is quite all right. I'm sure I may read Lady Louisa's when she is done."

"Oh no," Lady Louisa said, leaning forward. "I shall never lend this one out. It is signed by the author."

"Signed by the author?" Lady Cosgrove exclaimed. "However did you find an autographed copy?"

Seb shrugged. "I stumbled upon it last year. I thought Lady Louisa might enjoy it."

"Oh, I do," she said earnestly. "It is truly one of the most thoughtful gifts I have ever received."

"You must allow me to see it," Lady Wimbledon said to Lady Louisa. "Mrs. Gorely is one of my very favorite authors. Such imagination!"

Seb wondered just how many signed Gorely books he might believably have stumbled upon. Clearly this was a better gift than anything else he could afford. He decided he'd better lay the foundation for his story now:

"I found a complete autographed set at a bookshop last autumn," he said, rather pleased with his inventiveness. He now had three more opportunities for autographed gifts. Who knew when they might come in handy?

"I really cannot ask you to break up the set," Lady Louisa murmured, *clearly* hoping that he would tell her it was no bother.

"It's no bother," he assured her. "It is the least I

can do in exchange for such a wonderful seat for the opera." He took this opportunity to engage Miss Winslow in the conversation. "You are very fortunate to sit here for your first opera."

"I am looking forward to it," she said.

"Enough so that you don't mind sitting next to me?" he said in a low voice.

He saw her try not to smile. "Indeed."

"I am told I am quite charming," he told her.

"Are you?"

"Charming?"

"No." She tried again not to smile. "Told that you are so."

"Ah. Occasionally. Not by my family, of course."

This time she did smile. Sebastian was absurdly pleased.

"Naturally, I live to pester them," he said.

She laughed. "You must not be the eldest child."

"Why would you say that?"

"Because we hate pestering."

"Oh we do?"

She blinked with surprise. "You *are* the oldest?"

"Only, I'm afraid. Such a disappointment for my parents."

"Ah, well, that explains it."

A parry he could not resist. "Pray tell."

She turned to him, clearly engaged in the conversation. Her expression was perhaps a touch supercilious, but he found he liked a crafty look in her eye.

"Well," she said, officiously enough so that if he hadn't known she was the eldest child before, he would have been certain of it now. "As an only child you would have grown up bereft of company, and thus never have learned how to properly interact with your peers."

"I did go to school," he said mildly.

She waved this off. "Nevertheless."

He waited a moment, and then echoed, "Nevertheless?"

She blinked.

"Surely there is more to your argument."

She thought about that for a moment. "No."

He waited a moment again, and this time she added, "Need there be?"

"Apparently not, if you are the eldest child and large enough to beat your siblings to a pulp."

Her eyes widened, and then she burst out laughing, a lovely, throaty sound that wasn't musical in the least. She did not laugh delicately, Miss Winslow.

He loved it.

"I beat no one who did not deserve it," she told him, once she'd regained her composure.

He felt himself chuckling along with her. "But Miss Winslow," he said, affecting an earnest expression, "we have only just met. How can I trust your judgment in such a matter?"

She gave him a wicked grin. "You can't."

Sebastian's heart lurched dangerously. He couldn't seem to take his eyes off the corner of her mouth, that little spot where her skin dimpled and turned up. She had wonderful lips, full and pink, and he rather thought he'd like to kiss them again, now that he'd had a chance to see her by the light of day. He wondered if it would feel different, having a perfectly colored portrait of her in his mind as he kissed her.

He wondered if it would feel different, knowing her name.

He tilted his head, as if the motion might bring her into sharper focus. It did, somehow, and he realized that yes, it would feel different.

Better.

He was saved from having to ponder the meaning of this by the appearance of his cousins. Harry and Olivia arrived with pink cheeks and slightly mussed hair, and after greetings were exchanged all around, the not-quite-newlyweds took seats in the back row.

Sebastian settled happily into his seat. It wasn't as if he was alone with Miss Winslow; there were six others in the box, not to mention hundreds below in the opera house, but they were alone in their row, and for now, it felt like enough.

He turned to look at her. She was peering out over the edge of the box, her eyes alight with excitement. Sebastian tried to remember the last time he'd felt such anticipation. He'd been in London since his return from the war, and this—the parties, the operas, the liaisons—had all become routine. He enjoyed it all, of course, but he did not think he could say that there was anything he truly *anticipated*.

She turned, then. Looked at him and smiled.

Until now.

Chapter Ten

$\mathscr{A}$nnabel's breath caught as the lights of the Royal Opera House dimmed. She'd been looking forward to this night since she'd arrived in town, could hardly wait to relate all the details in a long missive to her sisters back home. But now, as the curtains lifted to reveal a strangely barren set, she realized that she didn't just want this performance to be breathtaking, she *needed* it.

Because if it wasn't amazing, if it wasn't everything she'd dreamed of, it was not going to distract her from the gentleman in the seat next to her, whose every movement seemed to somehow disrupt the air just enough to make her skin tingle.

He didn't even have to touch her and she tingled. This was very, very bad news.

"Are you familiar with the story?" came a warm voice in her ear.

Annabel nodded, even though she had only a

cursory knowledge of the libretto. Her program had contained a synopsis, which Louisa had told her was mandatory for anyone who did not understand German, but Annabel had not had time to read it carefully before Mr. Grey had arrived. "I know a little," she whispered. "Some."

"That is Tamino," he said, pointing to the young man who had entered the stage. "Our hero."

Annabel started to nod, then gasped as a monstrous serpent took the stage, writhing and hissing. "How did they *make* that?" she could not help but murmur.

But before Mr. Grey could offer an opinion, Tamino fainted with fear.

"I've never found him very heroic myself," Mr. Grey said.

She glanced over at him.

He gave a little one-shouldered shrug. "A hero really shouldn't swoon on the first page."

"The first page?"

"The first scene," he amended.

Annabel was inclined to agree. She was far more interested in the odd feather-coated man who had arrived on the scene, along with three ladies who promptly killed the snake. "No cowards they," she murmured to herself.

Beside her she heard Mr. Grey smile. She *heard* him smile. How that was possible she did not know, but when she stole a glance at his profile, she saw it was true. He was watching the singers, his chin slightly lifted as he gazed over the crowd below, and his lips were curved into a small smile of kinship.

Annabel drew in a breath. Here in the half-light of the theater, she was reminded of how she'd first seen him, on the darkened heath. Had that been only one night earlier? It seemed strange that a mere twenty-four hours had passed since their accidental meeting. She felt different inside, changed far more than one day ought to allow.

She let her eyes fall on his lips. His smile had melted away, and now he looked intent, concentrating on the unfolding drama. And then—

He turned.

She almost looked away. But she didn't. She smiled. Just a little.

He smiled back.

She moved her hands against her belly, which was doing all sorts of strange flips and wiggles. She should not be flirting with this man. It was a dangerous game that could go nowhere, and she knew better, truly she did. But she couldn't seem to help herself. There was something so compelling, so infectious about him. He was her personal pied piper, and when she was near him, she felt . . .

She felt different. Special. As if she might possibly exist for some reason other than to find a husband and produce a baby and do it specifically in that order, with the proper person, as picked out by her grandparents, and—

She turned back to the stage. She didn't want to think about this now. This was supposed to be a good night. A *wonderful* night.

"Now he's going to fall in love," Mr. Grey whispered in her ear.

She didn't look back at him. She didn't trust herself to. "Tamino?" she murmured.

"The ladies are going to show him a portrait of Pamina, the daughter of the Queen of the Night. He will fall instantly in love."

Annabel leaned forward, not that she was going to be able to see the portrait from up in the box. She knew the tale was just a fantasy, but really, that had to be a remarkable portraitist.

"I always wondered about the portraitist," Mr. Grey said. "He must be incandescently talented."

Annabel turned sharply and blinked.

"What is it?" he asked.

"Nothing," she said, feeling vaguely dazed. "Just . . . I was thinking the same thing."

He smiled again, but this time it was different. Almost as if . . . No, it could not be that. He could not be smiling at her as if he'd found a kindred spirit. Because they could not be kindred spirits. Annabel could not allow it. It would be unbearable.

Determined to enjoy the opera more than she was enjoying Mr. Grey's intermittent narration, she turned her attention back to the stage, allowing herself to be swept up in the story. It was a ludicrous tale, really, but the music was so wonderful she didn't care.

Every few minutes Mr. Grey would continue his commentary, which Annabel had to admit aided her understanding immensely. His words were part narration and part observation, and Annabel could not help but be entertained. She would hear the rustle of his clothing as he leaned in, then feel the heat of his skin as his lips approached her ear. Then came his words, always astute, frequently amusing, tickling her ear, making her heart skip.

It had to be the most wonderful way to experience the opera.

"This is the final scene," he whispered, as some sort of judicial proceeding began on stage.

"Of the play?" she asked in surprise. The hero and heroine hadn't even met each other yet.

"Of the first act," he told her.

"Oh." Of course. She turned front again, and within a few minutes, Tamino and Pamina finally clapped eyes on each other and instantly embraced . . .

. . . and were separated.

"Well," Annabel said as the curtain went down, "I suppose there wouldn't be much of a second act if they weren't torn apart at the end of the scene."

"You seem suspicious of the romance," Mr. Grey said.

"You must admit, it is a bit far-fetched that he should fall in love with her portrait, and she should fall in love with his . . ." Annabel felt her brow furrow. "Why *did* she fall in love with him?"

"Because Papageno told her he was coming to save her," Louisa said, leaning forward.

"Oh, of course," Annabel replied, rolling her eyes. "She fell in love because a man wearing feathers told her she would be saved by a man she'd never met."

"You don't believe in love at first sight, Miss Winslow?" Mr. Grey asked.

"I did not say that."

"Then you *do* believe?"

"I don't believe or not believe," Annabel replied, not trusting the glint in his eye. "I myself have not witnessed it, but that does not mean it does not exist. And it was not love at first sight. How can it be love at first sight if she has not even *seen* him?"

"It is difficult to argue with such logic," he murmured.

"I should hope so."

He chuckled at that, then frowned as he looked toward the back row. "Harry and Olivia seem to have disappeared," he said.

Annabel twisted and looked over her shoulder. "I hope nothing is wrong."

"Oh, I assure you that nothing is *wrong*," Mr. Grey said cryptically.

Annabel blushed, not entirely sure what he meant, but certain nonetheless that it could not be proper.

Mr. Grey must have seen her go pink, because he chuckled, then leaned toward her with a mischievous gleam in his eye. There was something dangerously intimate in his expression, as if he *knew* her, or as if he would know her, or wanted to know her, or—

"Annabel," Louisa said loudly, "will you come with me to the retiring room?"

"Of course." Annabel had no particular need to "retire," but if there was one thing she had learned in London, it was that one never refused an invitation to accompany another lady to the retiring room. Why this was so, she was not certain, but she'd declined once and had been told that it had been very bad form.

"I await your return," Mr. Grey said, standing.

Annabel nodded and followed Louisa out. They were barely two steps out of the box when Louisa grabbed her upper arm and whispered urgently, "What have you been talking about?"

"With Mr. Grey?"

"Of course with Mr. Grey. The two of you were practically touching heads the entire performance."

"That can't be true."

"I assure you, it can. And you were sitting in the front. Everyone will have seen it."

Annabel began to feel nervous. "What do you mean by everyone?"

Louisa looked furtively about. Crowds were beginning to spill out from the boxes, everyone dressed in their finest opera attire. "I don't know if Lord Newbury is in attendance," she whispered, "but if not, he'll surely hear about this soon."

Annabel swallowed nervously. She did not wish to jeopardize her impending match with the earl, but at the same time . . .

She desperately did.

"It is not Lord Newbury I'm worried about," Louisa continued, looping her arm through Annabel's to bring her closer. "You know I pray that the match will fall through."

"Then—"

"Grandmama Vickers," Louisa cut in. "And Lord Vickers. They will be livid if they think you have purposefully sabotaged the courtship."

"But I—"

"They couldn't possibly think anything else." Louisa swallowed and lowered her voice when she saw someone make a curious turn in their direction. "*Sebastian Grey*, Annabel."

"I know!" Annabel retorted, grateful to have finally got a word in. "You're one to talk. You've been flirting with him all night."

Louisa looked stricken, but only for a moment. "Oh, my heavens," she said. "You're jealous."

"I am not."

"You are." Her eyes lit up. "This is wonderful. And a disaster," she added, almost as an afterthought. "It's a wonderful disaster."

"Louisa." Annabel wanted to rub her eyes. She was suddenly exhausted. And not quite sure that this rather crafty-looking lady in front of her was her normally shy cousin.

"Stop. Listen." Louisa looked about and let out a frustrated groan. She pulled Annabel into an alcove and yanked a velvet curtain around them to afford them a bit of privacy. "You have to go home."

"What? Why?"

"You have to go home right now. There will be enough of a scandal as it is."

"All I did was talk with him!"

Louisa placed her hands on Annabel's shoulders and looked her straight and hard in the eyes. "It's enough. Trust me."

Annabel took one look at her cousin's grave expression and gave a nod. If Louisa said she had to go home, then she had to go home. She knew this world better than Annabel. She understood how to navigate the murky waters of London society.

"With any luck, someone else will make a scene in the second act, and they'll forget all about you. I'll tell everyone you've taken ill, and then—" Louisa's eyes filled with alarm.

"What?"

She shook her head. "I shall just have to make certain that Mr. Grey remains for the entire performance. If he departs early as well, everyone will assume you've gone off together."

The blood drained from Annabel's face.

Louisa gave her head a shake. "I can do it. Don't worry."

"Are you sure?" Because Annabel wasn't. Louisa was not known for her assertiveness.

"No, I can," Louisa said, sounding as if she were convincing herself as much as Annabel. "He's actually much easier to talk to than most men."

"I'd noticed," Annabel said weakly.

Louisa sighed. "Yes, I expect you had. Very well, you must go home, and I will go . . ."

Annabel waited.

"I will go with you," Louisa finished decisively. "That's a much better idea."

Annabel could only blink.

"If I go with you, no one will suspect anything, even if Mr. Grey departs as well." Louisa gave her a sheepish shrug. "It's an advantage of a sterling reputation."

Before Annabel could inquire as to what that said about *her* reputation, Louisa cut in with: "You're an unknown quantity. But me . . . No one ever suspects me of anything."

"Are you saying that they should?" Annabel asked carefully.

"No." Louisa shook her head, almost wistfully. "I never do anything wrong."

But as they made their way from their curtained hideaway, Annabel could have sworn she heard Louisa whisper, "Sadly."

Three hours later Sebastian walked into his club, still rather annoyed by how the evening had turned out. Miss Winslow, he was told, had taken ill during the intermission and departed with Lady Louisa, who had insisted upon accompanying her.

Not that Sebastian believed a word of it. Miss Winslow had been such a picture of health, the only way she could have taken ill was if she'd been attacked by a leper in the stairwell.

The Ladies Cosgrove and Wimbledon, freed of their duties as chaperones, had departed as well, leaving their guests alone in the box. Olivia immediately moved to the front row, setting a program on the chair next to her for Harry, who had gone off to the lobby.

Sebastian had remained for the second act, mostly because Olivia had insisted upon it. He'd been all prepared to go home and write (the leper in the stairwell had given him all sorts of ideas), but she had positively yanked him into the seat next to her and hissed, "If you depart everyone will think you've left with Miss Winslow, and I will not allow you to ruin the poor girl in her first season."

"She left with Lady Louisa," he protested. "Am I really thought so reckless that I'd engage in a *ménage a trois* with that?"

"*That*?"

"You know what I mean," he said with a scowl.

"Everyone will think it a ruse," Olivia explained. "Lady Louisa's reputation may be unimpeachable, but yours is not, and the way you were carrying on with Miss Winslow during the first act . . ."

"I was *talking* with her."

"What are you talking about?" It was Harry, returned from the lobby, needing to get past them to his seat.

"Nothing," they both snapped, adjusting their legs to let him by.

Harry's brows rose, but he merely yawned. "Where did everyone go?" he asked, sitting down.

"Miss Winslow took ill," Olivia told him, "and Lady Louisa accompanied her home. The two aunts departed as well."

Harry gave a shrug, since he was generally more interested in the opera than gossip, and picked up his program.

Sebastian turned to Olivia, who had resumed her glare. "Are you still scolding me?"

"You should have known better," Olivia said in a hushed voice.

Sebastian glanced over at Harry. He was immersed in the libretto, seemingly oblivious to the conversation.

Which, knowing Harry, meant he heard every word.

Sebastian decided he didn't care. "Since when have you become Miss Winslow's champion?" he asked.

"I'm not," she said, shrugging her elegant shoulders. "But it is obvious she is new to town and in need of guidance. I applaud Lady Louisa for taking her home."

"How do you know Lady Louisa took her home?"

"Oh, Sebastian," she said, giving him an impatient look. "How can you even ask?"

And that was the end of it. Until he arrived at the club.

Which was when all hell broke loose.

Chapter Eleven

"*Y*ou bastard!"

Sebastian was normally an observant fellow, blessed with quick reflexes and a healthy sense of self-preservation, but his mind had been uncharacteristically stuck on a single topic—the curve of Miss Winslow's lips—and he had not been paying much attention to his surroundings as he entered the club.

Thus he had not seen his uncle.

Or his uncle's fist.

"What the hell?"

The force of the blow slammed Sebastian into a wall, which led his shoulder to be only slightly less painful than his eye, which was probably already turning black.

"Since the moment you were born," his uncle seethed, "I have known you to be without morals or discipline, but *this*—"

This? What *this?*

"This," his uncle continued, his voice shaking with fury, "is beneath even you."

Since the moment I was born, Seb thought with something that was almost exasperation. *Since the moment I was born*. Well, his uncle was right about that, at least. Back to his earliest memories, his uncle had been angry and hard, always insulting, always finding new ways to make a boy feel small. Sebastian had later realized that the rancor was inevitable. Newbury had never liked Sebastian's father, who had been but eleven months his junior. Adolphus Grey had been taller, more athletic, and better-looking than his older brother. Probably smarter, too, although Sebastian had to admit, his father had never been one for books.

As for Seb's mother, Lord Newbury had thought her appallingly beneath the family.

Sebastian, he considered the spawn of the devil.

Seb had learned to live with it. And occasionally live up to it. Really, he hadn't much cared. His uncle was a nuisance, rather like a pesky, albeit large, insect. The strategy was the same: avoid, and if that proved impossible, swat.

But he didn't say this. Because really, what would be the point? Instead he staggered to his feet, dimly aware that an audience was gathering. "What the devil are you talking about?"

"Miss Vickers," Newbury hissed.

"Who?" Seb asked distractedly. He should probably pay more attention to whatever his uncle was blathering on about, but damn, his eye *really* hurt.

The bloody bruise would probably show for a week. Who knew the old bag had it in him?

"Her name ain't Vickers," someone said.

Sebastian removed his hand from his eye, blinking carefully. Bloody hell. His vision was still blurry. What his uncle lacked in muscle he made up for in heft, and he'd apparently put all of it behind his punch.

Several gentlemen were standing near, presumably hoping that a fight would break out, which of course it would not. Sebastian would never hit his uncle, no matter how roundly he deserved it. If he hit Newbury, it would surely prove too lovely a sensation to resist, and then Seb would have to beat him to a pulp. Which would be very bad form.

Besides, he did not lose his temper. Ever. Everyone knew that, and if they didn't, they should.

"Who, pray tell, is Miss Vickers?" Sebastian asked, molding his body into an insolent slouch.

"She's not a Vickers," someone said. "Her mother was a Vickers. Her father was someone else."

"Winslow," the earl bit off. "Her name is Winslow."

Seb felt his fingers begin to tingle. His right hand might have formed a fist. "What about Miss Winslow?"

"Do you pretend not to know?"

Seb shrugged, though the casual motion took all of his concentration. "I pretend nothing."

His uncle's eyes glittered nastily. "She will soon be your aunt, dear nephew."

The breath whooshed from Sebastian's body,

and he thanked whatever god or architect had made sure there was a wall nearby for him to lean a shoulder against.

Annabel Winslow was Lord Vickers's granddaughter. She was that lush, voluptuous creature Newbury was panting after, the one so fertile she sent birds into fits of song.

It all made sense now. He'd been wondering how a country miss should become such close friends with a duke's daughter. She and Lady Louisa were first cousins. Of course they would be friends.

He thought back to his conversation with *his* cousin, the bit about the fertile hips and singing birds. Miss Winslow's figure was every bit as spectacular as Edward had described. When Sebastian thought about the way Edward's eyes had glazed over when he'd described her breasts . . .

Seb tasted acid. He might have to hit Edward. His uncle was off-limits due to age, but Edward was fair game.

Miss Annabel Winslow was indeed a ripe piece of fruit. And his uncle was planning to marry her.

"You will stay away from her," his uncle said in a low voice.

Sebastian did not speak. He had no ready quip or retort, so he said nothing. It was better that way.

"Although God knows if I still want her, given her dubious lapse in judgment."

Sebastian focused on his breathing, which was quickening dangerously.

"You may have looks and youth," Newbury continued, "but I have the title. And I will be damned before you get your grasping hands on it."

Seb shrugged. "I don't want it."

"Of course you do," Newbury scoffed.

"I don't," Sebastian said carelessly. He was beginning to feel more himself. Amazing what a touch of insolence and attitude could do to restore a man. "I wish you would just hurry up and spawn yourself a new heir. The whole thing is bloody inconvenient."

Newbury's face grew even more florid, not that Sebastian would have thought it possible. "Inconvenient? You dare to call the earldom of Newbury inconvenient?"

Seb started to shrug again, then thought it would be better if he inspected his fingernails. After a moment, he looked back up. "I do. And *you* are a nuisance."

It was perhaps a bit over the line. Very well, it was a good mile over the line, and evidently Newbury agreed, because he blustered incoherently, sending spittle and God knows what else through the air, then finally hurled the contents of his glass into Sebastian's face. There wasn't much in it; presumably it had sloshed half out when he'd punched Seb earlier. But it was enough to sting a man's eyes, and enough to drip from his nose. And as Sebastian stood there, looking like a snot-nosed child in need of a handkerchief, he felt a rage build up inside of him. A rage like nothing he had ever experienced. Even in war, he'd been denied this bloodlust. He was a sniper, trained to be cool and calm, to pick off the enemy from afar.

He acted, but he didn't engage.

His heart pounded in his chest, his blood

rushed in his ears, and yet he still heard the collective gasp, still saw the men gathered around, waiting for him to retaliate.

And he did. But not with his fists. That would never do.

"Out of respect for your age and fragility," he said icily, "I will not strike you." He took a step away and then, quite unable to keep all of his fury in check, he turned back around and added, more in his usual offhanded tone, "Besides, I know you are desirous of a son. If I knocked you to the floor, and truthfully, we all know that I would . . ." Sebastian sighed, as if lamenting a sad, sad tale. "Well, I'm not sure your virility would survive the blow."

There was a deathly silence, followed by Newbury's ramblings and rantings, but Sebastian heard none of it. He simply turned on his heel and left.

It was easier that way.

By the following morning it was all over town. The first of the vultures arrived at Vickers House at the unseemly hour of ten. Annabel was up and about; she frequently was, having found it difficult to shed her country hours. She was so surprised to hear that two countesses were calling for her that she didn't even think to suggest to the butler that she might not be receiving.

"Miss Winslow," came the officious voice of Lady Westfield.

Annabel immediately rose and curtsied, then repeated the gesture toward Lady Challis.

"Wherever is your grandmother?" Lady Westfield asked. She strode into the drawing room with singular purpose. Her mouth was flattened into an unpleasant line, and her entire bearing seemed to suggest that she smelled something foul.

"She is still abed," Annabel answered, remembering that the Ladies Westfield and Vickers were good friends. Or perhaps just friends. Or maybe not that, but they spoke frequently.

Which counted for something, Annabel supposed.

"Then one can only imagine she does not know," Lady Challis said.

Annabel turned to Lady Challis, who was a good twenty-five years younger than her companion and yet still managed to boast a pinched and prickly mien.

"Does not know what, my lady?"

"Don't play coy, gel."

"I'm not." Annabel looked from face to sanctimonious face. What were they talking about? Surely a mere *conversation* with Mr. Grey did not warrant such censure. And she'd left during the intermission, just as Louisa had insisted she must.

"You are a bold girl," Lady Challis said, "playing the uncle off the nephew."

"I–I don't know what you mean," Annabel stammered. But of course she did.

"Stop that this instant," Lady Westfield snapped. "You are a Vickers, despite that awful man your mother married, and you are far too intelligent to get away with such cow-headed playacting."

Annabel swallowed.

"Lord Newbury is furious," Lady Westfield

hissed. "Furious. And I cannot say that I blame him."

"I made him no promises," Annabel said, wishing that her voice sounded a bit more firm. "And I did not know—"

"Do you have any idea the honor he bestowed upon you, just by offering his regard?"

Annabel felt her mouth open and close. And open and close. She felt like an idiot. A fish-faced, muted mule. If she'd been at home she'd have been quick to defend herself, ably summoning retort after retort. But she'd never faced down two furious countesses at home, staring her down with ice-chip eyes over their hard, elegant noses.

It was enough to make a girl want to sit down, were she permitted to sit down in the company of two standing countesses.

"Naturally," Lady Challis said, "he took measures to protect his reputation."

"Lord Newbury?" Annabel asked.

"Of course I mean Lord Newbury. The other one hasn't a care for his reputation and never has."

But somehow Annabel didn't think that was true. Mr. Grey was a known rogue, but there was more to him than that. He had a sense of honor, and she suspected he valued this very highly.

Or maybe she was being fanciful, romanticizing him in her mind. How well did she know him, anyway?

Not at all. Theirs was a two-day acquaintance. Two days! She had to regain hold on her common sense. Now.

"What did Lord Newbury do?" Annabel asked warily.

"He defended his honor, as well he should," Lady Westfield said in what Annabel judged to be an unsatisfactorily vague explanation. "Where is your grandmother?" she repeated, looking sharply about the room as if she might discover her hidden behind a chair. "Someone should wake her. This is not a trifling matter."

In the month she had been living in London, Annabel had seen her grandmother before noon on but two previous occasions. Neither had ended well.

"We try to wake her only for emergencies," she said.

"What the devil do you think this is, you ungrateful chit?" Lady Westfield all but yelled.

Annabel flinched as if struck, and she felt words forming in her mouth: *Yes, of course, my lady. Immediately, my lady.* But then she looked back up, right into Lady Westfield's eyes, and saw something so ugly, so *mean* that it was as if a bolt of electricity shot right up her backbone.

"I will not wake my grandmother," she said firmly. "And I do hope you haven't already done so with your yelling."

Lady Westfield drew back. "Think twice about the way you speak to me, Miss Winslow."

"I offer you no disrespect, my lady. Quite the opposite, I assure you. My grandmother is not herself before noon, and I'm sure, as her friend, that you do not wish to cause her discomfort."

The countess's eyes narrowed, and she looked over at her friend, who seemed equally unsure what to make of Annabel's statement.

"Tell her we called," Lady Westfield finally said, her voice clipped into harsh little syllables.

"I shall," Annabel promised her, dipping into a curtsy just low enough to be reverent without sinking into obsequiousness.

When had she learned such subtleties of curtsying? She must have absorbed more rarefied knowledge in London than she had realized.

The two ladies stalked out, but Annabel barely had time to collapse on the sofa before the butler announced another set of callers: Lady Twombley and Mr. Grimston.

Annabel's belly went queasy with alarm. She had been introduced to the pair only in passing, but they were well known to her. Horrible gossips, Louisa had said, insidious and cruel.

Annabel leaped to her feet, trying to catch the butler before he admitted them, but it was too late. She'd already received one set of guests; it was not his fault if he assumed she was "at home" for everyone. It would have made little difference, anyway; the drawing room was well within sight of the front door, and she could already see Lady Twombley and Mr. Grimston making their way forward.

"Miss Winslow," Lady Twombley said, entering in a graceful swish of pink muslin. She was an incredibly lovely young matron, with honey-blond hair and green eyes, but unlike Lady

Olivia Valentine, whose pale good looks radiated kindness and humor, Lady Twombley just looked shrewd. And not in a good way.

Annabel curtsied. "Lady Twombley. How kind of you to call."

Lady Twombley gestured toward her companion. "You have met my dear friend Mr. Grimston, have you not?"

Annabel nodded. "It was the—"

"Mottram ball," Mr. Grimston finished.

"Of course," Annabel murmured, surprised that he remembered. She certainly didn't.

"Basil possesses the most remarkable memory when it comes to young ladies," Lady Twombley said with a twitter. "It is probably why he is such an expert on fashion."

"Ladies' fashion?" Annabel asked.

"All fashion," Mr. Grimston replied, glancing disdainfully about the room.

Annabel would have liked to have resented him for the expression, but she had to agree—it was all a bit oppressively mauve.

"We see you appear in fine health," Lady Twombley said, lowering herself onto a sofa without being asked.

Annabel immediately followed suit. "Yes, of course, why wouldn't I be?"

"Oh my heavens," Lady Twombley's eyes became the picture of genteel shock and she placed a hand over her heart. "You haven't heard. Oh, Basil, she hasn't heard."

"Heard *what*?" Annabel ground out, although truth be told, she wasn't sure she wanted to know. If it gave Lady Twombley this much joy, it could not be good.

"If it had happened to me," Lady Twombley went on, "I should have taken to my bed."

Annabel looked over at Mr. Grimston to see if he might be willing to actually tell her what Lady Twombley was talking about, but he was busy looking bored.

"Such an insult," Lady Twombley murmured. "Such an insult."

To me? Annabel wanted to ask. But she didn't dare.

"Basil saw the whole thing," Lady Twombley said with a wave toward her friend.

Now approaching panic, Annabel turned to the gentleman, who sighed and said, "It was quite a to-do."

"What happened?" Annabel finally cried out.

Finally satisfied with the level of Annabel's distress, Lady Twombley said, "Lord Newbury attacked Mr. Grey."

Annabel felt the blood drain from her face. "What? No. That's not possible." Mr. Grey was young and supremely fit. And Lord Newbury was . . . not.

"Punched him right in the face," Mr. Grimston said, as if it were not anything out of the ordinary.

"Oh my goodness," Annabel said, her hand covering her mouth. "Is he all right?"

"One presumes," Mr. Grimston replied.

Annabel looked from Lady Twombley to Mr. Grimston and back again. Damn and blast, they were going to make her ask *again*. "What happened next?" she asked, not without irritation.

"Words were exchanged," Mr. Grimston said with a polite yawn, "then Lord Newbury threw his drink in Mr. Grey's face."

"I should have liked to have seen that," Lady Twombley murmured. Annabel shot her a horrified look, and she just shrugged. "What we cannot prevent," she said, "we might as well witness."

"Did Mr. Grey hit him in return?" Annabel asked Mr. Grimston, and to her own horror she realized she was a bit giddy inside. She shouldn't wish for one person to cause another pain, and yet—

The thought of Lord Newbury being knocked to the floor . . . after what he'd tried to do to her . . .

She had to try very hard to keep her eagerness off her face.

"He did not," Mr. Grimston said. "Others were surprised by his restraint, but I was not."

"He is quite a rogue," Lady Twombley said, leaning forward with a meaningful glint in her eyes, "but he's not a *rash* sort, if you know what I mean."

"No," Annabel bit off, thoroughly out of patience with her vague comments, "I don't."

"He cut him," Mr. Grimston said. "Not quite the cut direct. Even he wouldn't dare, I reckon. But I do believe he called into question his lordship's manhood."

Annabel gasped.

Lady Twombley laughed.

"The way I see it," Mr. Grimston continued, "one of two things is likely to occur."

For once, Annabel thought, she wasn't going to

have to prod. Judging from the rapacious gleam in his eye, there was no way Mr. Grimston was going to keep his thoughts to himself.

"It is quite possible," he continued, clearly pleased with the hanging-on-every-word silence that filled the room, "that Lord Newbury will marry you immediately. He will need to defend his honor, and the quickest way to do so would be to plow you well and good."

Annabel drew back, then felt even sicker as Mr. Grimston looked her up and down.

"You do look the sort to breed quickly," he said.

"Indeed," Lady Twombley added with a flick of her wrist.

"I beg your pardon," Annabel said stiffly.

"Or," Mr. Grimston added, "Mr. Grey will seduce you."

"What?"

This caught Lady Twombley's interest instantly. "Do you really think so, Basil?" she asked.

He turned to her, completely turning his back on Annabel. "Oh, to be certain. Can you think of a better way for him to exact his revenge against his uncle?"

"I'm going to have to ask the two of you to leave," Annabel said.

"Oh, I thought of a third!" Lady Twombley chimed, as if Annabel had not just attempted to evict her.

Mr. Grimston was all ears. "Really?"

"The earl could choose someone else, of course. Miss Winslow is hardly the only unmarried girl in London. No one would think less of him for looking elsewhere after what happened last night at the opera."

"Nothing happened at the opera," Annabel ground out.

Lady Twombley looked at her pityingly. "It doesn't matter if anything happened or not. Surely you realize that?"

"Go on, Cressida," Mr. Grimston said.

"Of course," she said, as if bestowing a gift. "If Lord Newbury chooses someone else, Mr. Grey will have little reason to pursue Miss Winslow."

"What happens then?" Annabel asked, even though she knew she should not.

They both looked at her with identically blank expressions. "Why, you'll be a pariah," Lady Twombley said, as if nothing could have been more obvious.

Annabel was speechless. Not so much at the words, but at the delivery. These people had come into her home—her grandparents' home, but really, it was hers for the time being—and insulted her in every possible manner. That they were most probably correct in their predictions only made it worse.

"We are so sorry to be the bearers of unpleasant news," Lady Twombley cooed.

"I think you should go," Annabel said, standing. She would have liked to have made the request in a quite different manner, but she was all too aware that her reputation was now hanging by a thread, and these people—these awful, horrible people—had the power to pull out their little scissors and cut.

"Of course," Lady Twombley said, coming to her feet. "You will be overset, I'm sure."

"You do look flushed," Mr. Grimston added. "Although that might just be the burgundy of your gown. You would do well to find a shade with a touch less blue to it."

"I shall take that under advisement," Annabel said tightly.

"Oh, you should, Miss Winslow," Lady Twombley said, sailing to the door. "Basil has such a cunning eye for fashion. Truly."

And just like that they were gone.

Almost.

They had just made it to the front hall when Annabel heard her grandmother's voice. At— good heavens, Annabel looked at the clock—half ten! What on earth could have got Lady Vickers out of bed at such an hour?

Annabel spent the next ten minutes standing near the open doorway, listening to her grandmother receive the gospel according to Grimston and Twombley. What joy, she thought flatly, to hear it all again. In such impeccable detail. Finally, the front door opened and closed, and one minute later Lady Vickers stormed into the room.

"I need a drink," she announced, "and so do you."

Annabel did not argue.

"Annoying weasely little pair they are," her grandmother said, tossing back her brandy in one gulp. She poured another, took a sip, then poured one for Annabel. "But they're right, dash it all. It's a fine mess you've got yourself into, my girl."

Annabel touched her lips to the brandy. Drinking at half ten. What would her mother say?

Her grandmother shook her head. "Foolish, foolish girl. What were you thinking?"

Annabel hoped that was a rhetorical question.

"Well, I suppose you didn't know any better." Lady Vickers topped off her glass and sat in her favorite chair. "You're lucky your grandfather is such a good friend to the earl. We'll save the match yet."

Annabel nodded dutifully, wishing . . .

Wishing . . .

Just wishing. For anything. For something good.

"Thank heavens Judkins had the sense to alert me to all your visitors," her grandmother went on. "I tell you, Annabel, it makes very little difference what sort of husband you take on, but a good butler is worth his weight in gold."

Annabel could not even begin to think of a response.

Her grandmother took another drink from her glass. "Judkins said Rebecca and Winifred were here earlier?"

Annabel nodded, assuming that meant the Ladies Westfield and Challis.

"We are going to be inundated. Just inundated." She looked over at Annabel with narrowed eyes. "I hope you're prepared."

Annabel felt something desperate uncurling in her belly. "Can't we say we're not at home?"

Lady Vickers snorted. "No, we can't say we're not at home. You got yourself into this mess, and you'll take it like a lady, which means holding your head high, receiving every guest, and remembering each word so that it might be dissected later for analysis."

Annabel sat, then stood when Judkins entered, announcing the next set of visitors.

"You'd best finish that brandy," her grandmother said to her. "You're going to need it."

Chapter Twelve

Three days later

"If you don't do something to repair what you've done, I shall never speak to you again."

Sebastian looked up from his eggs into the magnificently furious face of his cousin's wife. Olivia wasn't often angry, and truly, it was a sight to behold.

Although all things considered, he'd have rather beheld it turned upon someone else.

Seb looked toward Harry, who was reading the newspaper over his own breakfast. Harry just shrugged, the motion clearly indicating that he did not judge this to be his problem.

Sebastian took a sip of his tea, swallowed, then looked back up at Olivia with a carefully blank countenance. "I beg your pardon," he said cheerfully. "Were you speaking to me?"

"Harry!" she exclaimed, letting out a huff of indignation. But her husband just shook his head, not even looking up.

Olivia's eyes narrowed menacingly, and Seb decided he was quite glad not to be in Harry's future shoes, when he had to face down his wife that evening.

Although really, one would hope Harry would be shoeless by that point.

"Sebastian!" Olivia said sternly. "Are you even listening to me?"

He blinked her face into focus. "I hang on your every word, dear cousin. You know that."

She yanked out the chair across from him and sat down.

"Don't you want breakfast?" he asked mildly.

"Later. First I—"

"I would be happy to fix your plate," he offered. "You don't want to go without the proper sustenance in your condition, you know."

"My condition isn't the problem at hand," she said, pointing a long, graceful finger in his direction. "Sit."

Seb tilted his head quizzically. "I *am* sitting."

"You were thinking of getting up."

He turned to Harry. "How do you tolerate her?"

Harry looked up from the newspaper for the first time that morning and smiled slyly. "There are certain benefits," he murmured.

"Harry!" Olivia squeaked.

Sebastian was pleased to see that she blushed. "Very well," he said, "what have I done now?"

"It is Miss Winslow."

Miss Winslow. Seb tried not to frown as he thought of her. Which was ironic because he'd spent the better part of two days frowning as he tried *not* to think of her. "What about Miss Winslow?"

"You did not mention that she was being courted by your uncle."

"I did not know that she was being courted by my uncle." Did his words sound a little tight? That would not do. He needed to get a firmer grip on his aspect and attitude.

There was a beat of silence. And then: "You must be very angry with her."

"On the contrary," Sebastian said nonchalantly.

Olivia's pretty little lips opened in surprise. "You're *not* angry with her?"

Seb shrugged. "It requires far too much energy to be angry." He looked up from his food, giving her a bland smile. "I have better things to do with my time."

"You do? I mean, of course you do. But wouldn't you agree—"

Sebastian thought that he needed to do something about this niggle of irritation jabbing him under his ribs. It was really rather unpleasant, and he found it so much easier to glide along, letting insults roll off his back. But really, did Olivia think he sat about eating bonbons all day?

"Sebastian? Are you listening to me?"

He smiled and lied, "Of course."

Olivia let out a noise that was somewhere between a groan and a growl. But she plodded on. "Very well, you're not angry with her, although, in my opinion, you have every right to be. Still—"

"If you were being pursued by my uncle," Sebastian cut in, "wouldn't you wish for a few last moments of merriment? I say this not to be boastful—although I am rather good company, if I may say so myself—but I really don't think it can be disputed. I'm a far more pleasant companion than Newbury."

"He has a point," Harry said.

Olivia scowled. "I thought you weren't listening."

"I'm not," he replied. "I am merely sitting here while my ears are assaulted."

"How do you put up with him?" Sebastian murmured.

Olivia grit her teeth. "There are benefits," she ground out.

Although Sebastian rather thought Harry might not be getting any benefits that evening.

"So there it is," Sebastian said to Olivia. "I forgive her. She should have said something, but I understand why she did not, and I rather suspect that any one of us would have done the same."

There was a pause, and then Olivia said, "That is very generous of you."

He shrugged. "It's not good for the constitution to carry a grudge. Just look at Newbury. He'd not be nearly so fat and florid if he didn't hate me so much." He turned back to his breakfast, wondering what Olivia might make of that little leap of logic.

She waited approximately ten seconds before

continuing on. "I am relieved to hear that you do not harbor her any ill will. As I said, she is in need of your help. After your little scene at White's—"

"What?" Sebastian snapped, barely resisting the urge to slam his hand on the table. "Hold this minute. It was not *my* scene at all. If you wish to take someone to task, go find my uncle."

"Very well, I'm sorry," Olivia said, with enough discomfort that he believed her. "It was entirely your uncle's doing, I realize that, but the end result is the same. Miss Winslow is in a terrible spot, and you are the only person who can save her."

Sebastian took another bite of his food, then carefully wiped his mouth. There were at least ten things about Olivia's statement that he could have taken exception to, were he the sort of gentleman to take exception to statements made by females in a huff. The first being:

One: Miss Winslow's spot was not so terrible because **Two**: she was apparently very close to becoming the Countess of Newbury, which **Three**: came with all sorts of fortune and prestige, despite also coming with the Earl of Newbury, whom no one could possibly judge as a prize.

To say nothing of **Four**: Sebastian was the one sporting a black eye and **Five**: he was also the one who'd had a drink thrown in his face, all because **Six**: she had not seen fit to tell him that she was being courted by his uncle despite the fact that **Seven**: she knew damn well of the connection, because **Eight**: she had nearly passed out from shock when he'd told her his name that night on the heath.

But perhaps he really ought to focus more on the second part of Olivia's statement, the bit about his being the only person who could save Miss Winslow. Because **Nine**: he saw no reason why this might be the case, and **Ten**: he also didn't see why he should care.

"Well?" Olivia demanded. "Do you have any thoughts on the matter?"

"Quite a few, actually," he said equably. He went back to his food. After a few moments he looked back up. Olivia was gripping the table so hard her knuckles were turning white, and the look on her face . . .

"Careful there," he murmured. "You're going to curdle the milk."

"Harry!" she fairly yelled.

Harry lowered the newspaper. "While I do appreciate your soliciting my opinion, I am quite certain I have nothing to offer this conversation. I doubt I'd even recognize Miss Winslow if I stumbled across her in the street."

"You spent an entire evening in the opera box with her," Olivia said in disbelief.

Harry considered this. "I suppose I might recognize the back of her head, were that the view she offered to me."

Sebastian chuckled, then very quickly straightened his expression. Olivia was *not* amused. "Oh very well," he said, holding his hands toward her in supplication. "Tell me how this is all my fault and what I may do to fix it."

Olivia stared at him for one last endless second before saying quite primly, "I am glad you asked."

Harry choked on something down the table. Probably his laughter. Sebastian hoped it was his tongue.

"Do you have any idea what people are saying about Miss Winslow?" Olivia asked.

As Sebastian had spent the last two days holed up in his rooms, working on getting the fictional Miss Spencer out from under her fictional Scotsman's fictional bed, he did not, in fact, know what people were saying about Miss Winslow.

"Well?" Olivia demanded.

"I do not," he admitted.

"They are saying"—she leaned forward here, and her expression was such that Sebastian just barely resisted the urge to lean back—"that it is only a matter of time before you seduce her."

"She would not be the first lady about whom that has been said," Seb pointed out.

"It's different," Olivia said between her teeth, "and you know that it is. Miss Winslow is not one of your merry widows."

"I do love a good merry widow," he murmured, just because he knew it would vex her.

"People are saying," she ground out, "that you will ruin her just to thwart your uncle."

"I am quite certain that is not my plan," Sebastian said, "and I expect the rest of society will figure that out once they realize I have not even called upon her."

And he did not intend to. Yes, he quite liked Miss Winslow, and yes, he'd spent far too much of his waking hours pondering the various ways he'd like to tie her to a bed, but he had absolutely no intention of following through on that particular fantasy. He might have forgiven her, but he had no plans for any further contact. As far as he was concerned, if Newbury wanted her, Newbury could have her.

Which was what he said to Olivia, although with perhaps a bit more delicacy. This, however, only earned him a furious glare, followed by, "Newbury *doesn't* want her any longer. That is the problem."

"For whom?" Seb asked suspiciously. "If I were Miss Winslow, I'd see that as something more akin to a solution."

"You are not Miss Winslow, and furthermore, you are not a lady."

"Thank God," he said, with no small bit of feeling. Beside him, Harry rapped three times on the table.

Olivia scowled at both of them. "If you were a lady," she said, "you would understand what a disaster this is. Lord Newbury has not called upon her even once since your altercation."

Sebastian's brows rose. "Really?"

"Really. Do you know who *has* called upon her?"

"I do not," he replied, because it wasn't as if she was going to withhold the information, anyway.

"Everyone else. Everyone!"

"Quite a busy drawing room," he murmured.

"Sebastian! Do you know whom 'everyone' includes?"

He briefly considered a sarcastic answer, then decided, out of motives of pure self-preservation, that he ought to hold his tongue.

"Cressida Twombley," Olivia fairly hissed. "And Basil Grimston. They have been there three times."

"Three ti— How do you *know* this?"

"I know everything," Olivia said dismissively.

This, he believed. If Olivia had been in town before she'd met Miss Winslow in the park, none of this would have happened. She would have known that Annabel Winslow was Lady Louisa's cousin. She'd probably have known her birthday and favorite color as well. She certainly would have known that Miss Winslow was a Vickers granddaughter, and thus his uncle's prey.

And Sebastian would have steered himself far far away. That kiss on the heath would be nothing but a dim (albeit delightful) memory. He certainly would not have accepted the invitation to the opera, and he would not have sat next to her, and he would not know that her eyes—such a clear, focused gray—took on a hint of green when she dressed in that color. He would not know that her sensibilities were remarkably like his, or that she caught the inside of her lower lip between her teeth when she was concentrating on something. Or that she was not terribly good at sitting still.

Or that she smelled faintly of violets.

If he had but known who she was, none of those pesky bits of information would be jiggling about in his brain, taking up useful space from something important. Like a thorough analysis of roundarm versus underarm bowling in cricket. Or the precise wording of Shakespeare's sonnet "Alack! What poverty my Muse brings forth," which he'd been misquoting in his head for at least a year now.

"Miss Winslow has become a laughingstock," Olivia said, "and it is not fair. She did not do anything."

"Neither did I," Sebastian pointed out.

"But you have the power to fix things. She does not."

"Alack, what poverty my Position brings forth," he muttered.

"What?" Olivia said impatiently.

He waved his previous comment away. It wasn't worth trying to explain. Instead, he gave her a direct look and asked, "What would you have me do?"

"Call upon her."

Sebastian turned to Harry, who was still pretending to read his newspaper. "Didn't she just say that all of London thinks I plan to seduce her?"

"She did," Harry confirmed.

"Good *God*," Olivia blasphemed, with enough force to cause both men to blink. "The two of you are so obtuse."

They both stared at her, their very silence confirming her statement.

"Right now it looks as if *both* of you have abandoned her. The earl apparently does not want her, and by all appearances, neither do you. Heaven knows what the society ladies are tittering behind their hands."

Sebastian could well imagine. Most would say that Miss Winslow overreached, and society loved nothing more than to watch an ambitious female brought low.

"Right now people are calling upon her out of curiosity," Olivia said. *"And,"* she added with a meaningful narrowing of her eyes, "cruelty. But make no mistake, Sebastian. When all this is over, no one will have her. Not unless you do the right thing *right now."*

"Please tell me the right thing does not involve a proposal of marriage," he said. Because really, delightful though Miss Winslow was, he hardly thought he'd behaved in a fashion to warrant it.

"Of course not," Olivia said. "You need merely to call upon her. Show society that you still find her delightful. And you must be all that is proper. If you do anything that even hints of seduction, she will be ruined."

Sebastian started to make one of his usual flip comments, but a little jab of indignation began to uncurl within him, and by the time he opened his mouth it could not be denied. "Why is it," he wanted to know, "that people—people, I might add, who have known me for several years, some even for decades—believe me the sort of person who might seduce an innocent young lady for revenge?"

He waited for a moment, but Olivia had no answer. And neither, apparently did Harry, who had given up all pretense of reading his newspaper.

"This is not an idle question," Sebastian said angrily. "Have I ever behaved in a manner to suggest such a thing? Tell me what I have done to make myself out to be such a predatory villain. Because I must confess that I am at a loss. Do you know that I have never, not *once*, slept with a virgin?" He directed that comment at Olivia, mostly because he was in the mood to shock and offend. "Even when I *was* a virgin."

"Sebastian, that's enough," Harry said quietly.

"No, I don't think it is. What, I wonder, do people think I plan to do with Miss Winslow once I seduce her? Abandon her? Kill her and toss the body in the Thames?"

For a moment his cousins could do nothing but stare. It was the closest Sebastian had come to raising his voice since . . .

Since . . .

Since ever. Even Harry, who had known him since childhood, been through school and army with him, had never heard him raise his voice.

"Sebastian," Olivia said gently. She reached across the table to place her hand on his, but he shook her off.

"Is this what you think of me?" he demanded.

"No!" she said, her eyes filling with horror. "Of course not. But I *know* you. And—Where are you going?"

He'd already come to his feet and was rapidly making for the door. "To call upon Miss Winslow," he bit off.

"Well, don't go in *that* mood," she said, hurrying out of her chair.

Sebastian stopped in his tracks and gave her a look.

"I . . . er . . ." She looked over at Harry, who

had also risen to his feet. He answered her silent question in kind, merely quirking a brow and tilting his head to the door.

"Perhaps I will go with you," Olivia said. She swallowed, then quickly placed her hand on Sebastian's arm. "It will make it seem all the more proper, wouldn't you think?"

Sebastian gave her a curt nod, but the truth was, he didn't know what to think anymore. Or maybe he just didn't care.

Chapter Thirteen

"Brandy?" Lady Vickers asked, holding forth a glass.

Annabel shook her head. After the second day of receiving morning callers with her grandmother (who could not face any hour before noon without the proper libation) she had learned that it was best to stick to lemonade and tea until after dinner. "It will give me a stomachache," she said.

"This?" Lady Vickers asked, eyeing the glass curiously. "How odd. It makes me feel positively serene."

Annabel nodded. There was no other way to respond. She'd spent more time with her grandmother in the last few days than she had in the entire previous month. When Lady Vickers had told her to take the scandal like a lady, she'd been referring to herself as well, and apparently that meant sticking to one's granddaughter's side like glue.

It was, Annabel realized, quite the most tangible show of love her grandmother had ever displayed toward her.

"Well, I will say one thing," Lady Vickers proclaimed, "for all that it's a scandal, I have seen more of my friends than I have in years."

Friends? Annabel smiled weakly.

"I do think perhaps it's dying down," Lady Vickers continued. "There were thirty-three visitors the first day, thirty-nine the second, and only twenty-six yesterday."

Annabel's mouth fell open. "You've been counting?"

"Of course I've been counting. What have *you* been doing?"

"Ehrm . . . sitting here and trying to take it like a lady?"

Her grandmother chuckled. "You probably didn't think I could count so high."

Annabel spluttered and stammered and began to regret turning down that brandy.

"*Pfft.*" Lady Vickers dismissed her distress with a sharp wave of her hand. "I have all sorts of hidden talents."

Annabel nodded, but the truth was, she was not certain she wanted any more of her grandmother's talents to rise to the surface. In fact, she was sure of it.

"A lady must have her own private reserve of secrets and strength," her grandmother continued. "*Trust me.*" She took a sip of her drink, let out a contented exhale, and took another. "Once you are married you will understand what I mean."

Ninety-eight visitors, Annabel thought, doing the addition in her head. Ninety-eight people had called upon Vickers House, eager to see the latest scandal. Or spread it. Or tell her how much it had spread.

It had been awful.

Ninety-eight people. She slumped.

"Sit up straight!" her grandmother snapped.

Annabel obeyed. Maybe not quite ninety-eight. Several people had come more than once. Lady Twombley had been by *every day*.

And where had Mr. Grey been in all this? No one seemed to know. He had not been seen since the altercation at his club. Annabel was quite certain this was true, because she had been told this, no fewer than ninety-eight times.

But Annabel supposed she wasn't angry at Mr. Grey. None of this was his fault. She should have told him that she was being courted by his uncle. *She* was the one who could have prevented the scandal. That was the worst of it. She had spent the whole of three days feeling embarrassed and angry and small, and she had no one to blame but herself. If she had told him the truth, if not the moment she'd learned his name then at least when they'd met in Hyde Park . . .

"Visitors, my lady," the butler announced.

"Our first two of the day," Lady Vickers said dryly. Or was it mockingly? "Who is it, Judkins?"

"Lady Olivia Valentine and Mr. Grey."

"It's about damned time," Lady Vickers grunted.

And then, when Judkins had shown their guests in, she said it again. "It's about damned time. What has taken you so long?"

Annabel wanted to die of mortification.

"I took ill," Mr. Grey said smoothly, with a wry half smile that pointed up toward his eye.

His eye. It looked awful. Horribly red rimmed, a bit swollen, and with a blue-black bruise that spread from the underneath around to the outer corner. Annabel gasped aloud; she could not help it.

"I am rather frightening to behold," he murmured, taking her hand and leaning down to kiss it.

"Mr. Grey," she said, "I am terribly sorry about your eye."

He straightened. "I rather like it myself. It gives me the air of a perpetual wink."

Annabel started to smile, then tried not to. "A most gruesome wink," she agreed.

"And here I thought it was dashing," he murmured.

"Sit down," Lady Vickers said, pointing at the sofa. Annabel started toward the spot, but her grandmother said, "No. Him. You over there." Then she marched over to the doorway, called out, "Judkins, we are home to *no one*," and firmly shut the door.

Once Lady Vickers had finished directing everyone into her chosen seats, she wasted no time in starting the conversation. "What do you plan to do?" she asked, directing her question not to Mr. Grey but to his cousin, who had heretofore managed to remain silent throughout the exchange.

But Lady Olivia was unruffled. Clearly she also did not judge either of the two principals able to manage their own scandal. "That's why we're here," she said efficiently. "My cousin is aghast at the potential damage to your granddaughter's reputation and is most apologetic over any part he may have had in the scandal."

"As he should be," Lady Vickers said tartly.

Annabel stole a glance at Mr. Grey. To her relief, he looked somewhat amused. Maybe even a little bored.

"Of course," Lady Olivia said smoothly, "his involvement was completely inadvertent. As we all know, Lord Newbury threw the first punch."

"The *only* punch," Mr. Grey interjected.

"Yes," Lady Vickers said, acknowledging the point with a grand wave of her arm. "But who could blame him? He would have been overcome with shock. I have known Newbury all of my adult life. He is a man of delicate sensibilities."

Annabel very nearly snorted aloud at that. She looked over at Mr. Grey again, to see if he felt the same. Just as she did so, however, his eyes widened with alarm.

Wait a moment . . . *alarm?*

Mr. Grey swallowed uncomfortably.

"Yes," Lady Vickers said with an affected sigh, "but now the entire match has been put at risk. We did so want an earl for Annabel."

"*Eeep!*"

Annabel and Lady Olivia both looked over at

Mr. Grey, who had, if Annabel's ears did not deceive, just squeaked. He smiled tightly, looking as ill at ease as she had ever seen him. Not that she'd seen him terribly much, but he did seem the sort of gentleman who was rarely anything but utterly comfortable in his own skin.

He shifted in his seat.

Annabel looked down.

And saw her grandmother's hand on his thigh.

"Tea!" she practically shrieked, jumping to her feet. "We must have tea. Don't you think?"

"I *do*," Mr. Grey said with great feeling, using the opportunity to scoot himself as far away from Lady Vickers as the sofa would allow. It was only a few inches, but still, far enough so that she could not grab him without being ridiculously obvious about it.

"I adore tea," Annabel babbled, moving over to the bellpull to ring for it. "Don't you? My mother always said that nothing could be solved without a pot of tea."

"And does the opposite hold true?" Mr. Grey asked. "That anything can be solved *with* it?"

"We shall soon find out, shan't we?" Annabel watched with horror as her grandmother edged across the sofa toward him. "Oh *my!*" she said, with what was certainly too much emphasis. "It's become stuck. Mr. Grey, would you mind helping me with this?" She held out the bellpull, careful not to tug it into ringing.

He practically leaped to his feet. "I would be happy to. You know me," he said to the other ladies. "I *live* to rescue damsels in distress."

"It's why we're here," Lady Olivia said smoothly.

"Careful," Annabel said as he took the cord from her hands. "You don't want to pull too hard."

"Of course not," he murmured, then mouthed, *Thank you.*

They stood there for a moment, and then, confident that her grandmother and Lady Olivia were ensconced in their conversation, Annabel said, "I'm sorry about your eye."

"Oh, this," he said, waving it away.

She swallowed. "I'm also very sorry I didn't say anything. That was not well done of me."

He gave an oddly sharp one-shouldered shrug. "If I were being courted by my uncle, I'm not sure I would wish to advertise it, either."

She had a feeling she was supposed to laugh, but all she felt was a terrible desperation. She managed a smile—not a very good one—and said . . .

Nothing. Apparently the smile was all she could manage.

"Are you going to marry him?" Mr. Grey asked.

She looked down at her feet. "He has not asked."

"He will."

Annabel tried not to answer. She tried to think of something else to say, anything that would change the subject without being painfully obvious. She shifted her weight, then looked over at the clock, then—

"He wants an heir," Mr. Grey said.

"I know," she said quietly.

"He needs one quickly."

"I know."

"Most young ladies would be flattered by his regard."

She sighed. "I know." And so she looked up and smiled. It was one of those awkward sorts of smiles that are at least three fourths nervous laughter. "I am," she said. She swallowed. "Flattered, that is."

"Of course you are," he murmured.

Annabel stood still, trying not to tap her foot. Another one of those habits her grandmother deplored. But it was so *hard* to stand still when one wasn't feeling quite oneself. "It's a moot point," she said in a rush. "He has not called. I suspect he has moved on to another prospect."

"For which I hope you are grateful," Mr. Grey said quietly.

She did not reply. She couldn't. Because she *was* grateful. More than that, she was relieved. And she felt so bloody guilty for feeling that way. Marriage to the earl would have saved her entire family. She shouldn't feel grateful. She should be prostrate with grief that the match had fallen through.

"Mr. Gre-ey!" her grandmother trilled from across the room.

"Lady Vickers," he said solicitously, walking back to the seating area. He did not, however, sit.

"We think you must court my granddaughter," she announced.

Annabel felt her skin turn to beets, and she

would have loved to have crawled under a chair, but panic set in, and she hurried over, exclaiming, "Oh, Grandmother, you can't be serious." And then to Mr. Grey: "She's not serious."

"I'm serious," her grandmother said succinctly. "It's the only way."

"Oh no, Mr. Grey," Annabel put in, absolutely mortified that he was being ordered to court her. "Please don't think—"

"Am I that bad?" he said dryly.

"No! No. I mean, no, you know that you are not."

"Well, I'd hoped . ." he murmured.

Annabel looked over at the other two ladies for help, but they were offering none of it.

"None of this is your fault," Annabel said firmly.

"Nevertheless," he said grandly, "I cannot stand by while a damsel is in distress. What sort of gentleman would I be?"

Annabel looked over at Lady Olivia. She was smiling in a way that alarmed her.

"It's nothing *serious*, of course," Lady Vickers said. "All for show. You may part ways by the end of the month. Amicably, of course." She smiled wolfishly. "We would hate for Mr. Grey to feel he was not welcome here at Vickers House."

Annabel hazarded a glance at the gentleman in question. He looked a bit queasy.

"Please do sit again," Lady Vickers said, patting the spot on the sofa beside her. "You make me feel a most incompetent hostess."

"No!" Annabel burst out, without even beginning to ponder the ramifications of that one word.

"No?" her grandmother echoed.

"We should go for a walk," Annabel said.

"We should?" Mr. Grey said. "Oh, we should."

"Absolutely, you should," Lady Olivia said.

"The weather is fine," Annabel said.

"And everyone will see us and think we are courting," Mr. Grey finished. He took Annabel's arm with alacrity and announced, "And so we depart!"

They hurried from the room, not speaking a word until reaching the front steps, when Mr. Grey turned to her and let out a heartfelt, "Thank you."

"It was my pleasure," Annabel said, stepping lightly down to the pavement. She turned back and smiled. "I *live* to rescue gentlemen in distress."

Chapter Fourteen

 $\mathcal{B}$ efore Sebastian could respond with a suitably pithy statement, the front door of Vickers House opened and Olivia emerged. He glanced up at her and raised a brow.

"I am your chaperone," she explained.

Before he could respond pithily to *that*, she added, "Miss Winslow's maid has the afternoon free, so it was either me or Lady Vickers."

"We are delighted to have you," he said firmly.

"What *happened* in there?" Olivia asked, descending to the pavement.

Sebastian looked over at Miss Winslow, who was looking rather determinedly at a tree.

"I couldn't possibly discuss it," he said, turning back to Olivia. "It's far too painful."

He thought he heard Miss Winslow snort. He did like her sense of humor.

"Very well," Olivia said, making a shooing motion with her hand. "Go on ahead. I shall hang back, being chaperony."

"Is that a word?" Because really, he had to ask. After the *purview* incident, she had no right to be using improper vocabulary.

"If it's not, it should be," she announced.

Sebastian had all sorts of pithy replies to that, but unfortunately they all involved the revealing of his secret identity, such as it was. But as he was constitutionally unable to allow the comment to pass without saying *some*thing to needle Olivia, he turned to Miss Winslow and said, "This is her first time."

"Her first . . . ?" Miss Winslow twisted back toward Olivia, her face delightfully confused.

"As a chaperone," he clarified, taking her arm. "She'll be trying to impress you."

"I heard that!"

"Of course you did," he said agreeably. He leaned a little closer to Miss Winslow and whispered in her ear, "We shall have to work hard to be rid of her."

"Sebastian!"

"Hang back, Olivia," he called out. "Hang back."

"This doesn't seem right," Miss Winslow said. Her lips made quite an adorable frown, and Seb found himself pondering all the ways her pout might be melted into something a tad more seductive. Or seducible.

"Hmmm?" he murmured.

"It's not as if she's a maiden aunt," she said, following that with: "Lady Olivia, please. You must come forward and join us."

"I am quite certain that is not what Sebastian wants," Olivia said, but Seb noticed that she had quite the spring in her step as she came abreast. "Do not worry, Seb," she said to him. "Lady Vickers gave me her newspaper. I shall find a tidy little bench to sit upon, and the two of you may meander about all you wish."

She held out the newspaper, clearly intending for him to carry it, so he did. He never argued with females unless it was absolutely necessary.

They made their way to the park, chatting about nothing in particular, and true to her word, Olivia immediately found a bench and proceeded to ignore them. Or at least to do a cracking good job of pretending to ignore them.

"Shall we take a turn?" he asked Miss Winslow. "We can imagine this is an extremely large drawing room and walk the perimeter."

"That would be lovely." She looked back at Olivia, who was reading her newspaper.

"Oh, she's watching, don't worry."

"Do you think so? She looks quite engrossed."

"My dear cousin can most certainly read the newspaper and spy upon us at the same time. She could probably paint a watercolor and conduct an orchestra, as well." He cocked his head toward Miss Winslow in salute. "Women, I have learned, can do at least six things at once without pausing for breath."

"And men?"

"Oh, we are much too lugheaded. It's a miracle we can walk and talk at the same time."

She laughed, then motioned down at his feet. "You seem to be succeeding admirably."

He pretended to be amazed. "Well, look at that. I must be improving."

She laughed again, a lovely, throaty sound. He smiled over at her, since that was what one did when a lady laughed in one's presence, and for a moment he forgot where he was. The trees, the grass, the entire world just slipped away, and all he saw was her face, and her smile, and her lips, so full and pink, curved so deliciously at the corners.

His body began to thrum with a light, heady feeling. It wasn't lust, or even desire—he knew exactly how those felt. This was different. Excitement, perhaps. Maybe anticipation, although he was not sure for what. They were merely walking in the park. Still, he could not quite shake the feeling that he was waiting for something good.

It was an excellent sensation.

"I think I rather enjoy being rescued," he said as they strolled sedately toward Stanhope Gate. The weather was fine, Miss Winslow was lovely, and Olivia was now well out of earshot.

What more could a man want in an afternoon?

Except possibly the afternoon part. He squinted up at the sky. It was definitely still morning.

"I am so sorry about my grandmother," Miss Winslow said. With great feeling.

"Tut tut, don't you know you're not supposed to mention such things?"

She sighed. "Really? I can't even apologize?"

"Of course not." He grinned down at her. "You're supposed to sweep it under the rug and hope I did not notice."

Her brows rose dubiously. "That her hand was on your . . . er . . ."

He waved a hand, although the truth was, he was rather enjoying her blush. "I can't remember a thing."

For a moment her face was perfectly blank, and then she just shook her head. "London society baffles me."

"There is no sense to it, certainly," he agreed.

"Just look at *my* situation."

"I know. It's a shame. But it's the way things work. If I don't want you, and my uncle doesn't want you"—here he watched her, trying to gauge whether this was a disappointment—"neither will anyone else."

"No, I understand that," she said. "I find it monstrously unfair—"

"Agreed," he put in.

"—but I do understand it. But still, I suspect there are all sorts of nuances of which I am completely unaware."

"Oh, absolutely. For example, our performance here in the park—there are all sorts of details that must be played precisely right."

"I have no idea what you're talking about."

He adjusted his position so that he was more directly facing her. "It's all in how I look at you."

"I beg your pardon?"

He smiled down at her, gazing adoringly at her face. "Rather like this," he murmured.

Her lips parted, and for a moment she didn't breathe.

He loved that he could do this to her. Almost as much as he loved that he *knew* she didn't breathe. God, how loved being able to read women. "No, no," he admonished. "You can't look *back* at me like that."

She gave a dazed blink. "What?"

He leaned another inch down and mock whispered, "People are watching."

Her eyes widened, and he could tell the exact moment her brain snapped back to attention. She tried to be surreptitious as she looked to the left and then to the right, and then, slowly and with the utmost confusion, back at him. But really, she had no clue what she was doing.

"You're quite bad at this," he told her.

"I am utterly at a loss," she admitted.

"Probably why you have no idea what you're doing," he said smoothly. "Allow me to edify: We are in the park."

Annabel raised a brow. "I'm aware."

"With about a hundred or so of our closest acquaintances."

She turned her head again, this time toward Rotten Row, where several small groups of ladies were pretending not to look at them.

"Don't be so obvious," he said, giving a nod of greeting to Mrs. Brompton and her daughter Camilla, who were smiling at them in that *I acknowledge you but perhaps we should not converse* sort of way.

Annabel meant to get annoyed; really, who

looked at another person like that? But then she couldn't help but congratulate herself for having successfully interpreted a multifaceted expression.

However rude it might be.

"You look annoyed," Mr. Grey said.

"No." Well, maybe yes.

"You do understand what we are doing," he verified.

"I thought I did," she muttered.

"You may have noticed that you have become an object of speculation," he said.

Annabel fought the urge to snort. "You could say that."

"Why, Miss Winslow, do I detect a hint of sarcasm in your voice?"

"Just a hint."

He looked about ready to chuckle but did not. It was a common expression for him, she realized. He saw humor everywhere. It was a rare gift, that, and possibly why everyone liked to be near him. He was happy, and if one could be near a happy person, perhaps it would rub off. Happiness could be like a head cold. Or cholera.

Catching. She liked that. Catching happiness.

She smiled. She couldn't help it. She looked up at him, because she couldn't quite help that, either, and he looked down, his eyes curious. He was about to ask her a question, probably about why she'd suddenly started smiling like a loon, when—

Annabel jumped back. "Was that a gunshot?"

He didn't say anything, and when she looked at him closely, she realized he'd gone terribly pale.

"Mr. Grey?" She placed a hand on his arm. "Mr. Grey? Are you all right?"

He did not speak. Annabel felt her eyes widen, and even though she knew he could not possibly have been shot, she found herself looking him up and down, half expecting to see blood.

"Mr. Grey?" she said again, because she'd never seen him like this. And while she could not claim an extensive acquaintance, she knew that something was terribly wrong. His face was still and taut, and his eyes were somewhere else.

They were right there in his head, looking at a spot beyond her shoulder, and yet it was as if he wasn't there at all.

"Mr. Grey?" she said again, and this time she gave his arm a little squeeze, as if she might wake him up. He jumped, and his head snapped in her direction. He looked at her for several seconds before she thought he actually saw her, and even then he blinked several times before saying, "My apologies."

She did not know what to say to that. There was nothing he could possibly need to apologize for.

"It's that bloody competition," he muttered.

She knew better than to scold him for his language. "What competition?"

"Some stupid shooting contest. In the middle of Hyde Park," he snapped. "A pack of idiots. Who would do such a thing?"

Annabel started to say something. She felt her lips move, but nothing really came out. So she shut her mouth. Better to stay silent than to say something foolish.

"They were doing it last week as well," he muttered.

"I think they're just over the rise," Annabel said, motioning behind her. The shot had seemed rather close, actually. Nothing to make her go pale and shaky; a girl did not grow up in the country without hearing rifles discharged with a fair bit of regularity. Still, it had been rather loud, and she supposed that if one had returned from the war—

The *war*. That was what it had to be. Her father's father had fought in the colonies, and until the day he died he'd jumped every time he heard a loud noise. No one ever said a thing about it. The conversation would miss a beat, but never more than that, and then everything would go on as if nothing had happened. It had been unwritten rule in the Winslow family. And it had suited them all quite well.

Or had it?

It had suited the rest of the family, but what about her grandfather? He never quite lost the hollow look in his eyes. And he did not like to travel after dark. No one liked it, Annabel supposed, but they all did it when necessary. Except her grandfather. When night fell, he was in the house. Any house. More than once he'd ended up as someone's unexpected houseguest.

And Annabel wondered—had anyone ever asked him about it?

She looked up at Mr. Grey, suddenly feeling as if she knew him a great deal better than she had just a minute earlier.

But perhaps not well enough to say anything.

He dragged his gaze back to her face from whatever it was he was staring at, and he started to say something, but then—

Another gunshot.

"God *damn* it."

Annabel's lips parted in surprise. She looked this way and that, hoping no one had heard him curse. She did not mind, of course, she'd never been overly fussy about such things, but—

"Excuse me," he muttered, and then he took off in the direction of the shots, his gait long and purposeful. Annabel took a moment to react, then bounced to attention and hurried after him.

"Where are you going?"

He didn't answer, or if he did, she couldn't hear it because he did not turn around. And it was a stupid question, anyway, because it was perfectly clear where he was going: over to the shooting competition, although why, she had no idea. Was he going to scold them? Ask them to stop? Could he even do that? If people were shooting in the park, they would have had to get permission to do so. Wouldn't they?

"Mr. Grey!" she called out, trying to keep up. But he had long legs, and she had to move hers nearly twice as fast to match his stride. By the time she made it over to competition area, she was out of breath and perspiring under her corset.

But she soldiered on, chasing after him until she was but a few steps behind. He had stomped over to the gathering of participants—about a half dozen young men, none of them a day over twenty, if Annabel was any judge.

"What the devil do you think you are doing?" he demanded. Except that his voice was not raised. Which Annabel found odd, considering how obviously angry he was.

"Competition," one of the young gentlemen said, affecting the sort of annoyingly jaunty grin that always made Annabel roll her eyes. "We've been at it all week."

"So I've heard," Mr. Grey responded.

"We've got the area behind cleared out," the gentleman said, waving his arm toward the target. "Don't worry."

"And when will you be done?" Mr. Grey asked coolly.

"When someone hits dead center."

Annabel looked down toward the target. She had seen her fair share of shooting contests, and she could tell that it had been set uncommonly far away. And she suspected that at least three of the men had been drinking. They could be here all afternoon.

"D'you want to have a go at it?" another of the young men asked, holding a pistol out toward Mr. Grey.

He gave them a dry smile and reached for the gun. "Thank you."

And then, right before Annabel's extremely wide eyes, he lifted his arm, squeezed the trigger, and handed the gun back to its owner.

"There," he announced curtly. "You're done."

"But—"

"It's over," he said, then turned toward Annabel with an utterly placid face. "Shall we continue our stroll?"

Annabel got out a yes, but she wasn't sure it was terribly clear, as her head was snapping back and forth between Mr. Grey and the target. One of the young men had run out to see how he'd done and was presently yelling something and sounding extremely surprised.

"It was a bull's-eye!" he yelled, running toward them. "Dead center."

Annabel's lips parted in amazement. Mr. Grey hadn't even aimed. Or at least he hadn't *seemed* to aim.

"How'd you do that?" the young men were asking. And then one of them added, "Could you do it again?"

"No," he answered curtly, "and don't forget to clean up after yourselves."

"Oh, we're not done yet," one of the young men said—rather foolishly, in Annabel's opinion. Mr. Grey's tone was light, but only an idiot would have missed the hard glint in his eyes.

"We'll set up another target," he continued. "We have until half two. You don't really count, since you're not part of the games."

"Excuse me," Mr. Grey said smoothly to Annabel. He let go of her arm and walked back to the other men. "May I have your gun?" he asked one of them.

Silently it was handed over, and once again Mr. Grey lifted his arm, and with no apparent concentration, squeezed the trigger.

One of the wooden posts supporting the target splintered—no, it evaporated—and the entire thing went tumbling to the ground.

"Now you're done," Mr. Grey said, handing the gun back to its owner. "Good day."

He walked back to Annabel's side, took her arm, and said, before she could ask, "I was a sniper. In the war."

She nodded, fairly certain she now knew how the French had been defeated. She looked back at the target, now surrounded by men, then back at Mr. Grey, who appeared completely unconcerned. Then, because she couldn't stop herself, she turned back to target, dimly aware of his pressure on her arm as he tried to pull her away. "That was . . . that was . . ."

"Nothing," he said. "Nothing at all."

"I wouldn't call it nothing," she said gingerly. He didn't seem to want praise, but at the same time, she couldn't *not* say something.

He shrugged. "It's a talent."

"Er, a useful one, I should think." She wanted to look back one more time, but she wasn't going to be able to see anything, and anyway, *he* hadn't looked back even once.

"Would you like an ice?" he asked.

"I beg your pardon?"

"An ice. I'm feeling a bit warm. We could go to Gunter's."

Annabel made no response, still flummoxed by the abrupt change of conversation.

"We'll have to bring Olivia, of course, but she's good enough company." He frowned thoughtfully. "And she's probably hungry. I'm not sure she had breakfast this morning."

"Well, of course . . ." Annabel said, although not because she knew what he was talking about. He was looking at her expectantly, and she was clearly supposed to make a reply.

"Excellent. Gunter's it shall be." He grinned at her, his eyes sparkling in that now familiar way, and Annabel wanted to grab him by the shoulders and shake. It was as if the entire episode with the guns and target had never happened.

"Do you like orange?" he asked. "The orange is particularly good, second only to the lemon, although they don't always serve that."

"I like orange," she said, again because a response seemed appropriate.

"The chocolate is also quite delicious."

"I do like chocolate."

And so it went, a conversation about nothing at all, all the way to Gunter's. Where, Annabel was not particularly proud to say, she forgot all about the incident in the park. Mr. Grey insisted upon ordering one of every flavor, and Annabel insisted that it would be rude not to taste them all (except for rose, which she never could abide; it was a *flower*, for heaven's sake, not a flavor). Then Lady Olivia declared herself unable to tolerate the smell of the bergamot ice, which meant that of course Mr. Grey had to wave it under her nose. Annabel couldn't recall the last time she'd had so much fun.

Fun. Pure, simple, fun. A very good thing, indeed.

Chapter Fifteen

Two days later

By the time Annabel had finished dancing with Lord Rowton, which followed her dance with Mr. Berbrooke, which followed her dance with Mr. Albansdale, which followed her dance with a *different* Mr. Berbrooke, which followed her dance with Mr. Cavender, which followed her dance with—good heavens!— a Russian prince, which followed her dance with Sir Harry Valentine, which followed her dance with Mr. St. Clair, which (she had to take a breath here, just thinking about it!) followed her dance with Mr. Grey . . .

Suffice it to say that if she had not previously understood the fickle nature of London society, she did now. She did not know how many of the gentlemen had invited her to dance because Mr. Grey had asked them to, and how many had asked her because all of the other gentlemen seemed to be doing so, but one thing was clear: She was the latest rage. For this week, at least.

Their walk in the park had done its trick, as had the outing at Gunter's. Annabel had been seen by all the *ton* with Sebastian Grey acting (in his words) like a lovesick fool. He had made sure that all the biggest gossips had seen him kissing her hand, and laughing at her jokes, and, for those who approached them in conversation, gazing adoringly (but not lustfully) at her face.

And yes, he had actually used the word "lustfully." Which would have shocked her except that he had such an amusing way of saying things. All she could do was laugh, which, he informed her, was only fair because he could not have it getting out that he was laughing at her jokes and not vice versa.

Which made her laugh again.

They had repeated the charade the next afternoon, and the one after that, too, taking a picnic with Sir Harry and Lady Olivia. Mr. Grey had returned her to her grandparents' home with strict instructions not to arrive at the Hartside ball that evening until half nine at the earliest. The Vickers carriage rolled to a halt at nine forty-five, and when she stepped into the ballroom five minutes later, Mr. Grey just happened to be standing near the door, in conversation with a gentleman she did not recognize. When he saw her, however, he immediately broke away and came to her side.

That he walked past three extremely beautiful women to get there was not, Annabel suspected, an accident.

Two minutes later they were dancing. And five minutes after that she was dancing with the gentleman he'd been chatting with. And so on and so forth, straight through the Russian prince, both Berbrookes, to Lord Rowton. Annabel was not sure that she wished to live her life as the most popular girl in town, but she had to admit that for one evening at least, it was marvelously good fun.

Lady Twombley had approached, all venom and bile, but even she could not twist the gossip into anything unpleasant. She was no match for Lady Olivia Valentine, who (Annabel was informed) had casually mentioned that Mr. Grey might truly be smitten to three of her closest friends.

"The three with no discretion whatsoever," Sir Harry had murmured.

Lady Olivia, Annabel was coming to realize, had a very astute grasp on the mechanics of gossip.

"Annabel!"

Annabel saw Louisa waving to her, and as soon as she curtsied to Lord Rowton and thanked him prettily for the dance, she made her way over to her cousin's side.

"We are twins," Louisa declared, motioning to their gowns, which were of an almost identical pale sage hue.

Annabel could not help but laugh. Surely two cousins had never been made less alike.

"I know," Louisa said. "It's a dreadful color on me."

"Of course not," Annabel assured her, except that, maybe a little bit, it was.

"Don't lie," Louisa said. "As my cousin, it is your duty to tell the truth when no one else will."

"Very well, it is not your *best* color . . ."

Louisa sighed. "I am without color."

"Of course not!" Annabel exclaimed, except that tonight, in the sage green that looked so terrible on her, maybe a little bit, she was. Louisa's skin was always pale, but the dim light and the dress seemed to suck every last bit of pink from her cheeks. "I quite liked the blue you wore to the opera. It was very fetching on you."

"Do you think so?" Louisa asked, almost hopefully. "I *felt* fetching in it."

"Sometimes I think that is half the battle," Annabel told her.

"Well, *you* must be extremely fetching in sage," Louisa said. "You are quite the belle of the ball."

"It has nothing to do with the color of my dress," Annabel said, "as you well know."

"Mr. Grey has been very busy," Louisa stated.

"Indeed."

They stood for a moment, watching the rest of the crowd, and then Louisa said, "It was very good of him to intercede."

Annabel nodded and murmured her agreement.

"No, I mean it was *very* good of him."

Annabel turned to face her.

"He did not have to do it," Louisa said, her

voice not quite stern, but . . . almost. "Most gentlemen would not have done."

Annabel watched her cousin closely, searching
her face for some sort of hidden meaning. But
Louisa wasn't looking at her. Her chin was lifted,
and she was still glancing out over the crowd,
her head moving so very slightly, as if she were
looking for someone.

Or maybe just looking.

"What his uncle did . . ." Louisa said softly. "It
was inexcusable. No one would have faulted him
for striking back."

Annabel waited for more. An explanation. Instructions. Anything. Finally she let out a pent
up breath. "Please," she said. "Not you, too."

Louisa turned. "What do you mean?"

"Exactly that. *Please* just say what you mean. It
is exhausting trying to determine what everyone
is saying to me when it has nothing to do with
the words that are actually coming out of their
mouths."

"But I was," Louisa said. "You need to understand how remarkable his behavior has been.
After what his uncle did to him, and so publicly,
he could not have been blamed had he wished to
wash his hands of the entire affair and leave you
to your scandal."

"No, you see, *that*," Annabel exclaimed, relieved that Louisa had finally explained what
she meant, even if the topic was less than pleas-
ing. "*That* is what I was talking about. Perfectly
clear. *That* is what I wanted to hear."

"What did you want to hear?"

Annabel nearly jumped back a foot. "Mr. Grey!" she squeaked.

"At your service," he said, giving her a jaunty bow. He was wearing a patch over his injured eye, which on most men would have been ridiculous. He, however, looked utterly dashing and dangerous, and Annabel really wished she had not overheard two ladies commenting that they'd like to be plundered by *that* pirate.

"You look so intent," he said to her. "I must know what you were talking about."

Annabel saw no reason not to be almost completely honest. "Merely that I find it exhausting to interpret what everyone says here in London."

"Ah," he said, "you danced with Prince Alexei. Don't mind him. He has a very thick accent."

Louisa giggled.

Annabel fought the urge to shoot her a dirty look. "No one says what they actually mean," she said to Mr. Grey.

He regarded her with a remarkably blank expression, then said, "Did you expect it to be otherwise?"

Another snort emerged from the general vicinity of Louisa's mouth. Followed by several discreet and delicate coughs, since Louisa would never be so bold as to laugh loudly in public.

"I rather enjoy speaking in riddles," Mr. Grey said.

Annabel felt something pulse in her chest. It might have been surprise. Or maybe disappointment. She looked at him, quite unable to mask her expression, and said, "You do?"

His eyes held hers for a breathlessly long moment, and he said, sounding almost baffled, "No."

Annabel's lips parted, but she did not speak. She did not breathe. Something unusual had just passed between them, something remarkable.

"I think . . ." he said slowly. "I think I should ask you to dance."

Annabel nodded, almost dazed.

He held out his hand, then drew it back, signaling for her to wait where she was. "Don't move," he said. "I will be right back."

They were standing near to the orchestra, and Annabel watched as he made his way to the conductor.

"Annabel!" Louisa hissed.

Annabel started. She'd forgot that her cousin was there. She'd forgot that anyone was there. For a few perfect moments, the room had been empty. There had been nothing but her, him, and the soft whoosh of their breath.

"You've already danced with him," Louisa said.

Annabel nodded. "I know."

"People will talk."

Annabel turned and blinked, trying to set her cousin's face into focus. "People are already talking," she said.

Louisa opened her mouth as if she planned to say more, but then she just smiled. "Annabel Winslow," she said softly, "I do believe you are falling in love."

That snapped Annabel right out of her daze. "I am not."

"Oh, you are."

"I hardly know him."

"Apparently you know enough."

Annabel saw that he was making his way back, and something akin to panic rose in her chest. "Louisa, you hush your mouth. This is all for show. He is doing me a *favor*."

Louisa gave an uncharacteristically cavalier shrug. "If you say so."

"Louisa," Annabel hissed, but her cousin was stepping aside for Mr. Grey, who had returned.

"It is a waltz," he announced, as if he hadn't just asked the conductor to play one.

He held out his hand.

She almost took it. "Louisa," she said. "You should dance with Louisa."

He searched her face.

"And then with me," she said softly. "Please."

He bowed, then turned to Louisa, but she murmured her regrets, tilting her head gently in Annabel's direction.

"It has to be you, Miss Winslow," he said softly.

She nodded and stepped forward, allowing him to take her hand in his. Around her she heard whispers, and she felt stares, but when she looked up and saw him gazing down at her, his eyes so clear and gray, it all melted away. His uncle . . . the gossip . . . none of it mattered. She would not let it.

They walked to the center of the ballroom, and she turned to face him, trying to ignore the shiver of anticipation that slid through her when he placed his other hand at the small of her back.

Annabel had never understood why the waltz had once been considered so scandalous.

Now she knew.

He was holding her properly, a full twelve inches between them. No one could have found fault with their behavior. And yet Annabel felt as if the air around them had been heated, as if her skin had been rubbed with some strange, shimmering magic. Each breath seemed to fill her lungs differently, and she was acutely aware of her own body, of how it felt to be inside of it, of how each curve moved and flowed with the music.

She felt like a siren. A goddess. And when she looked up at him, he was staring down at her with a raw, hungry expression. He was aware of her body, too, she realized, and this made her even more tight and taut inside.

For one brief moment she closed her eyes, reminding herself that this was all a sham. They were playacting, rehabilitating her in the eyes of society. Merely by dancing with her, Mr. Grey was making her desirable. And if she felt desired—by him—then she needed to gain a clearer head. He was an honorable man, a generous one, but he was also a consummate actor on the societal stage. He knew exactly how to look at her, smile at her, so that everyone would think he was smitten.

"Why did you ask me to dance with your cousin?" he asked, but his voice sounded odd. Almost a little strangled.

"I don't know," she admitted. And she didn't. Or maybe she simply did not want to admit to herself that she had been scared. "She hadn't waltzed yet."

He nodded.

"And wouldn't it be good for the charade," she said, trying to think on her feet, "for you to dance with my cousin? You wouldn't bother with that if you intended only . . ."

"Only what?" he asked.

She licked her lips. They'd gone dry. "Seduction."

"Annabel," he said, surprising her with the use of her given name. "No man looks at you and thinks of anything *but* seduction."

She looked up at him, startled by the stab of pain his statement had brought. Lord Newbury had wanted her for her curves, for her generous breasts and wide, childbearing hips. And heaven knew she'd never quite got used to the lascivious looks she attracted from all but the most proper of gentlemen. But Mr. Grey . . . She'd thought, somehow, that he was different.

"What matters," he said quietly, "is whether they think of anything in addition to that."

"Do you?" she whispered.

He didn't answer right away. But then he said, almost as if he were figuring it out for himself, too, "I think I might."

Her breath caught, and she searched his face, trying to translate his statement into something she might understand. It did not occur to her that perhaps he didn't understand, either, that he might be just as mystified as she by this strange pull between them.

Or maybe he meant nothing at all. He was that rare kind of man who knew how to be friends with a woman. Perhaps that was all he meant, that he found her company amusing, that she was good for a laugh and a smile, and maybe even worth getting punched in the face.

Maybe that was all it was.

And then just like that, the dance was over. He was bowing, and she was curtsying, and they were walking back to the edge of the room, toward the lemonade table, for which Annabel was inordinately thankful. She was thirsty, but what she really needed was something in her hands, something to distract her, to keep her from fidgeting. Because her skin still felt hot, and her belly was jumping, and if she didn't have something to hold on to, she did not think she would be able to keep herself still.

He handed her a glass, and Annabel had just taken her first grateful sip when she heard someone calling his name. She turned and saw a matron of perhaps forty years moving toward them, waving her hand and trilling, "Oh, Mr. Grey! Mr. Grey!"

"Mrs. Carruthers," he said, giving her a respectful nod. "How lovely to see you."

"I just heard the most amazing bit of news," Mrs. Carruthers said.

Annabel braced herself for something dreadful, probably involving her, but Mrs. Carruthers focused all of her breathless attention on Mr. Grey and said, "Lady Cosgrove tells me you are in possession of autographed books by Mrs. Gorely."

That was all? Annabel was almost disappointed.

"I am," Mr. Grey confirmed.

"You *must* tell me where you got them. I am a

devoted fan, and I could not consider my library complete if I did not have her signature."

"Er, it was in a bookshop in, ah, Oxford, actually, I think."

"Oxford," Mrs. Carruthers said, visibly disappointed.

"I don't think it would be worth a trip to look for more," he said. "There was only the one set of autographed copies, and the bookseller told me that he had never seen others."

Mrs. Carruthers brought the knuckle of her index finger to her mouth, pursing her lips in thought. "It is so intriguing," she said. "I wonder if she is from Oxford. Perhaps she is married to a professor."

"Is there a professor there by the name of Gorely?" Annabel asked.

Mrs. Carruthers turned to her and blinked, as if only just then realizing she was there, standing beside Mr. Grey.

"So sorry," he murmured, and made the introductions.

"Is there?" Annabel asked again. "It would seem to me that that would be the most efficient way of determining if she is a professor's wife."

"It is unlikely that Gorely is her real name," Mrs. Carruthers explained officiously. "I cannot think of a lady who would allow her name to be put on a novel."

"If it's not her real name," Annabel wondered, "does the autograph even have value?"

This was met with silence.

"Furthermore," Annabel continued, "how do

you even know it's her signature? *I* could have signed her name on the title page."

Mrs. Carruthers stared at her. Annabel could not tell if she was aghast at her questions or merely annoyed. After a moment the older woman turned determinedly back to Mr. Grey and said, "Should you ever come across another autographed set, or even a single book, please purchase it and know that I will reimburse you."

"It would be my pleasure," he murmured.

Mrs. Carruthers nodded and walked away. Annabel watched her depart, then said, "I don't think I endeared myself to her."

"No," he agreed.

"I thought my question about the value of the signature was pertinent," she said with a shrug.

He smiled. "I am beginning to understand your obsession with people saying what they actually mean."

"It is not an obsession," she protested.

He quirked a brow. The movement was obscured by his eye patch, but that somehow made it all the more provoking.

"It's not," Annabel insisted. "It is common sense. Just think of all the misunderstandings that could be avoided if people merely spoke to one another instead of telling one person who might tell another who might tell another, who might—"

"You are confusing two issues," he cut in. "One is convoluted prose, the other is merely gossip."

"Both are equally insidious."

He looked down at her with a vaguely condescending air. "You're very hard on your fellow man, Miss Winslow."

She bristled. "I don't think it is too much to ask."

He nodded slowly. "All the same, I think I might have rather my uncle *hadn't* said what he meant Wednesday night."

Annabel swallowed, feeling a bit queasy. And certainly guilty.

"I suppose I appreciate his honesty. On a purely philosophical level, of course." He gave her precisely half a smile. "Practically speaking, however, I do think I'm prettier without the eye patch."

"I'm sorry," she said. It wasn't quite the right thing to say, but it was the best she could think of. And at least it wasn't wrong.

He waved off her apology. "All new experiences are good for the soul. Now I know exactly what it is like to be punched in the face."

"This is good for your soul?" she asked dubiously.

He shrugged, looking out over the crowd. "One never knows when one will need to know how to describe something."

Annabel found this to be an extremely odd statement, but she didn't say anything.

"Besides," he said breezily, "were it not for misunderstandings, we would be sadly lacking in great literature."

She looked at him questioningly.

"Where would Romeo and Juliet be?"

"Alive."

"True, but think of the hours of entertainment the rest of us would have lost."

Annabel smiled. She couldn't help it. "I prefer comedies myself."

"Do you? I suppose they are more entertaining. But then one would never experience the heightened sense of drama afforded by tragedies." He turned to her with that expression of his she was growing so accustomed to—the polite mask he wore for society, the one that labeled him a bored *bon vivant*, oxymoron though it was. And indeed, he let out a slightly affected sigh before saying, "What would life be without bleak moments?"

"Rather lovely, I think." Annabel considered her recent bleak moment, at the hands—or rather, paws—of Lord Newbury. She'd have been quite happy to have done without.

"Hmmm." That was all he said, or rather, hmmmed. Annabel felt a strange need to fill the silence, and she blurted out, "I was voted Winslow Most Likely to Speak Her Mind."

That caught his attention. "Really?" His lips twitched. "And who might we count among the electorate?"

"Er, the other Winslows."

He chuckled.

"There are eight of us," she explained. "Ten with my parents, well, nine now that my father has passed, but still, more than enough for a decent vote."

"I'm sorry about your father," he said.

She nodded, waiting for the familiar lump to form in her throat. But it didn't. "He was a good man," she said.

He nodded in acknowledgment, then asked, "What other titles have you won?"

She gave a guilty grimace. "Winslow Most Likely to Fall Asleep in Church."

He laughed loudly at that.

"Everyone's looking," she whispered urgently.

"Don't mind it. It's all to your benefit in the end."

Right. Annabel smiled awkwardly. This was all about their performance, wasn't it?

"Anything else?" he asked. "Not that anything could possibly be better than the last."

"I came in third for Winslow Most Likely to Outrun a Turkey."

He did not laugh this time, but this appeared to require a valiant effort on his part. "You *are* a country girl," he said.

She nodded.

"Is it so very difficult to outrun a turkey?"

"Not for me."

"Go on," he urged. "I find this fascinating."

"That's right," she said. "You have no siblings."

"A lack for which I have never been so bereft as tonight. Just think of the titles I might have won."

"Grey Most Likely to Join a Pirate Ship?" she suggested, with a nod toward his patch.

"Privateer, if you please. I'm much too refined for piracy."

She rolled her eyes a bit, then offered: "Grey Most Likely to Get Lost on a Heath?"

"You are a cruel woman. I knew where I was the entire time. I was thinking Grey Most Likely to Win a Fortune at Darts."

"Grey Most Likely to Open a Lending Library?" she tried.

He laughed. "Grey Most Likely to Butcher an Opera."

Her mouth fell open. "Do you sing?"

"I tried once." He leaned down confidentially. "It was a moment never to be repeated."

"Probably wise," she murmured, "assuming you wish to keep your friends."

"Or at the very least, allow my friends to keep their hearing."

She grinned, starting to feel giddy with the joke. "Grey Most Likely to Write a Book!"

He froze. "Why would you say that?"

"I–I don't know," she said, perplexed by his reaction. He was not angry, but he had gone utterly serious. "I suppose I think you have a way with words. Didn't I once say you were a poet?"

"Did you?"

"Before I knew who you were," she clarified. "On the heath."

"Oh, right." He pressed his lips together, thinking.

"And you showed great concern for *Romeo and Juliet*. The play, that is, not the characters. On that score you were remarkably uncaring."

"Someone needs to be uncaring," he said.

"Well put," she said with a snort.

"I do try."

Then she remembered. "Oh, and of course there is Mrs. Gorely!"

"There is?"

"Yes, you are such an admirer. I really should read one of her books," Annabel mused.

"Perhaps I will give you one of my autographed copies."

"Oh no, you mustn't do that. You should reserve those for true devotees. I don't even know if I will like it. Lady Olivia doesn't seem to."

"Your cousin does," he pointed out.

"True. But Louisa also likes those horrible Mrs. Radcliffe novels, which honestly, I can't abide."

"Mrs. Gorely is far superior to Mrs. Radcliffe," he said firmly.

"You've read both?"

"Of course. There is no comparison."

"Hmmm. Well, I should give it a try. Judge for myself."

"Then I shall give you one of my unautographed copies."

"You have multiple editions?" My goodness, she hadn't realized he was as big a fan as that.

He gave a little shrug. "I had them all before I found the autographed set."

"Oh, of course. I hadn't considered. Very well, which is your favorite? I shall start with that."

He thought about that for a moment, then said, with a shake of his head, "I couldn't possibly choose. I like different things about each of them."

Annabel grinned. "You sound like my parents, whenever we demanded to know which of us they loved best."

"It's rather similar, I suppose," he murmured.

"If you've given birth to a book," she retorted, pressing her lips together to keep from laughing.

But he wasn't. Laughing, that was.

She blinked with surprise.

And then he did laugh. More of a chuckle, she supposed, but it was odd, because it was as if he'd been five seconds behind the joke, which was unlike him. Wasn't it?

"More plain speaking, Miss Winslow?" he asked, a dry smile turning his question into something of an endearment.

"Always," she said cheerily.

"I think you might—" But then he stopped.

"What?" She was smiling as she said it, but then she saw that he was looking out over her head, toward the door. And he looked grim.

She wet her lips nervously and swallowed. And turned. Lord Newbury had entered the room.

"He looks angry," she whispered.

"He has no claim on you," Mr. Grey bit off.

"Neither do you," she said softly. She looked over toward the side door, the one that led to the ladies' retiring room. But Mr. Grey put his hand on her wrist and held firm.

"You can't run," he said. "If you do, everyone will assume you've done something wrong."

"Or," she returned, *hating* this rush of panic that was washing over her, "they might take one look at him and think that any sane young lady would give him a wide berth."

But of course they wouldn't. And she knew that. Lord Newbury was walking toward them with steely purpose, and the crowds were parting swiftly to allow him passage. Parting and then reforming, of course, facing in Annabel's direction. If there was going to be a scene, no one wanted to miss it.

"I will be right here next to you," Mr. Grey said under his breath.

Annabel nodded. It was amazing—and terrifying—how much comfort that gave her.

Chapter Sixteen

"Uncle," Sebastian said jovially, since he'd long since learned that was the most effective tone to employ, "how delightful to see you again. Although I must say, everything looks different through only one eye." He smiled blandly. "Even you."

Newbury gave him a hard stare, then turned to Annabel. "Miss Winslow."

"My lord." She curtsied.

"We shall have the next dance."

It was an order, not a request. Sebastian stiffened, waiting for Annabel to make a cutting reply, but she just swallowed and nodded. He supposed that was understandable. She had little power against an earl, and Newbury had always been an imposing, imperious presence. She probably had her grandparents to answer to, as well. They were friendly with Newbury; she could not shame them by refusing a mere dance.

"Make sure you return her to my side," Sebastian said, giving his uncle a completely insincere, close-lipped smile.

Newbury returned the expression with an icy glare, and in that instant Sebastian knew he'd made a terrible mistake. He should never have attempted to restore Annabel's position. She would have been far better off an outcast. She could have returned to her country life, found herself a squire who spoke as plainly as she did, and lived contentedly ever after.

The irony was almost too much to bear. Everyone assumed that Sebastian had gone after her because his uncle wanted her, but the truth had turned out to be the exact opposite.

Newbury *had* washed his hands of her. Until he thought that Sebastian might actually be serious. And now he wanted her more than ever.

Sebastian had thought there might be a limit to how much his uncle hated him, but apparently not.

"Miss Winslow and I have an understanding," Newbury said to him.

"Don't you think that is for Miss Winslow to decide?" Sebastian said lightly.

His uncle's eyes flared, and for a moment Sebastian thought he might try to strike him again, but Newbury had not been caught by surprise this time, and he must have had a better hold on his temper because he merely spat, "You are impertinent."

"I merely attempt to restore her to the bosom of society," Sebastian said softly. Reproachfully. If indeed Newbury had had an understanding with her, he should never have left her to the wolves.

At that, Newbury's gaze dropped to Annabel's bosom.

Sebastian felt sick.

Newbury looked back up, his eyes glowing with what could only have been described as pride of ownership.

"You don't have to dance with him," Sebastian said quietly. Hang her grandparents, hang all of society's expectations. No lady should have to dance with a man who looked at her that way in public.

But Annabel just looked at him with the saddest eyes and said, "I think I do."

Newbury gave him a triumphant smile, took her by the arm, and led her away.

Sebastian watched, burning inside, hating this feeling, hating that everyone was staring at him, waiting to see what he'd do.

He'd lost. Somehow, he'd lost.

He felt lost, too.

The following afternoon

Visitors. Annabel was plagued by them.

Now that both Lord Newbury and Mr. Grey seemed to be interested in her, all of society felt the need to see her for themselves. It did not seem to matter that those very same people had *seen* her earlier that week when she was an object of pity.

By early afternoon, Annabel was desperate to escape, so she'd made up some ridiculous story about needing a bonnet the exact color of her new lavender dress, and her grandmother had finally waved her hand and said, "Off with you! I can't listen to another moment of your nonsense."

That Annabel had never before shown such ardor for fashion did not seem to concern her. Nor did she notice that for someone who was so obsessed with matching a hue exactly, Annabel did not see the need to actually bring the dress with her to the milliner.

Then again, Lady Vickers was deep into her game of solitaire, and even deeper into her decanter of brandy. Annabel could have likely strapped an Indian headdress to her brow and she'd not have said a word.

Annabel and her maid, Nettie, had set out for Bond Street, taking the less-traveled roads to their destination. Annabel would have stayed on the less-traveled roads altogether if she could have done. But she couldn't very well return without something new that could be put on her head, so she trudged on, hoping the air might help her clear her thoughts.

It didn't, of course, and the crowds on Bond Street only made it worse. Everyone seemed to be out that day, and Annabel was bumped and jostled, distracted by the buzz of conversation and the whinnies of horses in the street. It was hot, too, and it felt as if there wasn't quite enough air to go around.

She was trapped. Lord Newbury had made it clear the night before that he still planned to marry her. It was only a matter of time before he made his intentions official.

She'd been so relieved when it seemed that he'd

decided he did not want her. She knew her family needed the money, but if he did not ask for her hand, she would not have to say yes. Or no.

She would not have to commit herself to a man she found repulsive. Or turn him down, and live forever with the guilt of her own selfishness.

To make matters worse, she'd received a letter that morning from her sister. Mary was the next oldest to Annabel, and they had always been close. In fact, if Mary had not taken ill with a lung ailment that spring, she would have come to London as well. "Two for the price of one," Lady Vickers had said, when she'd originally offered to see to the girls' debut. "Everything's cheaper that way."

Mary's letter had been cheerful and bright, filled with news of their home, and their village, and the local assembly, and the blackbird that had somehow got trapped in the church, flapping about and eventually perching on the vicar's head.

It was lovely, and it made Annabel so intensely homesick she could hardly bear it. Except that hadn't been all that was in Mary's letter. There were little bits about economizing, and the governess their mother had had to let go, and the embarrassing supper two weeks earlier when the local baronet and his wife had dropped by unannounced, and there was only one type of meat on the table.

Money was running out. Mary hadn't said it in so many words, but it was right there, clear as day. Annabel let out a deep, sorrowful breath as she thought of her sister. Mary was probably sitting at home, imagining that Annabel was attracting the attention of some dashingly handsome, impossibly wealthy nobleman. She'd bring him home, glowing with happiness, and he'd shower everyone with money until their problems were solved.

Instead, Annabel had an extremely wealthy, impossibly dreadful nobleman, and a probably poor, unbelievably handsome rogue. Who made her feel . . .

No. She couldn't think about that. It did not matter what Mr. Grey made her feel, because Mr. Grey did not plan to offer her marriage, and even if he did, he hardly had the means to help her support her family. Annabel did not ordinarily place stock in that sort of gossip, but at least twelve of the eighteen callers she'd endured that morning had seen fit to point out that his was a hand-to-mouth existence. Not to mention the scores who had come by after the altercation at White's.

Everyone had their own opinion of Mr. Grey, it seemed, but the one thing they all agreed upon was that he was not in possession of great wealth. Or really, any wealth at all.

And anyway, he had not proposed. Nor did he intend to.

With a heavy heart, Annabel turned the corner onto Brook Street, allowing Nettie to chatter on about the extravagantly plumed bonnets they'd seen in a Bond Street window. She was about six houses away from home when she saw a grand carriage approaching from the other direction.

"Wait," she said, holding her hand out to stop Nettie.

Her maid looked at her in askance, but she stopped. And she quieted.

Annabel watched with dread as Lord Newbury plopped down to the pavement and marched up the steps. There could be no doubt as to why he was there.

"Ow! Miss . . ."

Annabel turned to Nettie, realizing that she'd been gripping the poor girl's arm like a vise. "I'm sorry," she said in a rush, quickly letting her go, "but I can't go home. Not yet."

"Do you want a different bonnet?" Nettie looked down at the bundle she was carrying. "There was that one with the grapes, but I think it was too dark."

"No. I just—I just—I can't go home. Not yet." Utterly panic-stricken, Annabel grabbed Nettie's hand and tugged her back the way they'd come, not even pausing to breathe until they were out of sight of Vickers House.

"What is it?" Nettie asked, out of breath.

"Please," Annabel pleaded. "Please, don't ask." She looked around. She was on a residential street. She could not remain there all afternoon. "Ehrm, we'll go . . ." She swallowed. Where could they go? She didn't want to go back to Bond Street. She'd just left, and surely someone who had seen her would still be there to notice her reappearance. "We'll get a sweet!" she said, too loudly. "That's just the thing. Aren't you hungry? I'm famished. Aren't you?"

Nettie looked at her as if she'd gone mad. And maybe she had. Annabel knew what she had to do. She'd known it for over a week. But she just didn't want to do it that afternoon. Was it so much to ask?

"Come," Annabel said urgently. "There is a sweet shop just over . . ." Where?

"On Clifford Street?" Nettie suggested.

"Yes! Yes, I think there is." Annabel hurried forth, barely watching where she was going, trying to hold back the tears that were burning behind her eyes. She had to get hold of herself. She could not enter an establishment, even a humble sweet shop, looking like this. She needed to take a breath, and calm herself down, and—

"Oh, Miss Winslow!"

Annabel froze. Dear God, she did not want to talk to anyone. Please, not now.

"Miss Winslow!"

Annabel took a deep breath and turned. It was Lady Olivia Valentine, smiling at her as she handed something to her own maid and walked forward.

"How lovely to see you," Olivia said brightly, "I'd heard— Oh, Miss Winslow, whatever can be wrong?"

"It's nothing," Annabel lied. "I just—"

"No, it's clearly something," Olivia said firmly. "Here, come with me." She took Annabel's arm and led her back a few steps. "This is my home," she informed her. "You may rest here."

Annabel did not argue, grateful to have somewhere to go, grateful to have someone to tell her what to do.

"You need tea," Olivia said, settling her into a drawing room. "I need tea just looking at you." She rang for a maid and ordered a tea service, then sat beside her, taking one of Annabel's hands between hers. "Annabel," she said. "May I call you Annabel?"

Annabel nodded.

"Is there something I can help you with?"

Annabel shook her head. "I wish you could."

Olivia chewed nervously on her lower lip and then asked, her voice careful, "Was it my cousin? Did Sebastian do something?"

"No!" Annabel exclaimed. "No. No. No, please, he has not. He has been everything that is kind and generous. If it weren't for him . . ." She shook her head again, but she did it too quickly this time, and it jarred her so much that she had to put a hand on her forehead. "If it weren't for Mr. Grey," she said, once she felt settled enough to speak evenly, "I should be an outcast."

Olivia nodded slowly. "Then I can only assume it is Lord Newbury."

Annabel gave a tiny nod. She looked down at her lap, at her hands, one still clasped in Olivia's, the other clenched in a fist. "I'm being very silly, and very selfish." She took a breath and tried to clear her throat, but it came out as an awful choking sound. The sound one made right before one cried. "I just don't . . . want . . ."

She didn't finish the sentence. She didn't have to. She saw the pity in Olivia's eyes. "He has asked, then," Olivia said softly.

"No. Not yet. But he is at my grandparents' house right now. I saw his carriage. I saw him go in." She looked up. She didn't want to think about what Olivia might see in her face, in her eyes, but she knew she could not speak to her lap forever. "I am a coward. I saw him, and I ran. I just thought—if I don't go home, then he can't ask me to marry him, and then I can't say yes."

"Can't you say no?"

Annabel shook her head, utterly defeated. "No," she said, wondering why she sounded so exhausted. "My family . . . We need . . ." She swallowed, closing her eyes against the pain of it. "After my father died, it was very difficult, and—"

"It's all right," Olivia said, stopping her with a gentle squeeze of her hands. "I understand."

Annabel smiled through her tears, so grateful for this woman's kindness, and yet unable to stop thinking that she *couldn't* understand. Not Olivia Valentine, with her loving husband and wealthy, titled parents. She could not possibly know the pressure that was bearing down on Annabel's shoulders, the knowledge that she could save her family, and all she had to do was forsake herself.

Olivia let out a long breath. "Well," she said efficiently, "we can delay it all by a day, at least. You can remain here for the afternoon. I should like the company."

"Thank you," Annabel said.

Olivia patted her hand and then stood. She walked over to the window and looked out.

"You can't see my grandparents' house from here," Annabel said.

Olivia turned, smiling. "I know. I was just thinking. I do some of my best thinking at windows. Perhaps I shall take a walk in an hour or so. To see if the earl's carriage still sits in front of Vickers House."

"You shouldn't," Annabel said. "Your condition . . ."

"Does not prevent me from walking," Olivia finished with a cheeky expression. "In fact, I should enjoy the air. I was miserable for the first three months, and according to my mother, I'll likely be miserable for the last three, so I had better enjoy this middle time."

"It's the best part of a pregnancy," Annabel confirmed.

Olivia cocked her head to the side, giving Annabel a quizzical look.

"I am the oldest of eight. My mother was with child almost the whole of my youth."

"Eight? My heavens. I am one of but three myself."

"It is why Lord Newbury wishes to marry me," Annabel said flatly. "My mother was one of seven. My father, one of ten. Not to mention that according to gossip, I am so fertile that birds sing when I draw near."

Olivia winced. "You heard that."

Annabel rolled her eyes. "Even I thought it was funny."

"It's good you can have a sense of humor about it."

"One has to," Annabel said with a fatalistic shrug. "If one doesn't, then . . ." She sighed, unable to finish the statement. It was too depressing.

She slumped, letting her gaze settle on the ornate curve of the foot of a nearby end table. She stared at it until it grew fuzzy, then split into two. Her eyes must be crossing. Or she could be going

blind. Maybe if she went blind then Lord Newbury wouldn't want her anymore. Could one go
blind by keeping one's eyes crossed for days?

Maybe. It might be worth trying.

She tilted her head to the side.

"Annabel? Miss Winslow? Are you all right?"

"Fine," Annabel said automatically, still staring at the table.

"Oh, the tea is here!" Olivia exclaimed, clearly
relieved to break the awkward silence. "Here we
are." She sat down and placed a cup in a saucer.
"How do you take yours?"

Annabel reluctantly pulled her gaze from the
table and blinked, allowing her eyes to uncross.
"Milk please. No sugar."

Olivia waited for the tea to finish steeping, chat-
tering away about this and that and nothing in
particular. Annabel was happy—no, grateful—to
just sit and listen. She learned about Olivia's sister-
in-law, who didn't much enjoy coming to town, and
her twin brother, who was (on odd days) the spawn
of the devil. On even days, Olivia had said, her eyes
flicking heavenward, "I *suppose* I love him."

As Annabel sipped the hot liquid, Olivia told
her about her husband's work. "He used to translate *awful* documents. Just dreadfully boring.
One would think that papers for the War Office
would be filled with intrigue, but trust me, that
is not the case."

Annabel sipped and nodded, sipped and
nodded.

"He complains about the Gorely books all the

time," Olivia continued. "The writing really *is* dreadful. But I think he secretly loves translating them." She looked up, as if she'd just thought of something. "Actually, he has Sebastian to thank for the job."

"Really? How is that?"

Olivia's mouth opened, but it was several moments before she actually said, "Honestly, I don't quite know how to describe it. But Sebastian gave a reading for Prince Alexei. Who I believe you met last night."

Annabel nodded. Then frowned. "He gave a reading?"

Olivia looked as if she still couldn't quite believe it. "It was remarkable." She shook her head. "I still can't quite believe it. He had the housemaids in tears."

"Oh my." She really did need to read one of these Gorely books.

"At any rate, Prince Alexei fell in love with the story. *Miss Butterworth and the Mad Baron.* He asked Harry to translate it so that his countrymen can read it, too."

"It must be quite a story."

"Oh, it is. Death by pigeons."

Annabel choked on her tea. "You're joking."

"No. I swear to you, Miss Butterworth's mother is pecked to death by pigeons. And this, the poor woman, after being the only member of her family—except for Miss Butterworth, of course—to survive the plague."

"Bubonic?" Annabel asked, wide-eyed.

"Oh, no, sorry, it was pox. I *wish* it had been bubonic."

"I need to read one of those books," Annabel said.

"I can give you one." Olivia set her tea down and stood, walking across the room. "We have many copies here. Harry sometimes marks the pages, so we've had to buy multiples." She opened up a small cabinet and bent down to look inside. "Oh, dear, I forgot I'm getting a bit unwieldy."

Annabel started to rise to her feet. "Do you need help?"

"No, no." Olivia let out a little groan as she straightened. "Here we are. *Miss Sainsbury and the Mysterious Colonel.* I believe it is Mrs. Gorely's debut effort."

"Thank you." Annabel took the book and looked down at it, running her fingers over gilt letters on the front. She opened to the first page and read the opening.

> *The slanted light of dawn was rippling through the windowpane, and Miss Anne Sainsbury huddled beneath her threadbare blanket, wondering as she often did, how she would find money for her next meal. She looked down at her faithful collie, lying quietly on the rug by her bed, and she knew that the time had come for her to make a momentous decision. The lives of her brothers and sisters depended upon it.*

She slammed it shut.

"Is something wrong?" Olivia asked.

"No, just . . . nothing." Annabel drank more tea. She wasn't sure she wanted to read about a girl making momentous decisions just then. Especially not one who had brothers and sisters depending on her. "I think I will read it later," she said.

"If you want to read now I'm more than happy to leave you to your peace," Olivia said. "Or I could join you. I'm still only halfway through today's newspaper."

"No, no. I'll start it tonight." She smiled ruefully. "It will be a welcome distraction."

Olivia started to say something, but just then they heard someone entering the front door.

"Harry?" Olivia called out.

"Only me, I'm afraid."

Annabel froze. It was Mr. Grey.

"Sebastian!" Olivia called out, shooting a nervous glance at Annabel. Annabel shook her head frantically. She didn't want to see him. Not now, when she was feeling so fragile.

"Sebastian, I wasn't expecting you," Olivia said, hurrying toward the drawing-room door.

He stepped in, leaning down to kiss her cheek. "Since when do you expect me or not expect me?"

Annabel slouched down in her seat. Maybe he wouldn't see her. Her dress was almost the same blue as the sofa. Perhaps she'd blend in. Perhaps he'd gone blind from having crossed his eyes for days. Perhaps—

"Annabel? Miss Winslow?"

She smiled weakly.

"What are you doing here?" He walked swiftly

across the room, his brow knitted with concern. "Is something wrong?"

Annabel shook her head, unable to speak. She'd thought she had herself under control. She'd been *laughing* with Olivia, for heaven's sake. But one look at Mr. Grey and everything she'd been trying so hard to keep down rose right back up, pressing behind her eyes, clenching at her throat.

"Annabel?" he asked, kneeling down in front of her.

She burst into tears.

Chapter Seventeen

Sebastian had seen Annabel only once the previous evening after her dance with his uncle. Her eyes had been shuttered and she had seemed subdued, but there had been nothing that might have predicted *this*. She was sobbing as if the world were about to crash on her shoulders.

Seb felt as if he'd been punched in the stomach.

"Good God," he said, turning to Olivia. "What happened to her?"

Olivia pursed her lips and didn't say anything. She just tilted her head toward Annabel. Seb had the impression he had just been scolded.

"It's nothing," Annabel sobbed.

"It's not nothing," he said. He looked at Olivia again, giving her an urgent—and annoyed—expression.

"It's not nothing," Olivia confirmed.

Seb swore under his breath. "What did Newbury do?"

"Nothing," Annabel said, shaking her head. "He didn't do anything . . . because . . . because . . ."

Sebastian swallowed, not liking the queasy feeling building in his belly. His uncle did not have a reputation for baseness or cruelty, but nor had any woman ever had cause to call him gentle. Newbury was the sort who inflicted pain through carelessness, or more accurately, selfishness. He took what he wanted because he thought he deserved it. If his needs conflicted with someone else's, frankly, he didn't much care.

"Annabel," he said, "you have to tell me what happened."

But she was still crying, gulping down big huge breaths, and her nose . . .

He handed her his handkerchief.

"Thank you," she got out, and used it. Twice.

"Olivia," he snapped, whipping around to face her, "will you tell me what the hell is going on?"

Olivia walked over and crossed her arms, looking righteous as only a woman could. "Miss Winslow believes that your uncle is about to propose marriage."

He let out a long breath. He was not surprised. Annabel was everything his uncle wanted in a bride, moreso now that he thought Sebastian wanted her, too.

"Here now," he said, trying to be comforting. He took one of her hands and squeezed. "It'll all work out. I'd be crying, too, if he asked me to marry him."

She looked as if she might laugh, but then she just cried again.

"Can't you say no?" he asked. "Can't she say no?" he asked Olivia.

Olivia crossed her arms. "What do you think?"

"If I'd known what to think, I'd hardly have asked, would I?" he bit off, coming to his feet.

"She is the oldest of eight, Sebastian. Eight!"

"For the love of God," he exploded, "will you just say what you mean?"

Annabel looked up, momentarily silenced.

"I now understand your feelings precisely," he told her.

"There is no money left," Annabel said in a small voice. "My sisters have no governess. My brothers are going to be sent home from school."

"What about your grandparents?" Surely Lord Vickers had enough money to pay a few tuition bills.

"My grandfather hasn't spoken to my mother for twenty years. He never forgave her for marrying my father." She paused for a moment, taking a shaky breath and then using the handkerchief. "He only took me in because my grandmother insisted upon it. And she only did so because . . . well, I don't know why. I think she thought it would be amusing."

Seb looked over at Olivia. She was still standing there with her arms crossed, looking rather like a warrior mother hen. "Excuse me," he said to Annabel, and then he grabbed Olivia's wrist and dragged her across the room. "What would you have me do?" he hissed.

"I don't know what you're talking about."

"Stop playing games. You've been glowering at me since I arrived."

"She's upset!"

"I can see that," he snapped.

She poked him in the chest. "Well, then, do something."

"It isn't my fault!" And it wasn't. Newbury had wanted Annabel long before Sebastian had become embroiled in the affair. She'd likely be in the exact same position if Seb had never met her.

"She needs to marry, Sebastian."

Oh, for the love of God. "Are you suggesting that *I* propose to her?" he asked, knowing damn well that was what she was suggesting. "I have known her barely a week."

She stared at him as if he were a complete cad. Hell, he felt like one. Annabel was sitting across the room, whimpering into his handkerchief. A man would have to have a heart of stone not to want to help her.

But marriage? What sort of man married a woman he'd known for—how long had it been?— eight days? Society might think him foolish and flighty, but that was only because he liked it that way. He cultivated that image because . . . be-cause . . . well, hell, he wasn't sure why he did it. Maybe just because it amused him, too.

But he'd thought Olivia knew him better.

"I like Miss Winslow," he whispered. "I do. And I regret that she is in this ghastly situation. Lord knows, I know more than anyone what a miser-able existence it must be to live with Newbury. But it is not my doing. Nor is it my problem."

Olivia's eyes bored down on his, full of disappointment.

"You married for love," he reminded her.

Her jaw worked, and he knew he'd scored a hit. He wasn't, however, quite sure why he felt so guilty about it. Still, he could not stop now. "Would you deny me the same?" he asked.

Except . . .

He looked over at Annabel. She was staring forlornly out the window. Her dark hair was starting to come free of its pins, and one loose curl had made its way down her back, revealing the length to be a few inches below her shoulders.

It would be longer when it was wet, he thought absently.

But he would never see it wet.

He swallowed.

"You're right," Olivia said suddenly.

"What?" He looked back at her, blinking.

"You're right," she said again. "It was unfair of me to expect you to swoop in and save her. She's hardly the first girl in London to have to marry someone she doesn't like."

"No." He looked at her suspiciously. Was she up to something? She might be. Or she might not. Damn. He hated when he couldn't read a woman.

"It's not as if you can save them all."

He shook his head, but without much conviction.

"Very well," Olivia said briskly. "We can save her for this afternoon, at least. I've told her she may remain until evening. Surely Newbury will lose patience before then and go home."

"He's at her house right now?"

She gave a curt nod. "She was coming home from . . . well, I don't know where. Shopping, I suppose. She saw him get out of the carriage."

"And she is certain he was there to propose?"

"I don't believe she wished to remain long enough find out," Olivia answered acerbically.

He nodded slowly. It was difficult to put himself in Annabel's shoes, but he supposed he would have done the same.

Olivia looked over at the clock on the mantel. "I have an appointment."

This he did not believe for a second, but still he said, "I will stay with her."

Olivia let out a long exhale. "I suppose we'll need to send a note over to her grandparents. They are going to miss her at some point. Although knowing her grandmother, perhaps not."

"Say that you've invited her to visit," he suggested. "They cannot object to the connection." Olivia was one of London's most popular young matrons; anyone would be delighted to have her take their daughter—or granddaughter—under her wing.

Olivia nodded and went over to Annabel. Sebastian poured himself a drink, and then, after downing it in one swallow, poured himself another. And one for Annabel, too. By the time he brought them over, Olivia had said her good-byes and was heading out the door.

He held out the drink.

"She has an appointment," Annabel said.

He nodded. "Take it," he said. "You might not want it. But you might."

She took the glass, took a tiny sip, and set it down. "My grandmother drinks too much," she said, her voice a heartbreaking monotone.

He didn't say anything, just sat down in the chair closest to the sofa and made some sort of reassuring sound. He wasn't good with sad women. He didn't know what to say. Or do.

"She's not a bad drunk. She just gets a little silly."

"And amorous?" he asked, quirking a smile. It was a highly inappropriate comment, but he could not bear the sadness in her eyes. If he could make her smile, it would be worth it.

And she did! Just a little. But still, it felt like a victory.

"Oh, that." She covered her mouth with her hand and shook her head. "I am so sorry," she said with great feeling. "Honestly, I don't know when I have ever felt more embarrassed. I have never seen her do that before."

"It must be my charming aspect and hand-some visage."

She gave him a look.

"You're not going to say something about my modesty and discretion?" he murmured.

She shook her head, the sparkle starting to return to her eyes. "I've never been a very good liar."

He chuckled.

She took another sip of her drink, then set it down. But she didn't let go. Her fingers tapped against the glass, tracing short quick lines near the rim. She was a fidgeter, his Annabel.

He wondered why this pleased him. He was not

like that. He'd always been able to hold himself preternaturally still. It was probably why he was such a good shot. In the war he'd sometimes had to hold still for hours in his sniper's perch, waiting for the perfect moment to squeeze the trigger.

"I just want you to know . . ." she began.

He waited. Whatever it was she was trying to say, it wasn't easy.

"I just want you to know," she said again, sounding as if she was trying to muster her courage, "that I know this has nothing to do with you. And I don't expect—"

He shook his head, trying to save her from having to make a difficult speech. "Hush, hush. You don't have to say anything."

"But Lady Olivia—"

"Can be very meddlesome," he interjected. "Let us just, for now, pretend that—" He cut himself off. "Is that a Gorely book?"

Annabel blinked and looked down. She seemed to have forgotten it was sitting in her lap. "Oh. Yes. Lady Olivia lent it to me."

He held out his hand. "Which one did she give you?"

"Er . . ." She looked down. *"Miss Sainsbury and the Mysterious Colonel."* She handed it to him. "I assume you've read it."

"Of course." He opened the book to its first pages. *The slanted light of dawn*, he said to himself. He remembered so clearly writing those words. No, that was not true. He remembered *thinking* them. He'd thought out the entire opening before writing it down. He'd gone over it so many times, editing in his head until he'd got it just the way he wanted it.

That had been his moment. His very own point of division. He wondered if everyone's lives had a dividing point. A moment which sat clearly between *before* and *after*. That had been his. That night in his room. It hadn't been any different than the night before, or the one before that. He couldn't sleep. There was nothing out of the ordinary about that.

Except for some reason—some inexplicable, miraculous reason, he'd started thinking about books

And then he'd picked up a pen.

Now he got to be in his *after*. He looked at Annabel.

He looked away. He didn't want to think about her *after*.

"Shall I read it to you?" he asked, his voice sounding a little loud. But he had to do something to change the direction of his thoughts. Besides, it might cheer her up.

"All right," she said, her lips forming a hesitant smile. "Lady Olivia said you're a wonderful reader."

There was no *way* Olivia had said *that*. "She did, did she?"

"Well, not exactly. But she did say that you made the housemaids cry."

"In a good way," he assured her.

She actually giggled. He felt absurdly pleased.

"Here we are," he said. "*Chapter One*." He cleared his throat and went on. "*The slanted light of dawn was rippling through the windowpane, and Miss Anne Sainsbury huddled beneath her threadbare blanket, wondering as she often did, how she would find money for her next meal."*

"I can picture that exactly," Annabel said.

He looked up in surprise. And pleasure. "You can?"

She nodded. "I used to be an early riser. Before I arrived in London. The light is different in the morning. It's flatter, I suppose. And more golden. I've always thought—" She cut herself off, cocking her head to the side. Her brows knit together and she frowned. It was the most adorable expression. Sebastian almost thought that if he looked hard enough, he could actually *see* her thinking.

"You know exactly what I mean," she said.

"I do?"

"Yes." She straightened, and her eyes flashed with memory. "You said so. When I met you at the Trowbridge party."

"The heath," he said with a sigh. It seemed such a delightful, far-off memory now.

"Yes. You said something about the morning light. You said you—" She stopped, blushing furiously. "Never mind."

"I must say, now I *really* want to know what I said."

"Oh . . ." She shook her head quickly. "No."

"*Anna-bel*," he prodded, liking the way her name took on a musical lilt.

"You said you'd like to take a bath in it," she said, the words coming out in a single, mortified rush.

"I did?" Strange. He didn't remember saying that. Sometimes he got lost in his own thoughts. But it did sound like something he'd say.

She nodded.

"Hmmm. Well. I suppose I would." He tilted his head in her direction, the way he frequently did when about to deliver a *bon mot*. "I should want some privacy, though."

"Of course."

"Or maybe not *too* much privacy," he murmured.

"*Stop.*" But she didn't sound offended. Not quite.

He glanced at her when she thought he wasn't looking. She was smiling to herself, just a little bit. Enough for him to see her courage, her strength. Her ability to hold herself straight in the midst of adversity.

He stopped. What the hell was he thinking? All she had done was hold her own against his risqué comment. That was hardly akin to adversity.

He needed to be careful, else he'd build her up into something she wasn't. It was what he did almost every night, holed up in his room with pen and paper. He created characters. If he allowed his imagination to get the best of him, he'd turn her into the perfect woman.

Which wasn't fair to either of them.

He cleared his throat and motioned to the book. "Shall I continue?"

"Please."

"*She looked down at her faithful collie—*"

"I have a dog," she blurted out.

He looked up in surprise. Not that she had a dog. She seemed the sort who would. But he hadn't expected another interruption so quickly on the heels of the last. "You do?"

"A greyhound."

"Does he race?"

She shook her head. "His name is Mouse."

"You are a cruel woman, Annabel Winslow."

"It's a fitting name, I'm afraid."

"I don't suppose he was the winner in the Winslow Most Likely to Outrun a Turkey contest."

She chuckled. "No."

"You did say you'd come in third," he reminded her.

"We usually limit candidates to those of the human variety." Then she added, "Two of my brothers are quite fleet of foot."

He held up the book again. "Do you want me to continue?"

"I miss my dog," she said with a sigh.

Apparently not. "Er, your grandparents don't have one?" he asked.

"No. There is only Louisa's ridiculous hound."

He recalled the fat little sausage on legs he'd seen at the park. "He was quite stout."

She let out a little snort. "Who names a dog Frederick?"

"Eh?" She was jumping from topic to topic like a chickadee.

She sat up a little straighter. "Louisa named that dog Frederick. Don't you find that ridiculous?"

"Not really," he admitted.

"My *brother* is named Frederick."

He could not imagine why she was telling him all this, but it seemed to be taking her mind off her troubles, so he went along with it. "Is Frederick one of the fleet-footed ones?"

"He is, actually. Also the Winslow Most Likely Not to Become a Vicar." She motioned to herself with one hand. "I would have certainly beaten him at *that,* had the girls not been disqualified on religious grounds."

"Of course," he murmured. "Most likely to fall asleep in church and all that." Then it occurred to him to ask, "Did you actually do it? Fall asleep in church?"

She let out a weary sigh. "Every . . . single . . . week."

He chuckled. "We would have made quite a pair."

"You, too?"

"Oh, no. I never fell asleep. I was ejected for bad behavior."

She leaned forward, eyes sparkling. "What did you do?"

He leaned forward, smiling wickedly. "I'll never tell."

She drew back. "That's not fair."

He shrugged. "Now I just don't go."

"Ever?"

"No. Although to be honest, I probably *would* fall asleep." He would, too. Services were very poorly timed for people who did not sleep well at night.

She smiled, but there was something wistful in it, and she rose to her feet. He started to get up, but she held up a hand. "Please. Not on my account."

Sebastian watched as she walked to the window, resting her head against the glass as she peered out. "Do you think he's still there?" she asked.

He didn't pretend he didn't know exactly what she was talking about. "Probably. He's very tenacious. If your grandparents tell him they expect you to return soon, he'll wait."

"Lady Olivia said that she would drive past Vickers House after her appointment to see if his carriage is there." She turned around, and she didn't quite look at him as she said, "She didn't have an appointment, did she?"

He thought about lying. But he didn't. "I don't think so."

Annabel nodded slowly, and then her face seemed to crumple, and all he could think was, *Oh God, not more tears*, because he wasn't good with tears. Especially not *her* tears. But before he could think of an appropriately comforting thing to say, he realized—

"Are you laughing?"

She shook her head. While she was laughing.

He came to his feet. "What is so funny?"

"Your cousin," she sputtered. "I think she's trying to compromise you."

It was the most ludicrous thing he'd ever heard. And true.

"Oh, Annabel," he said, walking toward her with predatory grace. "I was compromised a long, long time ago."

"I'm sorry." She was still laughing. "I didn't mean to imply . . ."

Sebastian waited, but whatever it was she hadn't meant to imply was lost in a fresh gale of laughter.

"Oh!" She leaned against the wall clutching her middle.

"It wasn't that funny," he said. But he was smiling as he said it. It was impossible not to smile while she was laughing.

She had an extraordinary laugh.

"No, no," she gasped. "Not that. I was thinking of something else."

He waited. Nothing. Finally he said, "Care to tell me what?"

She let out a snort of laughter, possibly through her nose, and she clapped both hands over her mouth, nay, her entire face.

"You look like you're crying," he said.

"I'm not," was her muffled reply.

"I know. I just thought to tell you that, on the off chance someone comes in and thinks I made you weep."

She peeked through her fingers. "Sorry."

"What is so funny?" Because really, by now he had to know.

"Oh, it was just . . . last night . . . when you were talking to your uncle . . ."

He leaned against the back of the sofa, waiting.

"You said you wanted to restore me to the bosom of society."

"Not the most elegant turn of phrase," he allowed.

"And all I could think was—" She looked as if she were going to explode again. "I'm not so sure I like society's bosom."

"It's not my favorite bosom," he concurred, trying very hard not to look at hers.

This only seemed to make her laugh more, which made her quiver in rather bosomy areas.

Which had quite an effect on certain of *his* areas.

He stopped moving.

She covered her eyes in embarrassment. "I can't believe that I just said that."

He stopped breathing. He could only look at her, look at her lips, full and pink, still suspended in a smile.

He wanted to kiss her. He wanted to kiss her more than he wanted to breathe. He wanted to kiss her far more than he had sense, because if he'd been thinking sensibly, he would have stepped away. Walked out of the room. Found himself a very cold bath.

Instead he stepped toward her. Put his hand over hers, holding it gently in place over her eyes.

Her lips parted, and he heard a soft whisper of air rush across. Whether she'd exhaled or gasped, he didn't know. He didn't care. He just wanted her breath to be his breath.

He leaned forward. Slowly. He couldn't rush it, couldn't risk losing one second of it. He wanted to remember this. He wanted every last moment burned into his memory. He wanted to know what it felt like to be two inches away, and then one, and then . . .

He touched his lips to hers. One tiny, fleeting touch before pulling back. He wanted to see her, to know exactly what she looked like after a kiss.

To know exactly what she looked like waiting for another.

He wound his fingers through hers and slowly

pulled her hand from her eyes. "Look at me," he whispered.

But she shook her head, keeping her eyes closed.

And then he could wait no longer. He wrapped his arms around her, pulling her against him, and brought her lips to his. But it was so much more than a kiss. His hands stole around and down to her bottom, and he squeezed. He didn't know whether he was trying to press her against him or simply revel in the lushness of her body.

She was a goddess in his arms, soft and sumptuous, and he wanted to feel her, every inch. He wanted to touch and stroke and knead, and Good Lord, he almost forgot he was kissing her, too. But her body . . . her body was a thing of beauty. It was a bloody miracle in his arms, and when he finally lifted his mouth from hers to draw breath, he couldn't help it. He moaned and then moved down to her jaw, to her throat. He didn't just want to kiss her mouth. He wanted to kiss her everywhere.

"Annabel," he groaned, his fingers nimbly finding the buttons at the back of her frock. He was good. He knew exactly how to disrobe a woman. He usually did it slowly, savoring every moment, every new inch of flesh, but with her . . . he couldn't wait. He was like a madman, pushing each button through its hole until he'd got enough undone to push the dress down over her shoulders.

Her chemise was very plain, no silk, no lace, just thin white cotton. But it drove him wild. She didn't need embellishment. She'd been made perfectly.

With shaking fingers he went to the ties at her shoulders and tugged, barely able to breathe as the thin strips of fabric fell away.

He whispered her name, and then again, and again. He heard her moan, a soft little squeak of noise which grew deeper and huskier as his hand slid along her shoulder, down to the luscious curve of her breast. She was only lightly corseted, but the stays pushed her up, making her breasts impossibly high and round.

He nearly lost control of himself right then.

He had to stop this. It was madness. She was a proper young lady, and he was treating her like—

He pressed one final kiss against her skin, breathing in the hot scent of her, and then wrenched himself away.

"I'm sorry," he gasped. But he wasn't. He knew he should be, but he didn't think he could ever regret having held her so intimately.

He started to turn away, because he didn't think he could see her and not touch her again, but just before he did, he saw that her eyes were closed.

His heart dropped, and he rushed to her side. "Annabel?" He touched her shoulder, then her cheek. "What is wrong?"

"Nothing," she whispered.

His finger moved to her temple, right to the corner of her eye. "Why are your eyes closed?"

"I'm afraid."

"Of what?"

She swallowed. "Of myself." And then she

opened her eyes. "Of what I might want. And what I have to do."

"Did you not want me to . . ." Dear God, had she not wanted him? He tried to think. Had she returned the kiss? Had she touched him in return? He couldn't remember. He'd been so overwhelmed by her, by his own need, that he couldn't remember what she'd done.

"No," she said softly. "I wanted you to. That's the problem." She closed her eyes again, but just for a moment. She looked like she was trying to restore something within herself, and then she opened them again. "Could you help me?"

He started to say yes, that he'd help her. He'd do whatever was within his power to protect her from his uncle, to save her family and keep her brothers in school, but then he saw that she was motioning to the ties of her chemise, and he realized that all she actually wanted was help getting dressed.

So he did that. He tied her ties and buttoned her buttons, and he didn't say a word as she took a seat near the window and he found one by the door.

They waited. And they waited. And then finally, after what seemed like hours, Annabel stood and said, "She's back."

Sebastian rose to his feet, watching Annabel as she peered out the window at Olivia, alighting from her carriage. She turned, and it just came out of him:

"Will you marry me?"

Chapter Eighteen

Annabel nearly fell on her face. "What?"

"Not precisely the answer I'd been expecting," Sebastian murmured.

Still, she could not quite grasp it. "You want to marry me?"

He cocked his head to the side. "I believe I just inquired about it, yes."

"You don't have to," Annabel assured him, because . . . because she was an idiot, and that was clearly what idiots did when men asked to marry them. They told them they didn't have to.

"Are you saying no?" he asked.

"No!"

He smiled. "Then you are saying yes."

"No." Dear God, she felt dizzy.

He took a step toward her. "You're not speaking very plainly, Annabel."

"You purposefully caught me off guard," she accused.

"I caught myself off guard," he said softly.

She gripped the back of the chair she'd been sitting in. It was horribly uncomfortable piece of furniture, but it had been near the window, and she'd wanted to look out for Lady Olivia, and—oh for heaven's sake, why was she thinking about a stupid chair? Sebastian Grey had just asked her to *marry* him.

She glanced out the window. Lady Olivia was still in her carriage. She had two minutes, three at most. "Why?" she asked Sebastian.

"You're asking me why?"

She nodded. "I'm not a damsel in distress. Well, I *am*, but it is not your responsibility to rescue me."

"No," he agreed.

She'd been ready with an argument. Not a coherent one, but still, an argument. This, however, completely flummoxed her. "No?"

"You're right. It's not my responsibility." He walked over, seductively closing the distance between them. "It would, however, be my pleasure."

"Oh my."

He smiled.

"I'm back!" It was Lady Olivia, calling out from the hall.

Annabel looked up at Sebastian. He was standing very close.

"I kissed you," he said softly.

She could not speak. She could barely breathe.

"I kissed you in ways a husband kisses a wife."

Somehow he was even closer than before. Now she definitely couldn't breathe.

"I think," he murmured, his breath now close enough to heat her skin, "that you liked it."

"Sebastian?" It was Lady Olivia. "Oh!"

"Later, Olivia," he said, not even turning around. "And close the door."

Annabel heard the door shut. "Mr. Grey, I'm not sure—"

"Don't you think it's time to start calling me Sebastian?"

She swallowed. "Sebastian, I—"

"I'm sorry." It was Lady Olivia again, bursting in. "I can't."

"You *can*, Olivia," Sebastian ground out.

"No, I really can't. It's my house, and she's unmarried, and—"

"And I'm *asking* her to marry me."

"Oh!" The door shut again.

Annabel tried to keep her head, but it was difficult. Sebastian was smiling down at her as if he might like to nibble her from top to toes, and she was starting to feel the strangest sensations in areas of her body she'd almost forgotten she'd possessed. But she couldn't forget that Lady Olivia was almost certainly standing right outside the door, and she also couldn't forget that—

"Wait a moment!" she exclaimed, wedging her hands between them. She gave him a little push, and when that didn't work, turned it into a shove.

He stepped back, but he didn't stop smiling.

"You just said to her that you didn't want to marry me," she said.

"Hmmm?"

"Just a few hours ago. When I was crying. You said you'd known me barely a week."

He looked unconcerned. "Oh, that."

"Did you think I didn't hear?"

"I *have* known you barely a week."

She didn't reply, so Sebastian leaned down and stole a quick kiss. "I changed my mind."

"In"—she looked crazily around the room for a clock—"two hours?"

"Two and a half, actually." He gave her his most wicked smile. "But they were a rather momentous two and a half hours, wouldn't you agree?"

Olivia came crashing through the door. "What did you *do* to her?"

Sebastian groaned. "You'd make a terrible spy, did you know that?"

Olivia practically flew across the room. "Did you compromise her in my drawing room?"

"No," Annabel said quickly. "No. No. No, no, no. No."

That was quite a lot of no's, Seb thought peevishly.

"He kissed me," Annabel said to Olivia, "but that's all."

Sebastian crossed his arms. "When did you become such a prude, Olivia?"

"It's my *drawing room*!"

He didn't see a problem with that. "You weren't here," he pointed out.

"That's it," Olivia declared, stomping past him and taking Annabel's arm. "You're coming with me."

Oh no, she wasn't. "Where do you think you're taking her?" he demanded.

"Home. I just drove by. Newbury's gone."

Seb crossed his arms. "She hasn't given me an answer yet."

"She'll give it to you tomorrow." Olivia turned to Annabel. "You can give him your answer tomorrow."

"No. Wait a moment." Sebastian reached out and yanked Annabel back. Olivia was *not* going to take over his marriage proposal. Holding Annabel firmly at his side, he turned back to Olivia and said, "You were just hounding me to ask her to marry me, and now you're taking her away?"

"You were trying to seduce her."

"If I'd been trying to seduce her," he growled, "you'd have found a much different scene when you arrived."

"I'm still here," Annabel said.

"I may be the only woman in London who has never been in love with you," Olivia said, jabbing a finger toward Sebastian, "but that does not mean I don't know how charming you can be."

"Why, Olivia," he said, "such lovely compliments."

Annabel held up a hand. "Still here."

"She will make up her mind in the privacy of her own home, and not while you're looking at her with those . . . those . . . *eyes*."

For about two seconds Sebastian was silent. Then he doubled over with laughter.

"What?" Olivia snapped.

Seb elbowed Annabel, then jerked his head

toward Olivia. "I usually look at *her* with my nose."

Annabel pinched her lips together, obviously trying not to smile. She had an excellent sense of humor, his Annabel.

Olivia crossed her arms and turned to Annabel. "He's better than Lord Newbury," she said waspishly, "but only just."

"What's going on in here?" It was Harry, looking a bit rumpled, as if he'd been running his hand through his hair. There was an ink stain on his cheek. "Sebastian?"

Seb looked at his cousin, then at Olivia, and then started laughing so hard he had to flop into a chair.

Harry blinked and shrugged, as if this were nothing out of the ordinary. "Oh, good afternoon, Miss Winslow. Didn't see you back there."

"I told you you knew what she looked like," Olivia muttered.

"I'm looking for a quill," Sir Harry said. He went to a writing table and started looking through the drawers. "I snapped three of them today."

"You snapped three quills?" Olivia asked.

He pulled open another drawer. "It's that Gorely woman. Some of those sentences . . . Good God, they go on forever. I don't know that I have the skill to translate them."

"Try harder," Sebastian said, still trying to catch his breath.

Harry looked over at him. "What's wrong with you?"

Seb waved a hand in the air. "Just having a bit of fun at your wife's expense."

Harry looked over at Olivia, who merely rolled her eyes. He turned back to Annabel. "They can be a bit much at times. I do hope you've been made to feel welcome."

Annabel's skin flushed a delightful pink. "Er, very much so," she stammered.

Harry, however, was color blind, and thus oblivious to a woman's blush. "Ah, here we are." He held up a quill. "Don't mind me. Resume whatever it was you were—" He looked down at Sebastian and shook his head. "Er . . . doing."

"I will," Sebastian said solemnly. It sounded rather like wedding vows. He liked that.

"I should go home," Annabel said, watching Harry depart.

Sebastian stood, mostly recovered from his fit of laughter. "I will escort you."

"No, you won't," Olivia cut in.

"Yes, I will," he returned. And then he lifted his chin in the air and proceeded to look down his nose at her.

"What are you doing?" she burst out.

"I'm *looking* at you," he said, his voice almost singsong.

Annabel clapped a hand over her mouth.

"With my no-ose," he added, just in case Olivia hadn't got the joke the first time.

Olivia actually covered her face with her hands. And not because she was laughing.

Sebastian leaned sideways toward Annabel, not an easy maneuver when he was trying to keep his nose pointed at Olivia. "Not my favorite bosom," he whispered.

"I don't want to know what you just said," Olivia moaned from behind her hands.

"No," Seb agreed, "you probably don't." He resumed a normal standing position and grinned. "I shall escort Annabel home."

"Oh, go ahead," Olivia sighed.

Sebastian leaned down to Annabel and murmured, "I've exhausted her."

"You've exhausted *me*."

"Not yet I haven't."

Annabel blushed again. Sebastian decided he had never been so glad that he was not color blind, too.

"You have to give her at least a day to consider your proposal," Olivia insisted.

Sebastian quirked a brow in her direction. "Did Sir Harry give you a day?"

"That's not relevant," Olivia muttered.

"Very well," Sebastian said, turning back to Annabel, "I shall bow to my dear cousin's greater expertise. Harry was at least the twelfth man to propose to her. Whereas I have never even uttered the word 'marriage' in a woman's presence before today."

Annabel smiled at him. It felt rather like a sunrise.

"I will call upon you tomorrow for your reply," he said, feeling his own smile creep across his face. "But in the meantime . . ." He held out his arm. "Shall we depart?"

Annabel took a step toward him, then stopped. "Actually, I think I would like to walk home by myself."

"You would?"

She nodded. "I assume my maid is still here to accompany me. It's not far. And . . ." She looked down, chewing on her lower lip.

He touched her chin. "Speak plainly, Annabel," he whispered.

She did not quite look at him when she said, "It can be difficult to think clearly in your presence."

He decided to take that as a very good sign, indeed.

Annabel closed the front door carefully behind her and paused, listening. The house was quiet; maybe—hopefully—her grandparents had gone out. She set her book down on the entry table as she pulled off her gloves, then picked it back up, intending to head upstairs to her room. But before she could take three steps, her grandmother appeared in the doorway to the drawing room.

"There you are," Lady Vickers said, looking highly disgruntled. "Where the devil have you been?"

"Just out shopping," Annabel lied. "I saw some friends. We got an ice."

Her grandmother let out a beleaguered sigh. "You're going to ruin your figure."

Annabel gave a tight smile and held up the book Lady Olivia had lent her. "I'm going to my room to read."

Her grandmother waited until she had a foot on the stairs, then said, "You missed the earl."

Annabel swallowed uncomfortably and turned around. "He was here?"

Her grandmother narrowed her eyes, but if she suspected that Annabel had been avoiding Lord Newbury, she did not say so. She motioned with her head toward the drawing room, clearly expecting Annabel to follow. Annabel turned and did so, standing near the doorway while her grandmother walked over to the sideboard to pour herself a drink.

"It would have been a great deal more convenient if you had been here," Lady Vickers said, "but I'm pleased to say we've brought him up to scratch. He spent the better part of an hour with your grandfather."

"Did he?" Annabel's voice came out high and hollow.

"Yes, and *you'll* be pleased to know that I had my ear to the door the whole time." She took a sip and let out a contented sigh. "Your grandfather forgot to mention anything about your family in Gloucestershire, so I took it upon myself to intercede."

"Intercede?"

"I may be fifty-three—"

Seventy-one.

"—but I'm still sharp as a tack." Lady Vickers plunked her glass on the table and leaned forward, looking inordinately pleased with herself. "Newbury'll see to it that all four of your brothers have tuition through university, and he'll buy a commission for any who wants one. As for your sisters, I could only manage a piddling dowry, but it's more than you got." She took a long drink and chuckled. "And *you* landed an earl."

It was everything Annabel could have hoped for. All of her brothers and sisters would have security. They would have everything they needed.

"He doesn't want a long engagement," Lady Vickers said. "You know he wants a son, and fast. Oh, don't look at me like that. You knew this was coming."

Annabel shook her head. "I—I wasn't looking at you like anything. I was just—"

"Oh *God*," Lady Vickers groaned. "Do I have to have the *talk* with you?"

Annabel dearly hoped not.

"Euch. I did it with your mother and your aunt Joan. I'm going to need a far larger drink if I have to do it with you."

"It's all right," Annabel said quickly. "I don't need the talk."

That got her grandmother's attention. "Really?" she asked, suddenly very interested.

"Well, I don't need it right now," Annabel hedged. "Or maybe not . . . ever. From you," she continued, albeit more quietly.

"Eh?"

"I'm from the country," she said with false brightness. "Lots of . . . animals . . . and . . . er . . ."

"Look," Lady Vickers said. "You may know things about sheep that I'm sure I don't wish to hear about, but I still know a thing or two about marriage to an overweight nobleman."

Annabel sank into a chair. Whatever knowledge her grandmother was about to impart, she wasn't sure she could take it standing up.

"It all comes down to one thing," Lady Vickers

said, wagging a finger toward her. "When he's done, stick your legs straight up in the air."

The blood drained from Annabel's face.

"No, do it," her grandmother insisted. "Trust me. It'll help keep the seed in, and the sooner you start carrying, the sooner you can stop having to sleep with him. That, my dear, is the key to a successful marriage."

Annabel picked up her book and rose to her feet, moving as if in a daze. "I'm going to go lie down now."

Lady Vickers smiled. "Of course, dear. Oh! I almost forgot. We're leaving town this evening."

"What? Where?" And how would she let Sebastian know?

"Winifred is hosting an impromptu party in the country," she said, "and you are going."

"I am?"

"I have to go, too, the bloody, stupid . . ."

Annabel's mouth fell open as she listened to the stream of invective, impressive even for her grandmother.

"I hate the country," Lady Vickers grumbled. "It's a waste of perfectly good air."

"Do we have to go?"

"Of course we have to go, you nitwit. One of us had to take matters in hand."

"What do you mean?" Annabel asked carefully.

"She's a conniving little cow, but Winifred owes me a favor," her grandmother said sharply. "So she's made sure that Newbury will be in attendance. I couldn't stop her from inviting the other one, too, though."

"Seb—Mr. Grey?" Annabel asked, dropping her book.

"Yes, yes," Lady Vickers said, sounding much aggrieved. She waited for about half a second while Annabel fumbled about, dropping the book once more before finally managing to set it down on a table. "I suppose I can't blame her," she continued. "It'll be *the* invitation of the season."

"He's agreed to attend? Even knowing that his uncle will be there?"

"Who knows? She only sent out the invitations this afternoon." Lady Vickers gave a shrug. "He *is* a handsome one."

"What has that got to do with—" Annabel shut her mouth. She didn't want to know the answer.

"We leave in two hours," Lady Vickers said, finishing off her drink.

"Two hours? I can't possibly be ready by then."

"Of course you can. The maids have already packed up your things. Winifred doesn't live very far out of town, and the sun sets late this time of year. With good horses we can be there just after nightfall. And I'd much rather go this evening. I detest morning travel."

"You've been very busy," Annabel said.

Lady Vickers straightened her shoulders, looking quite proud of herself. "I have. You'd do well to emulate me. We'll get you that earl yet."

"But I—" Annabel froze, instantly silenced by the look on her grandmother's face.

"Surely," Lady Vickers said, her eyes narrowing to two icy chips, "you weren't about to say that you don't want him."

Annabel said nothing. She had never heard her grandmother speak in such a menacing tone. Slowly, she shook her head.

"Good. Because I know that you would not wish to do anything that might make life more difficult for your brothers and sisters."

Annabel actually took a step back. Could her grandmother be threatening her?

"Oh for God's sake," Lady Vickers snapped. "Don't look so petrified. Do you think I'm going to beat you?"

"No! Just that—"

"You'll marry the earl and carry on with the nephew on the side."

"Grandmother!"

"Don't look at me like a bloody Puritan. You couldn't hope for a better situation. If you have the wrong baby at least it all stays in the family."

Annabel was speechless.

"Oh, and by the by, Louisa is coming, too. That pinched-up old aunt of hers took a chill and can't chaperone her this week, so I said I'd take her along. We don't want her moldering in her room, do we?"

Annabel shook her head.

"Good. Get ready. We leave in an hour."

"You said two hours."

"Did I?" Lady Vickers blinked, then shrugged. "I must have lied. Better that than forgot, in any case."

Annabel watched openmouthed as her grandmother left the room. Surely this would go down as the strangest, most momentous day in her life.

Except that she had a feeling that tomorrow might be even stranger . . .

Chapter Nineteen

The following morning

Sebastian knew exactly why he had been invited to Lady Challis's house party. She had never liked him, and he had certainly never been invited to any Challis function before. But Lady Challis, for all her sanctimonious ways, was an extremely competitive hostess, and if she could arrange the party of the year by having Annabel, Sebastian, *and* the Earl of Newbury all under one roof, then by God she was going to do it.

Seb did not particularly relish being anyone's puppet, but he wasn't about to allow Newbury unfettered access to Annabel by refusing the invitation.

Besides, he had told Annabel he would give her a

day to consider his proposal, and meant to keep his promise. If she was going to be in Berkshire, in the home of Lord and Lady Challis, then so would he.

Seb was not a fool, though, and he knew that the Ladies Vickers, Challis, and whichever else of their cronies were in attendance would be cheering on Lord Newbury in the battle for Annabel. The most successful wars were never fought alone, so he dragged Edward out of bed and tossed him in the carriage to Berkshire. Edward hadn't been invited, but he was young, unmarried, and as far as Sebastian knew, in possession of all of his teeth. Which meant that he would never be turned away from a country house party. Never.

"Do Harry and Olivia know you've stolen their carriage?" Edward asked, rubbing his eyes.

"The correct term is commandeered, and yes, they know." Sort of. Sebastian had left a note.

"Who's going to be there?" Edward yawned.

"Cover your mouth."

Edward gave him a dirty look.

Sebastian lifted his chin as he peered impatiently out the window. The street was crowded, and the carriage was moving along at crawl. "Besides Miss Winslow and my uncle, I have no idea."

"Miss Winslow," Edward said with a sigh.

"Don't," Seb snapped.

"What?"

"Don't make that face when you're thinking about her."

"What face?"

"The one where you—" Seb went all stupid-eyed and let his tongue wag out the side of mouth. "That one."

"Well, you must admit, she's very—"

"Don't say it," Seb warned.

"I was going to say charming," Edward informed him.

"You were not."

"She has very nice—"

"*Edward!*"

"—eyes." Edward gave a smirky smile.

Sebastian glared at him, crossed his arms, and looked out the window. Then he uncrossed his arms, glared at Edward once more for good measure, and kicked him.

"What was that for?"

"For whatever inappropriate comment you were about to make."

Edward burst out laughing. And for once, Seb did not feel that he was being laughed *with*. This was definitely a laughing *at*.

"I have to say," Edward opined, "it's really rather amusing that you should fall in love with the woman your uncle wants to marry."

Sebastian shifted uncomfortably in his seat. "I'm not in love with her."

"No," Edward said mockingly, "you just want to marry her."

"Olivia told you?" Damn it, he'd told Olivia not to say anything.

"She did not," Edward said with a grin. "But you did."

"Whelp," Seb muttered.

"Do you think she'll say yes?"

"Why wouldn't she say yes?" Sebastian said defensively.

"Don't misunderstand, were I a woman, I can think of no one else I'd prefer to marry—"

"I believe I speak for men across the world when I say that I am relieved that that is not a consideration."

Edward pulled a face at the insult but took no offense. "Newbury can make her a countess," he reminded.

"I might be able to," Seb muttered.

"I thought you didn't care about the earldom."

"I don't." And he didn't. Except maybe now he did. "Not for myself, anyway."

Edward shrugged, his head tilting ever so slightly to the side. There was something familiar about the motion, something Sebastian could not quite place.

Until he realized it was a bit like looking into the mirror.

"She hates him," he blurted out.

Edward yawned. "She wouldn't be the first woman to marry a man she hated."

"He's three times her age."

"Again, not the first."

Seb finally threw out his hands in frustration. "Why are you saying all of this?"

Edward's face grew serious. "I merely believe in being prepared."

"So you think she will say no."

"Honestly, I have no idea. I've never even seen the two of you in the same room. But I would rather see you pleasantly surprised than heartbroken."

"My heart won't be broken," Seb grumbled. Because she wasn't going to say no. She'd told him she couldn't think clearly in his presence. If ever a woman wanted to say yes to a proposal of marriage it was Annabel.

But was wanting to say yes enough? Her grandparents would not be happy if she chose him over Newbury. And he knew that she was extremely concerned about her family's lack of money. But surely she would not forsake her own happiness to gain them a few coins. It wasn't as if they were teetering on the verge of the poor-house. They couldn't be, not with her brothers still in school. And Sebastian had money. Not as much as Newbury—oh very well, not even close—but he had some. Certainly enough to pay for her brothers' education.

Annabel likely did not know that, though. Most of society thought him an entertaining mooch. Even Harry thought he ate breakfast every day with the Valentines because he couldn't afford food of his own.

Sebastian owed his place in society to his good looks and charm. And because there was always the possibility his uncle would die before begetting a new heir. But no one thought Sebastian had any form of income. Certainly no one suspected that he had earned a tidy sum penning gothic novels under a woman's name.

Once the carriage escaped the snarled traffic of London, Edward fell right asleep. And stayed that way until they pulled up in front of Stonecross, the large Tudor manor that served as one of the Challis country seats. As Seb alighted, he found himself studying his surroundings with a careful eye.

It almost felt as if he were back in the war, scouting locations, watching the players. That was what he did. He observed. He had never been one of the soldiers at the front. He had never engaged in hand-to-hand combat, never looked the enemy in the eye. He had been removed from the action, always watching, taking his shots from afar.

And he never missed.

He had the two qualities found in all great snipers—excellent aim and endless patience. He took no shot unless it was perfect, and he never lost his head. Even the time Harry had been nearly killed, approached from behind by a French captain, Sebastian had held himself perfectly still. He'd watched, and waited, and he did not take the shot until the time was right. Harry had never known how close he had come to death.

Sebastian had vomited in the bushes.

Strange that he should feel so much like a soldier again. Or maybe not so strange. He'd been at war with his uncle his entire life.

At breakfast that morning, Lady Challis informed Annabel and Louisa that most of the guests, including Lord Newbury, were not due to arrive until late afternoon. She did not mention Sebastian, and Annabel did not ask. Such questions would be immediately reported to her grandmother, and Annabel dearly did not wish to repeat the sort of conversation they'd had the night before.

It was a lovely summer morning, so Annabel and Louisa decided to walk down to the pond, in no small part because no one else seemed to want to go. When they arrived, Louisa immediately picked up a stone and sent it skipping across the lake.

"How did you do that?" Annabel demanded.

"Skip a stone? Can't you?"

"No. My brothers always claimed no girl could."

"And you believed them?"

"Of course not. But I tried for years, and I was never able to prove them wrong." Annabel picked up a stone and tried to skip it. It sank instantly.

Rather like a stone.

Louisa gave her a lofty grin, picked up another stone, and let it fly. "One . . . two . . . three . . . four . . . *five!*" she crowed, counting the skips. "My record is six."

"Six?" Annabel asked, feeling very outdone. "Really?"

Louisa shrugged, looking for another stone. "My father ignores me in Scotland just as much as he does in London. The only difference is that instead of the season to occupy me, I have lakes and stones." She found a nice flat rock and picked it up. "I've had a great deal of time to practice."

"Show me how you—"

But Louisa had already sent it flying across the water. "One . . . two . . . three . . . *four.*" She let out an irritated snort. "I knew that rock was too heavy."

Annabel watched in disbelief as her cousin skipped three more stones across the lake, each of them bouncing five times. "I do believe I am jealous," she finally announced.

Louisa beamed. "Of me?"

"You don't even look strong enough to *lift* one of those stones, much less skip it across the lake."

"Now, now, Annabel," Louisa scolded, smiling all the while. "Let's not be mean."

Annabel feigned a scowl.

"I can't run fast," Louisa said. "I've been banned from all archery tournaments out of concern for the safety of the rest of the contestants, and I can't play cards worth a damn."

"*Louisa!*"

Louisa had cursed. Annabel could not believe she had cursed.

"But I can"—Louisa sent another stone across the pond—"skip stones like a master."

"So you can," Annabel said, duly impressed. "Will you show me how to do it?"

"No." Louisa gave her an arch look. "I like having something I'm so much better at than you."

Annabel stuck out her tongue. "You *say* you can do six."

"I can," Louisa insisted.

"I haven't seen it." Annabel walked over to a large rock and patted the top, making sure it was dry before she sat down. "I have all morning. And afternoon, too, now that I think on it."

Louisa scowled, then growled, then stomped off to find more stones. She did a five, then a four, then two more fives.

"I'm waiting!" Annabel called.

"I'm running out of good stones!"

"A likely excuse." Annabel looked down at her fingernails to see if she'd got any dirt under them when she'd picked up her one pathetic stone. When she looked back up, a stone was sailing across the surface. One . . . two . . . three . . . four . . . five . . . *six*!

"You did it!" Annabel exclaimed, jumping to her feet. "Six!"

"That wasn't me," Louisa said.

They both turned.

"Ladies," Sebastian said, bowing elegantly. He looked impossibly handsome in the mid-morning sunshine. Annabel had never realized just how much red he had in his hair. She had never seen him in the morning, she realized. They had met in the moonlight, and in the afternoon. At the opera she had seen him in the flickering light of a hundred candles.

The morning light *was* different.

"Mr. Grey," she murmured, feeling suddenly, unaccountably, shy.

"That was marvelous!" Louisa exclaimed. "What's your record?"

"Seven."

"Really?"

Annabel was not sure she'd ever seen her cousin so animated. Except possibly when she had been talking about those Gorely books. Which Annabel still needed to read. She'd started *Miss Sainsbury and the Mysterious Colonel* the night before but had only got through two chapters. Still, one could not help but be impressed by the adversity poor Miss Sainsbury had managed to overcome in just twenty-four pages. She'd survived cholera, an infestation of mice, and turned her ankle twice.

Annabel's problems didn't seem half so dreadful by comparison.

"Do you skip stones, Miss Winslow?" Sebastian asked politely.

"Much to my everlasting shame, no."

"I can do six," Louisa said.

"But not today," Annabel said, unable to resist the poke.

Louisa held up an irritated finger and stomped off to the edge of the bank, looking for another suitable stone. Sebastian walked over and stood near Annabel, his hands clasped lightly behind his back.

"Does she know?" he asked quietly, motioning with his head toward Louisa.

Annabel shook her head.

"Does anyone?"

"No."

"I see."

She wasn't sure what he thought he saw, because she certainly didn't.

"Rather sudden invitation to the country, wouldn't you say?" he murmured.

Annabel rolled her eyes. "I suspect my grandmother was behind it."

"And she invited me?"

"No, actually I believe she said she could not *prevent* your being invited."

He laughed at that. "I am so loved."

Annabel's heart skipped a beat.

"What is it?" he asked, taking in her suddenly startled expression.

"I don't know. I—"

"This!" Louisa announced, marching back over. She was holding aloft a round, flat stone. "This is the perfect skipping stone."

"May I see?" Sebastian asked.

"Only if you promise not to throw it."

"I give you my word."

She handed him the rock and he turned it over in his hand, testing the feel and weight of it. He gave it back with a little shrug.

"You don't think it's good?" Louisa asked, looking a bit put out.

"It's not *bad*."

"He's trying to prick your confidence," Annabel called.

Louisa gasped. "Is that true?"

Sebastian gave Annabel a lazy smile. "You know me so well, Miss Winslow."

Louisa stalked to the water's edge. "That was positively ungentlemanly of you, Mr. Grey."

Sebastian chuckled and leaned against the rock where Annabel was sitting. "I like your cousin," he said.

"I like her, too."

Louisa took a deep breath, assumed full concentration, and sent the stone forth, with what Annabel thought was an amazingly sharp flick of her wrist.

They all counted. "One . . . two . . . three . . . four . . . five . . . *six!*"

"Six!" Louisa shrieked. "I did it! Six! Ha!" This

was directed at Annabel. "I told you I could do six."

"Now you have to do seven," Sebastian said.

Annabel sputtered with laughter.

"Not today I don't," Louisa declared. "Today I glory in my sixdom."

"Sixdom?"

"Sixitude."

Annabel started to grin.

"Sixulation," Louisa proclaimed. "Besides," she added, cocking her head toward Sebastian, "I haven't seen you do seven."

He held up his hands in defeat. "It's been many, many years."

Louisa gave them both a regal smile. "On that note, I believe I shall take myself off to celebrate. I shall see the both of you later. Perhaps *much* later." And with that she departed, leaving Annabel and Sebastian quite alone.

"Did I say I like your cousin?" Sebastian mused. "I do believe I love her." He tilted his head toward. "Purely platonically, of course."

Annabel took a deep breath, but when she let it out, she felt shaky and nervous. She knew he wanted an answer, and he *deserved* one. But she had nothing. Just an awful, empty feeling inside.

"You look tired," she said. Because he did.

He shrugged. "I didn't sleep well. I rarely do."

His voice sounded odd to her, and she regarded him more closely. He wasn't looking at her; his eyes were fixed on some thoroughly random spot in the background. A tree root, by the looks of it. Then he looked down at his feet, one of which was pushing loose dirt around on the ground. There was something familiar about his expression, and then it came to her—he looked exactly as he had that day in the park, right after he'd shot apart the target.

And then hadn't wanted to talk about it.

"I'm sorry," she said. "I hate it when I cannot fall asleep."

He shrugged again, but the movement was starting to look forced. "I'm used to it."

She didn't say anything for a moment, and then she realized that the obvious question was: "Why?"

"Why?" he echoed.

"Yes. Why do you have trouble sleeping? Do you know?"

Sebastian sat down next to her, staring out over the water, where a few stone-skipped ripples still slid along the surface. He thought for a moment, then opened his mouth as if he might say something.

But he didn't.

"I find I have to close my eyes," she said.

That caught his attention.

"When I'm trying to sleep," she clarified. "I have to close my eyes. If I lie there, staring at the ceiling, I might as well admit defeat. I'm not going to fall asleep with my eyes open, after all."

Sebastian considered this for a moment, smiling wryly. "I stare at the ceiling," he admitted.

"Well, there's your problem."

He turned. She was looking at him, her expression open, her eyes clear. And while he was sitting there, thinking that he wished that were the problem, he suddenly thought—*well, maybe it is.* Maybe some of the most convoluted questions had simple answers.

Maybe *she* was his simple answer.

He wanted to kiss her. It hit him suddenly, overwhelmingly. Except he just wanted to touch his lips to hers. Nothing more. Just a simple kiss of gratitude, of friendship, maybe even of love.

But he wasn't going to kiss her. Not yet. She'd tilted her head to the side, and the way she was looking at him—he wanted to know what she was thinking. He wanted to know her. He wanted to know her thoughts and her hopes and her fears. He wanted to know what she was thinking about on the nights when she couldn't sleep, and then he wanted to know what it was she dreamed when she finally drifted off.

"I think about the war," he said softly. He'd never told anyone.

She nodded. Softly, a tiny movement he could barely see. "It must have been terrible."

"Not all of it. But the parts I think about at night . . ." He closed his eyes for a moment, unable to banish the acrid smell of gunpowder, the blood, and worst of all, the noise.

She put her hand on his. "I'm sorry."

"It's not as bad as it used to be."

"That's good." She smiled encouragingly. "What changed, do you think?"

"I—" But he didn't say it. He couldn't tell her. Not yet. How could he tell her about his writing when he didn't even know if she liked it? It had never bothered him that Harry and Olivia thought the Gorely books were so dreadful—well, not very much, at least—but if Annabel hated them . . .

It was almost too much to bear.

"I think it's only time," he said. "Heals all wounds, they say."

She nodded again, that tiny little motion he liked to think only he could detect. She looked at him curiously, her head tilting to the side.

"What is it?" he asked, watching her brow furrow.

"I think your eyes might be the exact same color as mine," she said wonderingly.

"What fine gray-eyed babies we shall have," he said, before he thought the better of it.

The lighthearted look fell from her eyes, and she looked away. Damn. He hadn't meant to push her. Not yet, anyway. Right now he was so simply *happy*. Perfectly and utterly comfortable. He'd told another human being one of his secrets and the heavens had not crashed to the ground. It was stunning how wonderful that felt.

No, that wasn't the right word. It was frustrating, that. He was in the business of finding the right words, and he didn't know how to explain it. He felt . . .

Lifted.

Weightless.

Rested. And at the same time, like he wanted to close his eyes, set his head on a pillow next to hers, and sleep. He'd never felt anything like it.

And now he'd gone and ruined it. She was staring at the ground, her cheeks pinched, and it was as if the color had gone out of her. She looked exactly the same, not pale, not flushed, and yet she was colorless.

It was coming from the inside. It broke his heart.

He could see it now—her life as his uncle's wife. It wouldn't break her, it would just slowly suck her dry.

He couldn't allow it. He simply could not allow it.

"I asked you to marry me yesterday," he said.

She looked away. Not down at her feet this time, but away.

She didn't have an answer. He was stunned at how much this stung. She wasn't even refusing him; she was just begging for more time.

Silently begging, he corrected. Perhaps it would be more accurately described as avoiding the question altogether.

Still, he'd asked her to *marry* him. Did she think he made such offers lightly? He'd always thought that when he finally proposed marriage, the woman in question would burst into happy tears, beside herself with bliss and joy. A rainbow would break out of the sky, butterflies would dance overhead, and all the world would join hands in song.

Or at the very least, she'd say yes. He hadn't thought himself the type of man to propose marriage to a woman who might say no.

He stood. He was too restless to sit now. All that peace, all that lovely weightlessness—gone.

What the hell was he supposed to do now?

Chapter Twenty

Annabel watched as Sebastian walked toward the water. He stood near the edge, almost close enough to get his shoes wet. He looked out toward the opposite shore, his posture stiff and unyielding.

It was so unlike him. It was so . . . wrong.

Sebastian was loose limbed, graceful. His every movement was a secret dance, every smile a silent poem. This was not right. It was not him.

When had she come to know him so well, that she could tell by the line of his back that he was not himself? And why did it hurt so much, to know that she knew this? That she knew *him*.

After what seemed an eternity, he turned around and said with heartbreaking formality, "From your silence I must deduce that you do not have an answer for me."

She moved her head in a tiny motion, just enough to say no.

"It does prick the confidence," he said, "to steal your phrase."

"It's all very complicated," Annabel said.

He crossed his arms and regarded her with a quirk of his brow. And just like that, he was back. The stiffness was gone, replaced by an easy confidence, and when he walked toward her, it was with an arrogant grace that mesmerized her.

"It's not complicated," he said. "It couldn't be simpler. I asked you to marry me, and you want to. All you have to do is say yes."

"I didn't say—"

"You want to," he said, with an unbelievably annoying degree of certainty. "You know that you do."

He was right, of course, but Annabel could not help but be provoked by his swagger. "You're rather sure of yourself."

He stepped toward her, smiling slowly. Seductively. "Shouldn't I be?"

"My family . . ." she whispered.

"Won't starve." He touched her chin, tipping her face gently toward his. "I'm not a pauper, Annabel."

"There are eight of us."

He considered this. "Very well, no one will starve, but you all might get a bit thin."

She let out a snort of laughter. She hated that he could make her laugh at such a moment. No, she loved it. No, she loved *him*.

Oh God.

She jumped back.

"What is it?" he asked.

She shook her head.

"Tell me," he prodded, and he took her hand, tugging her back toward him. "Something just happened. I saw it in your eyes."

"No, Mr.—"

"Sebastian," he reminded her, touching his lips to her forehead.

"Sebastian," she croaked. It was hard to speak when he was so close. It was hard to think.

His lips moved to her cheekbone, light and soft. "I have ways of making you talk," he whispered.

"Wh–what?"

He nibbled on her lower lip, then moved to her ear. "What were you thinking?" he murmured.

She could only moan.

"I shall have to be more persuasive." His hands moved to her back, sliding down until he cupped her bottom, pressing her against him. Annabel felt her head tilt back, away from his sensual on-slaught, but still, she could barely breathe. His body was so hard, and hot, and she could feel his arousal growing against her.

"I want you," he whispered. "And I know you want me."

"Here?" she gasped.

He chuckled. "I'm a bit more refined than that. But," he added, sounding thoughtful, "we *are* quite alone."

She nodded.

"None of the guests have arrived yet." He kissed the soft skin where her ear met the line of her jaw. "And I think it is safe to assume that your marvelous cousin will not disturb us."

"Sebastian, I—"

"We shall make her godmother to our children."

"What?" But she could barely gasp the word. His hand had found its way under her skirt and was moving relentlessly up her leg. And all she wanted—oh dear God, she was wicked—was to bend a little, and open a little, and make it easier for him to do whatever it was he wanted.

"She can teach them all to skip stones," he said, reaching the tender spot just above her knee. Annabel shuddered.

"Ticklish there?" he said with a smile. He moved higher. "We shall have lots of children, I think. Lots and lots and lots."

She needed to stop him. She needed to say something, to tell him that she had not decided yet, that she could not commit, not until she'd had a bit of time to think clearly, which she obviously could not do in his presence. He was talking about the future, about children, and she knew that her silence felt like an assent.

He ran one finger along the inside of her thigh. "I just don't think that we could possibly *not* have lots of children," he murmured. His lips found her ear again. "I shan't let you out of our bed."

Her knees buckled.

His finger slid even higher, reaching the hot crease where leg met her hip. "Shall I tell you what I plan to do there? In our bed?"

She nodded.

He smiled. She felt it against her ear, felt his lips move and tilt, heard his breath fill with joy. "First," he said softly, "I shall see to your pleasure."

A little moan escaped her lips. Or maybe it was a squeak.

"I will start with a kiss," he said, his voice hot and low against her skin. "But where, I wonder?"

"Where?" she whispered. It wasn't really a question, more of an echo of disbelief.

He touched her mouth. "On the lips? Maybe." His finger made a lazy trail down to her collarbone. "I do like this part of you. And these . . ." He cupped one of her breasts, moaning as he squeezed. "I could lose myself all day in these."

Annabel arched her back, wanting to give him more. Her body had taken over and it was desperate for him. She couldn't stop thinking about what he had done to her in the Valentines' drawing room. How he had touched her breasts. All her life she had hated them, hated how men stared and whistled and if they'd had too much to drink, seemed to think she was ripe for the picking.

But Sebastian had made her feel beautiful. He had loved her body, and this had made *her* love her body.

He dipped his hand into the bodice of her dress, slid his fingers under her chemise so he could skim them over her nipple. "You have no idea," he said in a husky voice, "how much I'm going to love you here."

Her breath caught, and she felt bereft as he

moved his hand again. It had been a most awkward position for him, and she could not help but think that if she could just push the whole bloody thing down, he could touch her everywhere. He could squeeze, and knead, and suckle.

"Oh my God," she moaned.

"What are you thinking about?" he whispered.

She shook her head. There was no way she could give voice to the wanton thoughts in her head.

"Are you thinking about where else I might kiss you?"

Dear God, she hoped he did not expect her to answer.

"I might kiss you somewhere else entirely," he teased. His other hand—the one on her leg—wrapped softly around her thigh and squeezed. "If I want to give you pleasure," he murmured, "to give you full pleasure, I think I'm going to have to kiss you here."

His finger dipped between her legs.

She almost jumped back. She would have, if his arm hadn't been wrapped so tightly around her.

"Do you like that?" he murmured, tracing tiny circles as he moved closer to her center.

She nodded. Or maybe she thought she nodded. But she definitely didn't say no.

A second finger joined the first, and with aching gentleness he teased her open, stroking her moist skin. Annabel felt her body begin to jerk and shudder, and she grabbed tightly to his shoulders, afraid that if she let go, she would simply collapse.

"You would taste like heaven, I think," he continued, clearly unwilling to stop until she had exploded in his arms. "I would lick you right here." He ran one fingertip lightly along her skin. "And then right here." He repeated the caress on the other side. "And then I would go *here*." He moved to her most sensitive nub of flesh, and she almost screamed.

His mouth pressed harder against her ear. "I'd lick that, too."

Annabel clutched him even harder, pressing her hips into his hand.

"But even that might not be enough," he whispered. "You are a discerning woman, and you might make me work for your pleasure."

"Oh, Sebastian," she moaned.

He chuckled lightly against her skin. "I might have to touch you a little more deeply." One of his fingers began to circle at her opening, then slid softly inside. "Like this. Do you like that?"

"Yes," she gasped. "Yes."

He began to move within her. "Do you like this?"

"Yes."

Oh, he was wicked, and she was wicked, and he was doing wicked things to her. And all she could think was that they were out of doors and anyone could come across them, and somehow that made it all the more delicious.

"Let go, Annabel," he whispered in her ear.

"I can't," she whimpered, clamping her legs around him. She was aching inside. He was making her ache, and she had no idea how to make it stop.

Or even if she wanted it to stop.

"Let go," he whispered again.

"I—I—"

He chuckled. "I'm going to speak very plainly, Anna—"

"Oh!"

She wasn't certain if she let go or not, but something inside her quite simply fell apart. She clung to his shoulders, holding on for dear life, and then, when she started to go limp, he scooped her into his arms and carried her to a soft patch of grass several yards away. She sat down, and then lay down, allowing the sun to warm her face.

"I love you in green," he said.

She didn't open her eyes. "I'm wearing pink."

"You'd look better if you took it all off," he said, dropping a kiss on her nose, "and it was just you and the grass."

"I don't know what you just did to me," she said. She sounded dazed. She didn't think she'd sounded so dazed in her life.

He kissed her again. "I can think of ten more things I'd like to do."

"I think that would kill me."

He laughed loudly at that. "Clearly we'll need to practice more. Build up your stamina."

She finally opened her eyes and looked at him. He was lounging on his side, his head propped against his hand. He had a clover in his hand.

He tickled her nose with it. "You're so beautiful, Annabel."

She sighed happily. She felt beautiful.

"Are you going to marry me?"

She closed her eyes again. She felt so perfectly languid.

"Annabel?"

"I want to," she said softly.

"Why do I think that's not quite the same thing as a yes?"

She let out another little sigh. The sun felt so nice on her face. She couldn't even bring herself to worry about freckles.

"What will I do with you?" he said aloud. She heard him move, and then his voice was much closer to her ear. "I can keep coming up with new ways to compromise you."

She giggled.

"Let me think. Number ten . . ."

"I do it, too," she said, still happily studying the insides of her eyelids. The sunlight made them orangey red. It was such a nice, warm color.

"Do what?"

"Count in tens. It's such a nice round number."

He nipped her earlobe. "I like nice round things."

"Stop." But even she didn't think she sounded like she meant it.

"Do you know how I know you're going to marry me?"

She opened her eyes for that. He sounded quite sure of himself. "How?"

"Look at you. So happy and content. If you weren't going to marry me, you'd be running about like a chicken—no, sorry, a turkey—yipping on about *what have I done* and *what have you done* and *what have we done?*"

"I'm thinking all those things," she told him.

He snorted. "Right."

"You don't believe me."

He kissed her. "Not for a second. But it hasn't been a full day yet, and I'm a man of my word, so I won't badger you." He stood and then held out his hand to her.

Annabel took it and rose to her feet, smiling with disbelief. "That wasn't badgering?"

"My dear Miss Winslow, I have not even begun to badger." And then his eyes took on a most devilish light. "Hmmm."

"What?"

He chuckled to himself as he led her up the hill to the path. "Has there ever been a Winslow Most Likely to Outrun a Badger competition?"

She laughed all the way back to Stonecross.

Chapter Twenty-one

Later that night

"Did you see him this afternoon?"

Annabel would have looked up at Louisa, who had just entered the room, except that Nettie had a viselike grip on her hair.

"Which him?" Annabel asked. "Ow! Nettie!"

Nettie yanked even harder, twisting a piece and pinning it into place. "Sit still and it won't take so long."

"You know which him," Louisa said, pulling up a chair.

"You wore blue," Annabel said, smiling at her. "It's my favorite color on you."

"Don't try to change the subject."

"She hasn't seen him," Nettie said.

"Nettie!"

"Well, you haven't," the maid declared.

"I haven't," Annabel confirmed. "Not since luncheon."

The midday meal had been served al fresco, and as there was no set seating, Annabel had ended up at a table for four with Sebastian, his cousin Edward, and Louisa. They had had a marvelous time, but halfway through, Lady Vickers had requested a private word with Annabel.

"What do you think you are doing?" she demanded, once they were off to the side.

"Nothing," Annabel had insisted. "Louisa and I—"

"This is not about your cousin," Lady Vickers bit off. She grabbed Annabel's arm, hard. "I am talking about Mr. Grey, who is not, may I point out, the Earl of Newbury."

Annabel could see that her grandmother's rising voice was attracting attention, so she lowered her own, hoping that her grandmother would follow suit. "Lord Newbury isn't even here yet," she said. "If he were, I would—"

"Sit with him?" Lady Vickers raised an extremely skeptical brow. "Hang on his every word and behave for all the world like a harlot?"

Annabel gasped and drew back.

"Everyone is staring at you," Lady Vickers hissed. "You can do whatever you want once you're married. I'll even tell you how to go about doing it. But for now, you will remain—and your reputation will remain—pure as the bloody driven snow."

"What do you imagine I have been doing?" Annabel said in a low voice. Surely her grandmother did not know what had happened by the pond. No one did.

"Have I taught you nothing?" Lady Vickers' eyes, as clear and sober as Annabel had ever seen them, settled hard on hers. "It doesn't matter what you do, it matters what people think you do. And you're staring at that man like you're in love with him."

But she was.

"I'll try to do better," was all Annabel said.

She finished her meal, because there was no way she would be seen running off to her room right after her grandmother publicly scolded her. But as soon as she'd finished eating, she excused herself and retired for the afternoon. She told Sebastian she needed to rest. Which was true. And that she did not want to be present when his uncle finally arrived.

Which was also true.

So she'd settled on her bed with *Miss Sainsbury*. And her mysterious colonel. And told herself that she deserved an afternoon to herself. She had a great deal to think about.

She knew what she wanted to do, and she knew what she *should* do, and she knew that these were not the same things at all.

She also knew that if she kept her head in a book for the entire afternoon, she might be able to ignore the whole awful mess for a few hours.

Which was remarkably appealing.

Maybe if she just waited long enough, something would happen, and all of her problems would disappear.

Her mother could find a long-lost diamond necklace.

Lord Newbury could find a girl with even bigger hips.

There could be a flood. A plague. Really, the world was full of calamities. Just look at poor Miss Sainsbury. In chapters three through eight she'd fallen off the side of a ship, was captured by a privateer, and nearly trampled by a goat.

Who was to say the same things might not happen to her?

Although, all things considered, the diamond necklace was a bit more appealing.

But a girl could hide for only so long, and so now she was sitting in front of the mirror, getting her hair yanked this way and that while Louisa filled her in on what she had missed.

"I saw Lord Newbury," Louisa said.

Annabel let out a groany sort of sigh.

"He was talking with Lord Challis. He . . . ah . . ." Louisa swallowed nervously and plucked at the lace adornment on her dress. "He said something about a special license."

"*What*? Ow!"

"Don't move so suddenly," Nettie scolded.

"What did he say about a special license?" Annabel whispered urgently. Not that there was any real reason to whisper. Nettie knew everything that was going on. Annabel had already promised two bonnets and a pair of shoes to keep quiet.

"Just that he had one. That was why he was so late. He came straight from Canterbury."

"Did you speak with him?"

Louisa shook her head. "I don't even think he saw me. I was reading in the library, and the door was open. They were in the corridor."

"A special license," Annabel repeated in a dull voice. A special license. It meant a couple could marry quickly, without posting banns. Three entire weeks could be saved, and the ceremony could take place anywhere, in any parish. At any time, even, although most couples still stuck to the traditional Saturday morning.

Annabel caught her own gaze in the looking glass. It was Thursday night.

Louisa reached out and took her hand. "I can help you," she said.

Annabel turned to her cousin. Something about her voice made her uneasy. "What do you mean?"

"I have—" Louisa stopped, looking up at Nettie, who was spearing Annabel with another pin. "I need to speak with my cousin privately."

"I only have this one last piece," Nettie said, giving it what Annabel deemed a more vigorous twist than necessary. She fixed it into place with a pin and left the room.

"I have money," Louisa said, just as soon as the door closed. "Not very much, but enough to help."

"Louisa, no."

"I never spend all of my pin money. My father gives me far more than I need." She gave a sad little shrug. "It's to make up for his absence in every other corner of my life, I'm sure. But that doesn't matter. The point is, I can send some to your family. It will be enough to keep your brothers in school for another term, at least."

"And the term after that?" Annabel said. Because there *would* be a term after that. And then another. And as generous as Louisa's offer was, it would not last forever.

"We'll deal with that when it comes. At the very least, we'll have bought you a bit of time. You can meet someone else. Or maybe Mr. Grey—"

"Louisa!"

"No, listen to me," Louisa interrupted. "Maybe he has money no one knows about."

"Don't you think he'd have said something if he did?"

"He hasn't—"

"No, he hasn't," Annabel cut in, hating the way her voice was cracking. But it was *hard*. It was hard to think about Sebastian and all of the reasons why she shouldn't marry him. "He said he's not a pauper and he said we wouldn't starve, but when I reminded him that there are eight of us, he made a joke about our growing thin!"

Louisa winced, then tried to dismiss it. "Well, we knew he wasn't as wealthy as the earl. But really, who is? And you don't need jewels and palaces, do you?"

"Of course not! If it weren't for my family, I'd—"

"You'd what? *What*, Annabel?"

I'd marry Sebastian.

But she dare not say it aloud.

"You must think of your own happiness," Louisa said.

Annabel let out a snort. "What do you think I've *been* thinking about? If I hadn't been thinking about my own happiness I'd have probably asked the earl to marry *me*."

"Annabel, you *cannot* marry Lord Newbury."

Annabel stared at her cousin in shock. It was the first time she had ever heard Louisa raise her voice.

"I won't let you do it," Louisa said urgently.

"Do you think I *want* to marry him?"

"Then don't."

Annabel clenched her teeth together in frustration. Not at Louisa. Just at life. "I don't have your choices," she finally said, trying to keep her voice even and calm. "I am not the daughter of the Duke of Fenniwick, and I don't have a dowry large enough to purchase a small kingdom in the Alps, and I wasn't raised in a castle, and—"

She stopped. The stricken look on Louisa's face was enough. "I didn't mean it that way," she mumbled.

Louisa was silent for a moment before saying, "I know. But do you know, I don't have *your* choices, either. Men have never fought over me at White's. No one has ever flirted with me at the opera, and I certainly have never been compared to a fertility goddess."

Annabel let out a little groan. "You heard that, too, eh?"

Louisa nodded. "I'm sorry."

"Don't be." Annabel shook her head. "It's funny, I suppose."

"No, it's not," Louisa said, but she looked as if

she was trying not to smile. She stole a glance at Annabel, saw that she was also trying not to smile, and gave up. "Yes, it is."

And they laughed.

"Oh, Louisa," Annabel said, once her laughter had melted into a wistful smile, "I do love you."

Louisa reached over and patted her hand. "I love you, too, cousin." Then she pushed back her chair and stood. "It's time to go down."

Annabel stood and followed her to the door.

Louisa walked out into the hall. "Lady Challis says there are to be charades after supper."

"Charades," Annabel repeated. Somehow that seemed ridiculously appropriate.

Lady Challis had instructed her guests to gather in the drawing room before supper. Annabel had waited until the last possible minute to head downstairs. Lord Newbury was not stupid; she had been avoiding him for several days, and she suspected he knew it. Sure enough, when she entered the drawing room, he was waiting near the door.

So, she noticed, was Sebastian.

"Miss Winslow," the earl said, intercepting her immediately, "we must talk."

"Supper," Annabel replied, managing a curtsy at the same time. "Er, I think it's almost time to go in."

"We have time," Newbury said curtly.

Out of the corner of her eye, Annabel could see Sebastian moving slowly toward her.

"I spoke to your grandfather," Newbury said. "It is all arranged."

It was all *arranged*? It was on the tip of Annabel's tongue to ask him if he even thought to ask *her*. But she held back. The second-to-last thing she wanted was to cause a scene in Lady Challis's drawing room. Not to mention that Lord Newbury would probably take that as an invitation to propose to her then and there.

Which *was* the last thing she wanted.

"Surely this is not the time, my lord," she hedged.

But Newbury's face tightened. And Sebastian was edging ever closer.

"I am making an announcement after supper," Lord Newbury told her.

Annabel gasped. "You can't do that!"

This seemed to amuse him. "Really?"

"You haven't even asked me," she protested. She nearly bit her tongue out of frustration. So much for not giving him the opening.

Newbury chuckled. "Is that the problem, then? Your pretty little pride has been pricked. Very well, I shall give you your hearts and flowers after supper." He smiled lasciviously, his lower lip jiggling with the exertion. "And perhaps you shall give something to me in return."

He put his hand on her arm, then let it slide down to her bottom.

"Lord Newbury!"

He pinched her.

Annabel jumped away, but the earl was already chuckling to himself and heading off to the dining room. And as she watched him go, she began to feel the strangest sensation.

Freedom.

Because finally, after avoiding and procrasti-
nating and hoping that something would happen
so that she would not have to say yes—or no—
to the man whose offer of marriage would solve
all her family's problems, she realized that she
simply could not do it.

Maybe last week, maybe before Sebastian . . .

No, she thought, as lovely and magnificent as
he was, as much as she adored him and hoped
he adored her, he wasn't the only reason she
couldn't marry Lord Newbury. He did, however,
provide a splendid alternative.

"What the hell just happened?" Sebastian demanded, at her side in an instant.

"Nothing," Annabel replied, and she almost
smiled.

"Annabel—"

"No, really. It was nothing. *Finally*, it was
nothing."

"What do you mean?"

She shook her head. Everyone was heading in
to supper. "I'll tell you later."

She was having far too much fun with her own
thoughts to share them, even with him. Who
would have thought that a pinch on the bottom
would be what finally made it all come clear? It
hadn't even been the pinch, actually, but the look
in his eyes.

Like he owned her.

In that moment she realized there were at least
ten reasons why she could never, ever commit
herself to that man in marriage.

Ten, but probably more like a hundred.

Chapter Twenty-two

*O*ne, Annabel thought happily as she took her seat at the table, Lord Newbury was simply too old. Not to mention that **Two**: he was so desperate for an heir that he'd probably injure her in the attempt, and certainly no woman with a broken hip could carry a baby for nine months. And of course there was—

"Why are you smiling?" Sebastian whispered.

He was standing behind her, supposedly on his way to his own seat, which was diagonal to hers, two seats closer to the head of the table. How anyone might think that her seat was on the way to his was beyond her, which brought her to a revision of **Three**: she seemed to have attracted the attention of the most charming and lovable man in England, and who was she to turn such a treasure away?

"I'm just happy to be down at the far end of the table with the rest of the peons," she whispered back. Lady Challis was nothing if not a stickler for propriety, and there would be no deviations from the order of rank when it came to her seating arrangements. Which meant that with nearly forty guests between Annabel and the head of the table, Lord Newbury seemed miles away.

Even more delightful, she had been seated directly next to Sebastian's cousin Edward, whose company she had so enjoyed at lunch. As it would be rude to remain lost in her own thoughts, she quickly decided to rename her brothers and sisters **Four** through **Ten**. Surely they loved her well enough not to want her to enter into such a hideous union on their behalf.

She turned to Mr. Valentine, beaming. Smiling so widely, in fact, that he actually seemed taken aback.

"Isn't it a marvelous evening?" she asked, because it *was*.

"Er, yes." He blinked a few times, then shot a quick look over to Sebastian, almost as if checking for approval. Or maybe just to see if he was watching.

"I am so glad that you are attending," she continued, gazing happily at the soup. She was hungry. Happiness always made her hungry. She looked back up at Mr. Valentine, lest he think she was pleased by the soup's attendance (although she was; she really was), and added, "I had not realized that you would be here." Her grandmother had obtained a guest list from Lady

Challis, and Annabel was certain there had been no Valentines on it.

"I was a very recent addition."

"I am sure Lady Challis was most pleased to have you." She smiled again; she couldn't seem to help herself. "Now then, Mr. Valentine, we must speak of far more important matters. I am sure you must know many terribly embarrassing stories about your cousin, Mr. Grey."

She leaned forward a bit, eyes gleaming. "I want to hear them *all*."

Sebastian could not decide if he was intrigued or enraged.

No, not true. He pondered rage for about two moments, then remembered he never got angry and decided he preferred intrigue.

He had almost interceded when Newbury had cornered Annabel in the drawing room, and in fact he'd had quite the most delicious urge to pinch his uncle on the eyelid after he'd pinched Annabel on the bum. But just as he stepped forward, Annabel had undergone the most remarkable transformation. For a few moments, it was almost as if she wasn't there, as if her mind had lifted off and gone to some faraway, blissful spot.

She'd looked lifted. Weightless.

Sebastian could not fathom what his uncle might have said to make her so happy, but he recognized the futility of trying to question her while everyone was filing in to supper.

So he decided that if Annabel wasn't going to

be furious about Newbury's pinch, then neither would he.

At supper she was positively incandescent, which, given the two-seats-down-and-across-the-tableness of their positions, was somewhat irksome. He could not enjoy her radiance, nor could he take credit for it. She did seem to be enjoying her conversation with Edward immensely, and Sebastian found that if he leaned just a bit to his left he could hear almost half of what they were saying.

He might have heard more, except that also to his left was the elderly Lady Millicent Farnsworth. Who was quite nearly deaf.

As he would surely be by the end of the evening.

"IS THAT DUCK?" she yelled, pointing at a slice of fowl which was, indeed, duck.

Sebastian swallowed, as if the motion might somehow dislodge her voice from his ear, and said something about the duck (which he had not yet tasted) being delicious.

She shook her head. "I DON'T LIKE DUCK." And then, in a blessed whisper, she added, "It gives me hives."

Sebastian decided then and there that until he himself was old enough to have sired grandchildren, this was more than he wanted to know about any woman over the age of seventy.

While Lady Millicent was busy with the beef burgundy, Sebastian craned his neck only slightly farther than was subtle, trying to hear what Annabel and Edward were talking about.

"I was a very recent addition," Edward said.

Sebastian presumed he was talking about the guest list.

Annabel gave him—Edward, that was; not Sebastian—another one of her brilliant smiles.

Sebastian heard himself growl.

"WHAT?"

He flinched. It was a natural reflex. He was fond of his left ear.

"Isn't the beef marvelous?" he said to Lady Millicent, pointing at it for clarification.

She nodded, said something about Parliament, and speared a potato.

Sebastian looked back at Annabel, who was chatting animatedly with Edward.

Look at me, he willed.

She didn't.

Look at me.

Nothing.

Look at—

"WHAT'RE YOU LOOKING AT?"

"Only admiring your fair skin, Lady Millicent," Seb said smoothly. He'd always been good on his feet. "You must be quite diligent about staying out of the sun."

She nodded and muttered, "I watch my money."

Sebastian was stupefied. What on earth had she thought he'd said?

"EAT THE BEEF." She took another bite. "IT'S THE BEST THING ON THE TABLE."

He did. But it needed salt. Or rather, *he* needed the salt cellar, which happened to be located directly in front of Annabel.

"Edward," he said, "would you please ask Miss Winslow for the salt?"

Edward turned to Annabel and repeated the request, although in Sebastian's opinion, there had been no need for his eyes to travel anywhere below her face.

"Of course," Annabel murmured, and she reached for the salt cellar.

Look at me.

She handed it to Edward.

Look at me.

And then . . . *finally.* He gave her his most melting smile, the kind that promised secrets and delight.

She flushed. From her cheeks, to her ears, to the skin on her chest, so delightfully displayed above the lacy trim of her bodice. Sebastian allowed himself a satisfied sigh.

"Miss Winslow?" Edward asked. "Are you unwell?"

"Perfectly well," she said, fanning herself. "Is it hot in here?"

"Perhaps a little bit," he said, obviously lying. He was wearing a shirt, cravat, waistcoat, and jacket, and he looked cool and comfortable as an ice chip. Whereas Annabel, whose dress was cut low enough so that half of her bosom was exposed to air, had just taken a long sip of wine.

"I think my soup was overly warm," she said, shooting a quick glare at Sebastian. He returned the sentiment with a tiny lick of his lips.

"Miss Winslow?" Edward asked again, all concern.

"I'm fine," she snapped.

Sebastian chuckled.

"TRY THE FISH."

"I believe I will," Seb said, smiling at Lady Millicent. He took a bite of the salmon, which really was excellent—Lady Millicent apparently knew her fish—then sneaked a glance over at Annabel, who still looked as if she'd dearly love a tall glass of water. Edward, on the other hand, had got that glazed look in his eyes, the one that appeared every time he thought about Annabel's—

Sebastian kicked him.

Edward snapped around to face him.

"Is something wrong, Mr. Valentine?" Annabel asked.

"My cousin," he bit off, "has uncommonly long legs."

"Did he kick you?" She turned quickly to Sebastian. *Did you kick him?* she mouthed.

He took another bite of fish.

She turned back to Edward. "Why would he do such a thing?"

Edward flushed to the tips of his ears. Sebastian decided to let Annabel figure that one out on her own. She turned and scowled at him, which he returned with: "Why, Miss Winslow, whatever can be the matter?"

"WERE YOU TALKING TO ME?"

"Miss Winslow was wondering what sort of fish we're eating," Sebastian lied.

Lady Millicent looked at Annabel as if she were an idiot, shook her head, and muttered something Sebastian couldn't quite grasp. He thought he heard salmon. Maybe beef, too. And he could have sworn she said something about a dog.

This concerned him.

He glanced down at his plate, making sure that he could identify every meat-like substance, and then, satisfied all was what it should be, took a bite of the beef.

"It's good," Lady Millicent said, giving him a nudge.

He smiled and nodded, relieved that she seemed to be speaking in a quieter voice.

"Should get some more. Best thing on the plate."

Sebastian wasn't sure about that, but—

"WHERE'S THE BEEF?"

And there went his ear.

Lady Millicent was craning her neck, looking this way and that. She opened her mouth to shout again, but Sebastian held up what he hoped was a silencing hand and signaled to a footman.

"More beef for the lady," he requested.

With a pained expression, the footman explained that there was none left.

"Can you get her something that *looks* like beef?"

"We have duck in a similar sauce."

"God, no." Sebastian had no idea how hivey Lady Millicent might get, or how long it would take for her to get there, but he fervently did not want to find out.

With an exaggerated gesture toward the far end of the table, he said something to her about a dog, and while she was looking the other way quickly slid the rest of his beef onto her plate.

Upon not locating a dog (or frog, hog, or log) near the bottom of the table, Lady Millicent turned back with an expression of some irritation, but Sebastian quickly held her off with: "They found one last portion."

She gave a grunt of pleasure and set back to eating. Seb hazarded a glance back at Annabel, who appeared to have been watching the entire exchange.

She was grinning from ear to ear.

Seb thought of all the ladies he'd met in London, the ones who would have looked on in horror, or disgust, or if they had any humor, would have been biting back their smiles, or trying to hide them behind a hand.

But not Annabel. She smiled like she laughed, magnificent and grand. Her eyes, greenish-gray turned pewter in the evening light, sparkled with shared mischief.

And he realized, right there across Lady Challis's heavily laden dining-room table, that he could never live without her. She was so beautiful, so gloriously womanly, his breath quite literally whooshed from his body. Her face, heart-shaped, and with that mouth that always looked as if it wanted to smile; her skin, not quite as pale as fashion wanted, but utterly perfect for her. She looked healthy, wind-kissed.

She was the type of woman a man wanted to come home to. No, she was *the* woman *he* wanted to come home to. He'd asked her to marry him . . . but why? He could barely remember. He'd liked her, he'd lusted for her, and God knew, he'd always loved saving females who needed saving. But he'd never asked one to marry him before.

Could his heart have known something his head hadn't quite grasped?

He loved her.

He *adored* her.

He wanted to crawl into bed with her every night, make love as if there would be no tomorrow, and then wake up in her arms the next morning, rested and sated, and ready to devote himself to the singular task of making her smile.

He lifted his glass to his lips, smiling into his wine. The flickering light of the candles was dancing across the table, and Sebastian Grey was happy.

At the end of the meal the ladies excused themselves so that the gentlemen might enjoy their port. Annabel found Louisa (who had, sadly, been stuck up near Lord Newbury at the head of the table) and the two walked arm in arm to the drawing room.

"Lady Challis says we shall read and write and embroider until the gentlemen rejoin us," Louisa said.

"Did you bring embroidery?"

Louisa grimaced. "I think she said something about providing it."

"The true purpose of the house party becomes clear," Annabel said dryly. "By the time we return to London, Lady Challis shall have an entirely new set of pillowcases."

Louisa giggled at that, then said, "I'm going to

ask someone to fetch my book. Shall I get yours as well?"

Annabel nodded, waiting while Louisa spoke to a housemaid. When she was through, they entered the drawing room, taking seats as close to the perimeter as they could. A few minutes later a maid arrived, carrying two books. She held out *Miss Sainsbury and the Mysterious Colonel*, and both ladies reached for it.

"Oh, how funny, we're reading the same book!" Louisa exclaimed, seeing that both volumes were the same title.

Annabel looked over at her cousin in surprise. "Haven't you read it already?"

Louisa shrugged. "I so enjoyed *Miss Truesdale and the Silent Gentleman* that I thought I would reread the other three." She looked down at Annabel's copy. "What part are you up to?"

"Ehrm . . ." Annabel opened the book and found her place. "I believe Miss Sainsbury has just thrown herself over a hedge. Or perhaps into the hedge."

"Oh, the goat," Louisa said breathlessly. "I loved that part." She held up her copy. "I'm still at the beginning."

They settled in with their books, but before either of them could turn a page, Lady Challis happened by. "What are you reading?" she asked.

"*Miss Sainsbury and the Mysterious Colonel*," Louisa answered politely.

"And you, Miss Winslow?"

"Oh, the same, actually."

"You're reading the same book? How darling!" Lady Challis motioned toward a friend across the room. "Rebecca, come look at this. They're reading the same book."

Annabel was not sure why this was deemed so remarkable, but she sat quietly and waited for Lady Westfield to come over.

"Cousins," Lady Challis declared. "Reading the same book."

"I've actually read it before," Louisa mentioned.

"What book is it?" Lady Westfield asked.

"Miss Sainsbury and the Mysterious Colonel," Annabel said again.

"Oh, yes. By Mrs. Gorely. I quite enjoyed that one. Especially when the pirate turned out to be—"

"Don't say anything!" Louisa exclaimed. "Annabel hasn't finished it."

"Oh yes, of course."

Annabel frowned, flipping through the pages. "I thought he was a privateer."

"It is one of my favorites," Louisa put in.

Lady Westfield turned her attention to Annabel. "And you, Miss Winslow, are you enjoying it?"

Annabel cleared her throat. She wasn't sure if she was precisely enjoying the book, but she did not dislike it. And there was something rather comforting about it. It reminded her of Sebastian, actually. Mrs. Gorely was one of his favorite authors, and she could see why. Bits of it almost sounded like him.

"Miss Winslow?" Lady Westfield repeated. "Are you enjoying the book?"

Annabel started, then realized she had not answered her question. "I think so. The story is quite entertaining, if a little implausible."

"A little?" Louisa said with laugh. "It's completely implausible. But that is what makes it so marvelous."

"I suppose," Annabel replied. "I just wish the writing were a little less florid. Sometimes I feel as if I am wading through adjectives."

"Oh, I've just had the most marvelous idea," Lady Challis exclaimed, clapping her hands together. "We shall save charades for another night."

Annabel let out a huge sigh of relief. She'd always hated charades.

"Instead, we shall have a reading!"

Annabel looked up at her sharply. "What?"

"A reading. We already have two copies right here. I'm sure I have another in our library. Three ought to be more than enough."

"You plan to read from *Miss Sainsbury*?" Louisa inquired.

"Oh, not me," Lady Challis said, placing a hand over her heart. "The hostess never takes a role."

Annabel was quite sure this was not true, but there wasn't much she could do about it.

"Will you be one of our players, Miss Winslow?" Lady Challis asked. "You have such a *theatrical* look about you."

Among other items of which Annabel was quite sure: this was not a compliment. But she agreed to read because, once again, there wasn't much she could do about it.

"You should ask Mr. Grey to take part," Louisa suggested.

Annabel determined to kick her later, since she could not reach her at the moment.

"He is a great fan of Mrs. Gorely," Louisa continued.

"Is he?" Lady Challis murmured.

"He is," Louisa confirmed. "We discussed our mutual admiration for the author recently."

"Very well, then," Lady Challis decided. "It shall be Mr. Grey. And you, too, I think, Lady Louisa."

"Oh. No." Louisa blushed furiously, which on Louisa was furious indeed. "I couldn't. I'm—I'm terrible at such things."

"No time like the present to practice, don't you think?"

Annabel had been looking forward to a bit of revenge against her cousin, but even she thought this was too cruel. "Lady Challis, I'm sure we can find someone else who would like to take part. Or perhaps Louisa can be our director!"

"Do you need one?"

"Er, yes. I mean, of course we must. Doesn't all theater require a director? And what is a reading if not theater?"

"Very well," Lady Challis said with a dismissive wave. "You may sort it out amongst yourselves. If you'll excuse me, I'm going to see what is taking the gentlemen so long."

"Thank you," Louisa said, as soon as Lady Challis had departed. "I could never have read in front of everyone."

"I know," Annabel said. She wasn't particularly

looking forward to reading from *Miss Sainsbury* in front of the entire party, either, but at least she had had some practice at that sort of thing. She and her siblings had frequently performed theatricals and readings at home.

"What section shall we perform?" Louisa asked, thumbing through the book.

"I don't know. I'm not even halfway through yet. But don't," Annabel said sharply, "make me the goat."

Louisa chuckled at that. "No, no, you shall be Miss Sainsbury, of course. Mr. Grey will be the colonel. Oh dear, we'll need a narrator. Perhaps Mr. Grey's cousin?"

"I think it would be much funnier if Mr. Grey played Miss Sainsbury," Annabel said, all nonchalance.

Louisa gasped. "Annabel, you are evil."

Annabel shrugged. "I can be the narrator."

"Oh, no. If you're going to make Mr. Grey be Miss Sainsbury, you must be the colonel. Mr. Valentine will be the narrator." Louisa frowned. "Or perhaps we ought to ask Mr. Valentine if he wishes to take part before assigning him a role."

"I didn't get a choice," Annabel reminded her.

Louisa considered that. "True. Very well, let me find an appropriate passage. How long do you suppose the reading ought to be?"

"As short as we can possibly get away with," Annabel said firmly.

Louisa flipped open her book and then flipped over several pages. "That may be difficult if we're avoiding the goat."

"Louisa . . ." Annabel warned.

"I assume your ban also extends to sheep?"

"To all four-legged creatures."

Louisa shook her head. "You're making this very difficult. I have to eliminate all of the shipboard scenes."

Annabel leaned over her shoulder, murmuring, "I haven't got to that point yet."

"Milking goats," Louisa confirmed.

"What are you ladies looking at?"

Annabel looked up, then melted a bit inside. Sebastian was standing over them, presumably seeing nothing but their bent heads as they pored over the book.

"We will be performing a scene," she said, with an apologetic smile. "From *Miss Sainsbury and the Mysterious Colonel.*"

"Really?" He immediately sat beside them. "Which scene?"

"I'm trying to decide," Louisa informed him. She looked up. "Oh, by the way, you are Miss Sainsbury."

He blinked. "Really."

She made a small motion with her head toward Annabel. "Annabel is the colonel."

"A little bit backwards, don't you think?"

"It will be more amusing that way," Louisa said. "It was Annabel's idea."

Sebastian turned the full force of his gaze to Annabel. "Why," he murmured dryly, "am I not surprised?"

He sat down very close to her. Not touching; he would never be so indiscreet to do so in so public a place. But it *felt* as if they were touching. The air between them had grown heated, and her skin began to prick and shiver.

In an instant she was back by the pond, his hands on her skin, his lips everywhere. Her heart began to race, and she really, *really* wished she'd thought to bring a fan. Or a glass of punch.

"Your cousin shall be the narrator," Louisa announced, completely oblivious to Annabel's overheated state.

"Edward?" Sebastian said, sitting back as if he were completely unaffected. "He'll enjoy that."

"Really?" Louisa smiled and looked up. "I just need to find the right scene."

"Something dramatic I hope?"

She nodded. "But Annabel has insisted that we not include the goats."

Annabel wanted to make a pithy comment, but she hadn't quite got her breathing under control.

"I don't know that Lady Challis would appreciate livestock in her drawing room," Sebastian agreed.

Annabel finally managed to breathe evenly, but the rest of her was feeling very odd. Shivery, as if her limbs were desperate to move, and there was a tightness beginning to coil within her.

"I never even considered a live goat," Louisa said with a laugh.

"You could try to draft Mr. Hammond-Betts," Sebastian suggested. "His hair *is* rather fluffy."

Annabel tried to focus her eyes on a spot right in front of her. They were talking right over her, about *goats*, for heaven's sake, and she felt as if she might burst into flame at any moment. How could they not notice?

"I don't imagine he would take kindly to the request," Louisa said with a bit of giggle.

"Pity," Sebastian murmured. "He does look the part."

Annabel took another shallow breath. When Sebastian dropped his voice like that, soft and husky, it made her positively squirm.

"Oh, here we are," Louisa said excitedly. "What do you think of this scene?" She reached past Annabel to hand the book to Sebastian. Which of course meant that he had to reach past Annabel, too.

His hand brushed her sleeve. His thigh leaned into hers.

Annabel jumped to her feet, knocking the book out of whatever person's hand it was in (she didn't know; didn't care, either). "Excuse me," she squeaked.

"Is something wrong?" Louisa asked.

"Nothing, I, ehrm, just . . ." She cleared her throat. "I'll be right back." And then: "If you'll excuse me." And then: "Just a moment." And then: "I—"

"Just *go*," Louisa said.

She did. Or rather, she tried. Annabel was in such a hurry she wasn't paying attention to where she was going, and when she reached the doorway she only just managed to avoid crashing into the gentleman entering the room.

The Earl of Newbury.

The giddiness bubbling along inside Annabel died in an instant. "Lord Newbury," she murmured, dipping into a respectful curtsy. She did not wish to antagonize him; she merely wished to *not* marry him.

"Miss Winslow." His eyes swept across the room before coming back to hers. Annabel noticed that his jaw tightened when he spied Sebastian, but other than that, the only expression on his face was one of satisfaction.

Which naturally made Annabel nervous.

"I shall make the announcement now," he told her.

"What?" Somehow she managed to make that not come out as a shriek. "My lord," she said, trying to sound placating, or if not that then at least reasonable, "surely this is not the time."

"Nonsense," he said dismissively. "I believe we are all here."

"I haven't said yes," she ground out.

He turned to her with a withering glare. And then said nothing else, as if nothing else was necessary.

He did not even think her worthy of a response, Annabel fumed. "Lord Newbury," she said firmly, placing a hand on his arm, "I forbid you to make an announcement."

His face, already florid, turned nearly to purple, and a vein began to bulge in his neck. Annabel removed her hand from his arm and took a cautious step back. She did not think he would strike her in so public a setting, but he *had* punched Sebastian in front of their entire club. It seemed wise to distance herself.

"I have not said yes," she said again, because he

was not responding. He was just looking at her with a thunderous expression, and for a moment she feared he might actually have an apoplectic fit. Never in her life had she witnessed another human being so angry. Spittle was popping from the corners of his mouth, and his eyes were huge and froglike in his head. It was horrific. *He* was horrific.

"You don't get to say yes," he finally spat out. But his voice remained a harsh whisper. "Or no. You have been bought and sold, and next week you're going to spread your legs and do your bloody duty by me. And you will do it again and again until you produce a healthy boy. Are we clear?"

"No," Annabel said, making sure that her voice, at least, was perfectly clear, "we are not."

Chapter Twenty-three

"Let's see, Lady Louisa, which scene have you chosen?" Sebastian grinned as he reached for *Miss Sainsbury*, which had fallen to the carpet after Annabel knocked it from his hands. What fun that he should be doing a recitation from his own work. A bit absurd that he should be playing Miss Sainsbury, but he had enough confidence in his manhood that he felt he could carry it off with aplomb.

Besides, he was rather good at this sort of thing, if he did say so himself. Never mind that the last time he'd read for an audience he'd fallen off a table and dislocated his shoulder. He didn't regret it in the least. He'd had the housemaids in tears. Tears!

It had been a beautiful moment.

He scooped up the book, straightening to hand

it back to Louisa so that she could find her place again, but when he caught her worried expression, he paused. Then he turned, following her gaze.

Annabel was standing near the doorway. So was his uncle.

"I hate him," Louisa whispered vehemently.

"I'm not terribly fond of him myself."

Louisa grabbed his arm with a force he would not have imagined she possessed, and when he turned to face her, he was startled by the ferocity in her eyes. She was such a colorless thing, and yet at that moment, she was positively ablaze.

"You cannot let her marry him," she said.

Sebastian turned back toward the door, his eyes narrowing. "I don't intend to."

He waited, though, to see if the situation would right itself. For Annabel's sake, he did not wish to cause a scene. He was well aware that Lady Challis had planned the house party with the Grey-Winslow-Newbury love triangle as the main source of entertainment. Anything that even hinted of scandal would be on every London gossip's tongue within days. Unsurprisingly, every eye in the room was set firmly on Annabel and Lord Newbury.

When they weren't stealing glances at Sebastian.

Truly, he'd had every intention of staying put. But when his uncle began to shake and seethe, his skin mottling with fury as he hissed something at Annabel, Sebastian could not stand by.

"Is there a problem?" he asked in a cool, smooth voice, coming to stand slightly behind and to the side of Annabel.

"This is none of your concern," his uncle spat.

"I beg to differ," Sebastian said quietly. "A lady in distress is always my concern."

"The lady is my affianced bride," Newbury snapped, "and therefore she will never be your concern."

"Is that true?" Sebastian asked Annabel. Not because he believed it might be; rather he wished to give her the opportunity to make a public denial.

She shook her head no.

Sebastian turned back to his uncle. "Miss Winslow seems to be under the impression that she is *not* your affianced bride."

"Miss Winslow is an idiot."

Sebastian's gut tightened, and his fingers got a strange, tingly feeling, the sort that forced one's hands into fists. Still, he kept his demeanor cool, merely raising a brow as he commented dryly, "And yet you wish to marry her."

"Stay out of this," his uncle warned.

"I could," Seb murmured, "but I'd feel so guilty in the morning, allowing a perfectly lovely young lady to meet such a terrible end."

Newbury's eyes narrowed. "You never change, do you?"

Sebastian kept his face remarkably blank as he said, "If you mean I'm eternally charming . . ."

His uncle's jaw tightened, nearly to the point of shaking.

"Winsome, even, some would say." Sebastian knew he was pushing it, but it was so damned hard to resist. There was such a sense of déjà vu in these arguments. They never changed. His uncle went on about what a pathetic excuse for a human being he was, and Sebastian stood there, bored, until he was done. Which was why, when Newbury started into his latest rant, Sebastian merely crossed his arms, widened his stance, and prepared to wait it out.

"All your life," Newbury raged, "you've been shiftless and without direction, whoring about, failing at school—"

"Well, now, that's not true," Seb cut in, feeling the need to defend his reputation in front of such a large audience. He'd never been at the top of his class, but he damn well hadn't been at the bottom, either.

But his uncle had no intention of bringing his tirade to an end. "Who do you think paid for that bloody education of yours? Your father?" He chortled with disdain. "He never had two shillings to rub together. I paid his bills his entire life."

For a moment Sebastian was taken aback. "Well, then, I suppose I must thank you," he said quietly. "I did not know."

"Of course you didn't know," his uncle shot back. "You don't pay attention to anything. You never have. You just trot about, sleeping with other men's wives, running away, leaving the country, and the rest of us have to take responsibility for all your pranks."

Now *that* was too much. But when Sebastian got angry, he got insolent. And flip. And actually quite funny. He turned to Annabel and held his hands out as if to say—*how can this be?* "And here I thought I was joining the army. King and country and all that."

A small crowd had gathered around them. Apparently Lady Challis and her guests had given up all pretense of discretion.

"I do hope I'm not mistaken," he added turning to onlookers with a carefully constructed expression of incredulity on his face. "I shot an awful lot of people in France."

Someone snickered. Someone else covered a laugh with a hand. But no one, Sebastian noticed, made any move to intervene. He wondered if he would have done so, were he an onlooker.

Probably not. The tableau would have been far too entertaining. The earl, spluttering with fury; the nephew, poking fun. It was what they expected of him, Sebastian imagined. His wit was dry, his charm legendary, and he never lost his temper.

Newbury's face turned an even more astonishing shade of magenta. He knew that if Sebastian held the humor, Sebastian held the crowd. In the end, most would side with rank and wealth, but for now, in this moment, the earl was a buffoon. And Sebastian knew he hated it.

"Don't stick your nose where it does not belong," his uncle bit off. He jabbed a thick, sausagy finger at Sebastian, coming within a few inches of his chest. "You didn't even care about Miss Winslow until you heard I was planning to marry her."

"Actually, that's not true," Sebastian said, almost affably. "And in fact, I would counter that you had decided to be done with her until you thought *I* might be interested."

"The last thing I'd want is one of your trollops. Which she"—he jerked his head toward Annabel, who had been watching the entire exchange with openmouthed horror—"is in fast danger of becoming."

That tightening in Sebastian's gut did another twist. "Careful," he warned, his voice dangerously soft. "You're insulting a lady."

Lord Newbury rolled his bloodshot eyes. "I'm insulting a whore."

And that was it. Sebastian Grey, the man who walked away from confrontation; the man who'd spent the war far from the action, picking off the enemy one by one; the man who found anger to be such a tedious emotion . . .

He went berserk.

He didn't think, he barely felt, and he had no idea what anyone was saying or doing around him. His entire being shrank and twisted, and the hideous, primitive cry that came from his throat—he had no more control over that than he did the rest of his body, which launched forward, practically flying through the air as he knocked his uncle to the floor.

They crashed through a table, Lord Newbury's heft splintering the wood, and two candelabras, both fully lit, went tumbling down.

There was a shriek, and Sebastian had a dim awareness of someone stamping out flames, but the entire bloody house could have been on fire and it would not have stopped him from his one singular goal.

Wrapping his hands around his uncle's throat.

"Apologize to the lady," he growled, jamming his knee right where it would hurt most.

Newbury let out a howl at the insulting blow.

Sebastian's thumbs rested longingly on his uncle's windpipe. "That didn't sound like an apology."

His uncle glared up at him and spit.

Sebastian did not even flinch. "Apologize," he said again, each syllable clipped and hard.

All around him people were yelling, and someone actually grabbed one of his arms, trying to haul him off his uncle before he killed him. But Sebastian could not make out anything they were saying. Nothing could possibly register above the hot roar of rage rushing through his head. He'd served in the army. He'd shot dozens of French soldiers from his sniper's perch, but *never* had he wanted to see another man dead.

But oh Lord, he did now.

"Apologize or so help me God I will kill you," he spat. He tightened his hands, feeling almost gleeful as his uncle's eyes bulged and face grew purple, and—

And then he was yanked off him and held back, and he heard Edward grunting with exertion as he hissed, "Get hold of yourself."

"Apologize to Miss Winslow," Sebastian snarled at his uncle, trying to shake loose. But Edward and Lord Challis were holding firm.

Two other gentlemen helped Lord Newbury to a sitting position, still on the floor amidst the rubble of the table they'd broken. He was gasping for air, and his skin was still an awful shade of pink, but he had enough hatred in him to try to spit at Annabel, harshly rasping, "Whore."

Sebastian let out another roar and hurled himself at his uncle, dragging both Edward and Lord Challis with him. They all lurched forward a few steps, but Sebastian was restrained before he could reach his uncle.

"Apologize to the lady," he bit off.

"No."

"*Apologize!*" Sebastian roared.

"It's all right," Annabel said. Or maybe she said it. Even she could not quite break through the haze of rage rushing through his skull.

He yanked forward, trying once again to reach his uncle. His blood was pounding and his pulse was racing, and his entire body was itching for a fight. He wanted to hurt. He wanted to maim. But he was held back by Edward and Lord Challis, and so instead he gathered his breath and said, "Apologize to Miss Winslow or so help me God, I will have satisfaction."

Several heads whipped around to face him. Had he just suggested a duel? Even Sebastian wasn't sure.

But Lord Newbury just lumbered to his feet and said, "Get him away from me."

Sebastian held his ground, despite the urging of the two men trying to pull him back. He watched as Newbury brushed off his sleeves, and all he could think was—it wasn't right. It could not end this way, with his uncle just walking away. It wasn't fair, and it wasn't right, and Annabel deserved better.

And so he said it. Clearly, this time. "Name your seconds."

"No!" Annabel cried out.

"What the hell are you doing?" Edward demanded, yanking him aside.

Lord Newbury turned slowly around, staring at him in shock.

"Are you mad?" Edward whispered, hushed but urgent.

Sebastian finally shook off Edward. "He has insulted Annabel and I demand satisfaction."

"He is your *uncle*."

"Not by choice."

"If you kill him—" Edward shook his head frantically. He looked over at Lord Newbury, then at Annabel, then at Newbury, then finally gave up and turned to Sebastian with an expression of utter panic. "You're his heir. Everyone would think you'd killed him for the title. You'll be thrown into gaol."

More likely he'd hang, Sebastian thought grimly. But all he said was, "He insulted Annabel."

"I don't care," Annabel said quickly, wedging herself next to Edward. "Honestly, I don't."

"I care."

"Sebastian, *please*," she pleaded. "It will only make things worse."

"Think," Edward urged. "There is nothing to be gained. Nothing."

Sebastian knew they were right, but he could not quite calm himself down enough to accept it. All his life his uncle had insulted him. He'd called him names—some fair; most not. Sebastian had brushed it off because that was his way. But when Newbury had insulted Annabel . . .

That could not be borne.

"I know I'm not a—what he called me," Annabel said softly, placing her hand on his arm. "And I know you know it, too. That is all that matters to me."

But Sebastian wanted revenge. He couldn't help it. It was petty and it was childish, but he wanted his uncle to *hurt*. He wanted him humiliated. And it just so happened that this objective was in complete accord with the only other goal in his life, which was to make Annabel Winslow his wife.

"I withdraw my challenge," he said loudly.

There was a collective exhale. The room, it seemed, had tensed and tightened, every shoulder drawn up to the ears, every set of eyes wide and worried.

Lord Newbury, still standing in the doorway leading out to the corridor, narrowed his eyes.

Sebastian wasted no time. Taking Annabel's hand, he dropped to one knee.

"Oh my goodness!" someone gasped. Someone else said Newbury's name, maybe to prevent him from leaving again.

"Annabel Winslow," Sebastian said, and when he gazed up at her, it wasn't with one of his hot, melting smiles, the kind he knew made female hearts bounce and skip, from age nine to ninety. It wasn't his dry half smile, either, the kind that said he knew things, secret things, and if he leaned down and whispered in your ear, you might know them, too.

When he looked up at Annabel, he was just a man, looking at a woman, hoping and praying that she loved him the way he loved her.

He brought her hand to his lips. "Will you do me the very great honor of becoming my wife?"

Her lips trembled, and she whispered, "Yes." And then, more loudly, "Yes!"

He rose to his feet and swept her into his arms. All around him people were cheering. Not everyone, but enough to make the moment a little bit theatrical. Which Seb belatedly realized wasn't what he wanted. He did not deny a little burst of joy at having so publicly bested his uncle (he'd never be so pure of heart that he could deny *that*), but as he held Annabel, smiling into her hair, several people began to chant, "Kiss! Kiss!" and he realized that he didn't want to do this in front of an audience.

This moment was sacred. It was theirs, and theirs alone, and he did not want to share it.

They would have their moment again, he vowed, even as he released Annabel and smiled cheerfully at Edward and Louisa and all the rest of Lady Challis's guests.

Later. They would have their moment later. Alone.

If he were writing the story, Sebastian decided, that was how he'd do it.

Chapter Twenty-four

Someone was in her room.

Annabel froze, barely breathing beneath the blankets on her bed. She'd had a terrible time falling asleep; her mind had been racing, and she was far too excited and giddy at having finally decided to throw caution to the wind and marry Sebastian. But sheer determination—and her trick of keeping her eyes closed at all times—had finally won out, and she'd fallen asleep.

But it must not have been a very deep sleep, or maybe it was just that it had only been a few minutes since she'd drifted off. Because something had woken her. A noise, maybe. Perhaps just the movement in the room. But someone was definitely there.

Maybe it was a thief. If that was the case, she'd do best to stay utterly still. She had nothing of value; all her earbobs were paste, and even her copy of *Miss Sainsbury and the Mysterious Colonel* was a third edition.

If it was a thief, he'd realize this and move on.

If it wasn't a thief—Bloody hell, then she was in very dire straits. She'd need a weapon, and all she had within arm's reach was a pillow, a blanket, and a book.

Miss Sainsbury again. Somehow Annabel didn't think it was going to save her.

If it wasn't a thief, should she try to sneak out of bed? Hide? See if she could make it to the door? Should she do anything? Should she? Should she? What if—? But maybe—

She squeezed her eyes shut, just for a moment, just to try to calm herself. Her heart was racing, and it was taking every ounce of her will to keep her breathing quiet and under control. She had to think. Keep her head. The room was dark, very much so. The curtains were thick, and they covered the windows completely. Even on a full-moon night—which this was not—barely a glimmer of light would sneak in around the edges. She couldn't even see the outline of the intruder. The only clues she had as to his location were the soft sounds of his feet on the carpet, the occasional tiny creak of the floor underneath.

He was moving slowly. Whoever was in the room was moving slowly. Slowly, but . . .

Closer.

Annabel's heart began to pound so loudly she thought the bed might shake. The intruder was moving closer. He was definitely approaching the bed. This was no thief, this was someone out to cause mischief, or malice, or pain, or good God, it didn't matter—she just had to get out of there.

Praying that the intruder was as blind in the dark as she was, she slid slowly across the bed, hoping he would not hear her movement. He was approaching on the right, so she moved left, carefully swinging her legs over the side and—

She screamed. But she didn't. There was a hand over her mouth, and an arm around her neck and any sound she might have made was lost in a terrified choking sob.

"If you know what's good for you, you'll be quiet."

Annabel's eyes flew open with terror. It was the Earl of Newbury. She knew his voice, and even his smell, that awful sweaty odor, flavored with brandy and fish.

"If you scream," he said, sounding almost amused, "someone will come running in. Your grandmother, perhaps, or your cousin. Isn't one of them right in the next room?"

Annabel nodded, the motion bringing her chin up and down over his beefy forearm. He was wearing a shirt, but still, he felt sticky. And she felt sick.

"Imagine that," he said with a malicious chuckle. "In comes the respectable and pure Lady Louisa. She would scream, too. A man between a woman's legs . . . Surely she'd be shocked."

Annabel said nothing. She couldn't have, anyway, with his hand over her mouth.

"Then the whole house would come running. What a scandal that would be. You'd be ruined. Your little idiot of a fiancé wouldn't have you, then, now, would he?"

That wasn't true. Sebastian would not abandon her. Annabel knew that he would not.

"You'd be a fallen woman," Newbury went on, clearly relishing his tale. He slid his arm down just far enough to palm her breast and squeeze. "Of course, you've always looked the part."

Annabel let out a little moan of distress.

"You like that, do you?" he chuckled, squeezing harder.

"No," she tried to say, but his hand blocked her.

"Some would say you'd have to marry me," Newbury continued, idly patting her breast, "but I wonder, would anyone think I had to marry *you*? I could just say you weren't a virgin, that you'd been playing uncle and nephew against each other. What a crafty woman you must be."

Unable to take it anymore, Annabel jerked her head to one side, then the next, trying to dislodge his hand. Finally, with a little laugh, he lifted it away. "Remember," he said, bringing his flabby lips close to her ear, "don't make too much noise."

"You know it isn't true," Annabel whispered roughly.

"Which bit? About your virginity? Are you saying you're not a virgin?" He whipped the covers away and flipped her onto her back, straddling her roughly. Each of his hands landed hard against her shoulders, pinning her down. "My, my, that changes everything."

"No," she cried softly. "About my playing—" Oh, what was the use? There could be no reasoning with him. He was out for revenge. On her, on Sebastian, probably on the whole world. He'd been made a fool of that night, in front of more than a score of his peers.

He was not the sort of man who could brush that off.

"You're a foolish, foolish girl," he said, shaking his head. "You could have been a countess. What were you thinking?"

Annabel held still, conserving her energy. She couldn't possibly break free while he had his full weight on her. She needed to wait until he moved, until she could catch him off balance. Even then, she would need all of her strength.

"I was so sure I'd found just the right woman."

Annabel stared at him in disbelief. He sounded almost regretful.

"All I wanted was an heir. Just one measly little son so that that moronic nephew of mine does not inherit."

She wanted to protest, to tell him all the ways she thought Sebastian was utterly brilliant. He had an amazing imagination, and he was marvelously clever in conversation. No one could outwit him. No one. And he was funny. Dear heavens, he could make her laugh like no one in the world.

He was perceptive, too. And observant. He saw everything, noticed everyone. He understood people, not just their hopes and dreams, but *how* they hoped and dreamed.

If that wasn't brilliance, she didn't know what was.

"Why do you hate him so much?" she whispered.

"Because he's an ass," Lord Newbury said dismissively.

That's not an answer, Annabel wanted to say.

"It doesn't matter, anyway," he continued. "He flatters himself if he thinks I sought a wife just to thwart his ambitions. Is it so wrong for a man to want his title and home to go to his own son?"

"No," Annabel said softly. Because maybe if she acted like his friend, he wouldn't hurt her. And because it *wasn't* so wrong to want what he wanted. The wrongness came in the way he went about it. "How did he die?"

Lord Newbury went still.

"Your son," she clarified.

"A fever," he said curtly. "He cut his leg."

Annabel nodded. She'd known several people who had got fevers the same way. A deep cut always provoked vigilance. Did it fester? Turn red? Hot? A wound that did not heal properly usually led to a fever, and a fever led all too often to death. Annabel had often wondered why some wounds healed neatly and quick, and others did not. There seemed no rhyme or reason to it, just an unfair, capricious hand of fate.

"I'm sorry," she said.

For a moment she thought he believed her. His hands, hard and firm at her shoulders, slackened ever so slightly. And his eyes—it might have been a trick of the dim light, but she thought they might have softened. But then he snorted and said, "No you're not."

The irony was, she was, or at least she had been. She'd had some sympathy for him, but that was banished when his hands moved to her throat.

"This is what he did to me," Lord Newbury

said, his words coming out like steam between his teeth. "In front of everyone."

Dear God, was he going to strangle her? Annabel's breathing quickened, and every nerve in her body felt primed for flight. But Lord Newbury had to be twice as heavy as she was, and no amount of panic-driven strength was going to help her to topple him.

"I'll marry you!" she blurted out, just as his fingers tightened over her windpipe.

"What?"

Annabel choked and gasped, unable to speak, and he loosened his grip.

"I'll marry you," she pleaded. "I'll jilt him. And I'll marry you. Please just don't kill me."

Lord Newbury let out a loud laugh, and Annabel shot a panicked look to the door. He was going to wake everyone, just as he'd warned her not to.

"Did you think I was going to kill you?" he asked, actually lifting one of his hands from her throat so that he could wipe a tear from his eye. "Oh, that's funny."

He was mad. That was all Annabel could think, except that she knew he *wasn't* mad.

"I won't kill you," he said, still sounding terribly amused. "I would be the first anyone would suspect, and while I doubt I'd be punished, it would be so inconvenient."

Inconvenient. Murder. Maybe he was mad.

"Not to mention it might give other young ladies pause. You're not the only one I've had my eye on. Stinson's youngest is a bit lacking up top, but her hips look healthy enough for childbearing. And she doesn't speak unless spoken to."

Because she's *fifteen*, Annabel thought wildly. Good Lord, he wanted to marry a *baby*.

"She wouldn't be as much fun to plow as you, but I don't need a wife for that." He leaned down, his eyes unnaturally bright in the dim light. "Maybe I'll even have *you*."

"No," Annabel whimpered, before she could stop herself. And sure enough, he smiled, taking great pleasure in her distress. He hated her, she realized. He hated her now like he hated Sebastian. Blindly, irrationally.

Dangerously.

But as he leaned toward her, his face coming closer to hers, he lifted his body from her hips and belly. Annabel took a deep, quick gasp at the decompression, and then, realizing instinctively that this might be her only chance, she yanked one of her legs up, bending at the knee. She caught him hard between the legs, and he howled in pain. It wasn't quite enough to completely disable him, though, and so she did it again, even harder, then brought her arms up and shoved. Lord Newbury let out an awful cry, but Annabel brought her knee up again, this time to use her legs to push against him, and finally she threw him off of her and ran from the bed.

He hit the carpet with a thud and a curse. Annabel ran for the door but he caught her by the ankle.

"Let . . . go of me," she ground out.

His response was: "You little bitch."

Annabel tugged and yanked, but he wrapped a second hand around her calf and held firm, pulling against her in an effort to bring his un-wieldy body upright.

"Let go!" she cried out. If she could just break loose, she knew she was safe. If she could outrun a turkey, damn it, she could outrun, in the words of her grandmother, an overweight nobleman.

She pulled hard, almost breaking free. They both lurched forward, Lord Newbury sliding along the carpet like some horrible beached monster. Annabel nearly toppled forward; luckily she was close enough to a wall to throw out her arms and stop herself from going down. That was when she realized she was near the fireplace. With one arm braced, she reached out blindly with the other, nearly crying out in triumph when her hand connected with the hard iron handle of the poker.

Quickly moving it to a two-hand grasp, she twisted around so that she was facing him again. He was trying to rise, not an easy task with both hands around her left ankle.

"Let go of me," she growled, raising the poker above her head. "Let go of me or I swear I'll—"

His hand went slack.

Annabel jumped back, edging along the wall toward the door, but Lord Newbury wasn't moving. At all.

"Oh my God," she breathed. "Oh my God."

And then she said it again, because she didn't know what else to say. Or do.

"Oh my God."

Sebastian moved quietly through the house, making his way toward Annabel's room on the second floor. He was an expert in the art of late night assignations, a skill he happily realized he would no longer need.

It was, he supposed, a science as well as an art. One needed to do one's research ahead of time—determining the location of the room, ascertaining the identity of its neighbors' occupants, and of course, traveling the route ahead of time to test the floor for squeaks or bumps.

Sebastian did like to be prepared.

He hadn't been able to do his usual route rehearsal; there hadn't been any appropriate time to do so after he proposed to Annabel. But he did know which room she was in, and he knew that her grandmother was sleeping to the north and her cousin to the south.

Across the hall was Lady Millicent, certainly a stroke of good luck. She wouldn't hear him unless he exploded a cannon outside her door.

The only thing he didn't know was whether there were any connecting doors between the trio of bedrooms. But this did not worry him. It was an important detail, but nothing he needed to learn ahead of time. It would be easy enough to check once he was inside.

Stonecross's floors were well maintained, and Sebastian made not a sound as he approached Annabel's door. He put his hand to the knob. It felt slightly damp. Curious. He shook his head. At what hour did Lady Challis have her maids polishing?

He turned the knob very slowly, vigilant for squeaks. Like everything else in the house, it worked perfectly, moving clockwise without a sound. He pushed the door open, preparing to slip in through the barest of cracks and then nudge it closed behind him.

But when he stepped inside, it took less than a second to know that something was not right. The breathing was not that of gentle sleep. It was harsh, and labored, and—

He pushed the door open wider to let more light in.

"Annabel?"

She was standing not far from the fireplace, a poker raised clutched in her hands. On the floor was Lord Newbury, utterly still.

"Annabel?" he said again. She looked to be in shock. She did not turn to him, did not acknowledge his arrival in any way.

He rushed to her side, carefully taking the poker from her fingers.

"I didn't hit him," she said, never once taking her eyes from the body from the floor. "I didn't even hit him."

"What happened?" He looked at the poker despite her statements. There was no blood on it, nothing to indicate a blow.

"I think he's dead," she said, still in that strange monotone whisper. "He was holding my ankle. I was going to hit him if he didn't let go, but then he let go, and—"

"His heart," Sebastian said, cutting her off so she did not have to say more. "It was probably his heart." He set the poker down, carefully placing it in its spot in the tool stand. The metal clinked together, but the sound was muted, and he did not think it would attract attention.

Moving back to Annabel, he took her hand, then touched her face. "Are you all right?" he asked carefully. "Did he hurt you?" He was terrified for the answer, but he had to ask. He had to know what had happened if he was going to help her.

"He was—he came in and—" But she could barely choke out the words, and when he wrapped his arms around her, she collapsed instantly, all the strength pouring from her before he could blink.

"Shh . . ." he crooned, cradling her lovingly. "It's all right. I'm here. I'm here now."

She nodded against his chest, but she didn't cry. She trembled, and she gasped for air, but she didn't cry. "He didn't—he didn't get to—I got away before—"

Thank God, Sebastian silently prayed. If his uncle had raped her . . . by God he would have brought him back from the dead just so that he could kill him again. Sebastian had seen rape in the war, not directly, but he'd seen the eyes of the women who had been brutalized. They had looked dead inside, and Sebastian had realized that in a way, they, too, had been killed, just like the men who'd gone off to battle. It was worse for the women. Their bodies lived on, with dead souls inside.

"What are we going to do?" she asked.

"I don't know," he admitted. "I'll think of something." But what? He knew how to handle himself in almost any situation, but this . . . the dead body of his uncle in the room of his fiancée . . .

Good God. This was beyond even him.

Think. He had to think. If he were writing this . . .

"First we shut the door," he said firmly, trying to sound as if he knew what he was doing. He gently removed his arms from around Annabel, making sure that she could stand on her own, and then moved swiftly to the door. He closed it firmly, then strode across the room to light a candle.

Annabel was standing where he'd left her, hugging her arms to her body. She looked freezing.

"Do you need a blanket?" he asked, and it seemed the most ludicrous question, under the circumstances. But she was cold, and he was a gentleman, and some things were just too deeply ingrained to be ignored.

She shook her head.

Seb planted his hands on his hips and stared down at his uncle, lying motionless, facedown on the carpet. He wasn't sure how he'd thought it would end between the two of them, but definitely not like *this*. Damn. What was he supposed to do now? "If I were writing this . . ." he muttered, trying to summon whatever creative corner of his imagination he usually reserved for his characters. "If I were writing this . . ."

"What did you say?"

He turned back to Annabel. He'd been so lost in his own thoughts he'd almost forgot she was there. "Nothing," he said, giving his head a shake. She probably thought he was babbling utter nonsense.

"I'm better now," she announced.

"What?"

She made a motion with her hand, a little bit of a twist, a little bit of a wave. "I have my head. Whatever we need to do, I can do it."

He blinked, surprised by her quick recovery. "Are you certain? I can—"

"I'll cry when we're done," she said sharply.

"I love you," he said, thinking this had to be the least appropriate time imaginable to tell her. But there was something about her standing there in her plain cotton nightgown, matter-of-fact and capable as a goddess. How could he not love her?

"Have I told you that?" he added.

She shook her head, her lips trembling into a smile. "I love you, too."

"Good," he said simply, because this wasn't the time for hearts and flowers. But he could not resist adding, "It would be bloody inconvenient for me if you didn't."

"I think we need to get him back to his own room," she said, looking down at Newbury with a queasy expression.

Sebastian nodded, grimly estimating his uncle's weight. It would not be easy, even with both of them. "Do you know where his room is?" he asked.

She shook her head. "Do you?"

"No." Damn.

"We can put him in the saloon," she suggested. "Or anywhere else there might be drink. If he was drunk, then maybe he would have fallen over." She swallowed. "Hit his head?"

Sebastian let out a long breath, planting his hands on his hips as he looked down at his uncle. He looked even more hideous in death than he had in life. Big, bloated . . . At least no one would doubt that his heart might have given out, especially after the excitement of the day. "His head, his heart," he muttered. "It doesn't matter. I feel unhealthy just looking at him."

He stood still for another moment, putting off the inevitable, and then finally he squared his shoulders and said, "I'll grab him under the arms. You take the legs. We'll have to roll him over first."

They got him onto his back, then moved to their spots and tried to lift. "Dear God in heaven," Sebastian grunted, the words flying from his mouth.

"This isn't going to work," Annabel said.

"It has to work."

They lifted and dragged, heaving with exertion, but they couldn't get the body to clear the floor for more than a few seconds at a time. There was no way they would be able to move him all the way to the saloon without making enough noise to wake someone.

"We're going to have to get Edward," Sebastian finally said.

Annabel's eyes flew to his in question.

"I would trust him with my life."

She nodded. "Maybe Louisa . . ."

"Couldn't lift a feather."

"I think she's stronger than she looks." But Annabel realized she sounded more hopeful than anything else. She bit her lip and looked back down at Newbury. "I think we need all the help we can get."

Sebastian started to nod, because they *did* need all the help they could get. But as it turned out, the help that did arrive came in the most surprising form . . .

Chapter Twenty-five

"What the devil is going on in here?"

Annabel froze. Not in horror. It was something far, far worse than horror.

"Annabel?" her grandmother snapped, marching in through the connecting door between their rooms. "It sounds like a herd of elephants. How do you expect a woman to get any sleep when—Oh." She stopped in her tracks, taking in the sight of Sebastian. Then she looked down and saw the earl. "Bloody hell."

She made a sound that Annabel could not quite interpret. Not a sigh, really; more of a grunt. Of supreme irritation.

"Which one of you killed him?" she demanded.

"Neither," Annabel said quickly. "He just . . . died."

"In your room?"

"I didn't invite him *in*," she ground out.

"No, you wouldn't." And damn if her grand-mother didn't sound almost regretful. Annabel could only stare at her in shock. Or maybe wonder.

"What are you doing here?" Lady Vickers asked, turning her frosty glare to Sebastian.

"Exactly what you think, my lady," he said. "Unfortunately, my timing was not what it could have been." He looked down at his uncle. "He was like this when I arrived."

"Better this way," Lady Vickers muttered. "If he'd come in with you on top of her . . . Good Lord, I can't even imagine the commotion."

She ought to blush, Annabel thought. She really ought. But she couldn't summon the will. She wasn't sure anything could embarrass her now.

"Well, we'll have to get rid of him," her grand-mother said, using the same voice Annabel imag-ined she would have used about an old sofa. She cocked her head toward Annabel. "I must say, this all worked out nicely for *you*."

"What are you saying?" Annabel asked, horrified.

"He's the earl now," Lady Vickers responded, flicking her fingers in Sebastian's direction. "And he'll be a damn sight more palatable than Robert here."

Robert, Annabel thought, looking down at Lord Newbury. She hadn't even known his given name. It seemed strange, somehow. The man had wanted to marry her, he'd attacked her, and then he'd died at her feet. And she hadn't even known his name.

For a moment they all just stared down at him. Finally, Lady Vickers said, "Damn, he's fat."

Annabel slammed a hand against her mouth,

trying not to laugh. Because it wasn't funny. It was *not* funny.

But she *really* wanted to laugh.

"I don't think we will be able to get him down to the saloon without waking half the house," Sebastian said. He looked over at Lady Vickers. "I don't suppose you know where his room is."

"At least as far as the saloon. And right next to the Challises. You'll never get him in without waking them up."

"I was going to wake my cousin," Seb told her. "With one more person we might be able to do it."

"We won't be able to move him with five more people," Lady Vickers retorted. "Not quietly, anyway."

Annabel stepped forward. "Maybe if we . . ."

But her grandmother cut her off with a sigh worthy of the Covent Garden stage. "Go ahead," she said, waving an arm to the connecting door. "Put him in my bed."

"What?" Annabel gasped.

"We'll just have to let everyone think he died having his way with me."

"But—but—" Annabel gaped at her grandmother, then looked at Lord Newbury, and then at Sebastian, who appeared to be speechless.

Sebastian. Speechless. Apparently, this was what it took.

"Oh for heaven's sake," Lady Vickers said, clearly irritated with their lack of action. "It's not as if we haven't done it before."

Annabel sucked in her breath so hard she choked. "You . . . *what*?"

"It was years ago," her grandmother replied, snapping her hand in the air as if batting away a fly. "But everybody knew about it."

"And you wanted me to *marry* him?"

Lady Vickers planted her hands on her hips and stared Annabel down. "Do you really think now is the time to make complaints? Besides, he wasn't that bad, if you know what I mean. And your uncle Percival turned out quite nicely."

"Oh my God," Annabel moaned. "Uncle Percy."

"Is apparently *my* uncle Percy," Sebastian said, shaking his head.

"Cousin, I should think," Lady Vickers said briskly. "Now then, are we going to move him or not? And I still haven't heard either one of you thanking me for throwing myself on the bayonet here, so to speak."

It was true. As much as her grandmother had got her into this mess, insisting that Annabel marry Lord Newbury in the first place, she was certainly doing her best to get her out of it. There would be a terrific scandal, and Annabel didn't even want to begin to imagine the cartoons and caricatures that would appear in the gossip papers. Although somehow she suspected her grandmother wouldn't mind a little notoriety in her old age.

"Thank you," Sebastian said, apparently finding his voice first. "It is much appreciated, I am sure."

"Come along, come along." Lady Vickers made little *get to it* motions with her hands. "He's not going to move himself into my bed."

Sebastian grabbed his uncle under the arms again, and Annabel moved to his feet, but as she wrapped her hands around his ankles and began to lift, she heard a very peculiar sound. And when she looked up, her eyes wide with horror at what this had to mean . . .

Newbury's eyes opened.

Annabel shrieked, and she dropped him.

"Almighty God," her grandmother cried out. "Did neither of you check to see if he was even dead?"

"I just assumed," Annabel protested. Her heart was racing, and she couldn't seem to slow her breathing down. She sagged against the edge of the bed. It was like the time her brothers had thrown sheets over their heads and jumped out in front of her on All Hallows' Eve, only a thousand times worse. A thousand thousand.

Lady Vickers turned her glare on Sebastian.

"I believed her," he said, setting Lord Newbury's head gently back down on the carpet. They all peered over him. His eyes had closed again.

"Is he dead again?" Annabel asked.

"If you're lucky," her grandmother said acerbically.

Annabel shot a frantic look at Sebastian. He was already staring at her, with an expression that clearly said, *You didn't check?*

She tried to answer with her own widened eyes and hand signals, but she had a feeling she wasn't making herself clear, and finally Sebastian just said, "What are you *saying*?"

"I don't know," she moaned.

"You two are worthless," Lady Vickers grumbled. She marched forward and then crouched down. "Newbury!" she barked. "Wake up."

Annabel chewed on her lip and glanced nervously at the door. They had long since stopped trying to be quiet.

"Wake up!"

Lord Newbury started to make a moaning, mumbling sort of sound.

"Robert," Lady Vickers snapped, "wake up." She slapped him across the face. Hard.

Annabel looked up at Sebastian. He seemed as stunned as she was, and just as happy to let her grandmother take the lead.

Lord Newbury's eyes opened again, fluttering like a sick cross between butterflies and jellyfish. He choked and gasped, trying to prop himself up on his elbows. He looked at Lady Vickers, his eyes making a few last incredulous blinks before he said, "Margaret?"

She slapped him again. "Idiot!"

He fell back down. "What the hell?"

"She is my granddaughter, Robert," Lady Vickers hissed. "My granddaughter! How dare you!"

Every now and then, Annabel thought, her grandmother's love for her shone through. Usually in the most peculiar ways.

"She was supposed to marry me," Lord Newbury sputtered.

"And now she's not. That doesn't give you license to *attack* her."

Annabel felt Sebastian's hand slip into hers, warm and comforting. She gave it a squeeze.

"She tried to kill me," Newbury said.

"I did not!" Annabel lurched forward, but Sebastian tightened his grip on her hand, holding her back.

"Let your grandmother take care of this," he murmured.

But Annabel could not let the insult pass. "I was defending myself," she said hotly.

"With a poker?" Newbury countered.

Annabel turned to her grandmother in disbelief. "How else would you have me defend myself?"

"Really, Robert," Lady Vickers said, dripping with sarcasm.

He finally managed to heave himself into a sitting position, grunting and groaning all the while. "For God's sake," he snapped. "Will someone come and help me?"

No one did.

"I'm not strong enough," Lady Vickers said with a shrug.

"What's *he* doing here?" Lord Newbury said, jerking his head toward Sebastian.

Sebastian crossed his arms and glowered. "I don't think you are in any position to be asking questions."

"Clearly I must take charge," Lady Vickers announced, as if she had been doing anything but. "Newbury," she barked, "you are to go back to your room and depart first thing in the morning."

"I will not," he said in a huff.

"Worried everyone will think you slunk away with your tail between your legs, eh?" she said shrewdly. "Well, consider the alternative. If you're still here when I wake up, I'll tell everyone you spent the night with *me*."

Lord Newbury blanched.

"She generally sleeps late," Annabel said helpfully. Her spirits were starting to return, and after all that Lord Newbury had done to her, she could not resist a little poke. Beside her she heard Sebastian smother a laugh, so she added, "But I don't."

"Furthermore," Lady Vickers continued, giving Annabel a glare for having dared to interrupt, "you will put a halt to this ridiculous quest for a bride. My granddaughter is marrying your nephew and you're going to let him inherit."

"Oh no—" Lord Newbury started to rage.

"Silence," Lady Vickers snapped. "Robert, you're older than I am. It's unseemly."

"You were going to let me marry her," he pointed out.

"That's because I thought you would *die*."

He looked a bit taken aback at that.

"Let it go gracefully," she said. "For the love of God, look at you. If you take a wife, you'll probably injure the poor thing in the process. Or die on top of her. And you two—" She whipped around to face Sebastian and Annabel, who were both trying not to laugh. "This isn't funny."

"Well, actually," Sebastian murmured, "it is a bit."

Lady Vickers shook her head, looking as if she'd dearly like to be rid of all of them. "Get out of here," she said to Lord Newbury.

He did, making all sorts of angry sounds as he went. But they all knew that he would be gone by morning. He would probably resume his search for a bride; he wasn't so cowed by Lady Vickers as *that*. But any threat he might pose to Sebastian and Annabel's marriage was gone.

"And *you*," Lady Vickers said dramatically. She was facing both Annabel and Sebastian, and it was difficult to tell who she meant. "*You*."

"Me?" Annabel asked.

"Both of you." She let out another of those dramatic sighs, then turned to Sebastian. "You are going to marry her, aren't you?"

"I will," he said solemnly.

"Good," she grunted. "I don't know that I could manage another disaster." She patted her chest. "My heart, you know."

Annabel rather suspected that her grandmother's heart would outbeat her own.

"I'm going to bed," Lady Vickers announced, "and I don't want to be disturbed."

"Of course not," Sebastian murmured, and Annabel, sensing that some sort of filial comment was required, added, "May I get you anything?"

"Silence. You may get me silence." Lady Vickers looked over at Sebastian again, this time with narrowed eyes. "You do understand my meaning, don't you?"

He nodded, smiling.

"I'm going to my room," Lady Vickers announced. "The two of you may do whatever you wish. But *don't* wake me up."

And with that, she left, shutting the connecting door behind her.

Annabel stared at the door, then turned to Sebastian, feeling quite dazed. "I think my grandmother may have just given me permission to ruin myself."

"I'll do all the ruining tonight," he said with a grin. "If you don't mind."

Annabel looked back at the door, then back at him, her mouth hanging open. "I think she might be mad," she finally concluded.

"*Au contraire*," he said, coming up behind her. "She has clearly proven herself the sanest among us." He leaned down and kissed her on the back of her neck. "I do believe we are alone."

Annabel turned around, twisting in his arms. "I don't feel alone," she said, motioning with her head over at the door to her grandmother's room.

He wrapped his arms around her and moved his lips to the hollow above her collarbone. For a moment Annabel thought he was dismissing her concerns and trying to be intimate, but then she realized he was laughing. Or at the very least, trying not to. "What?" she demanded.

"I keep picturing her listening at the door," he answered, his words muffled.

"That's funny?"

"It is." He sounded like he wasn't sure why, though.

"She had an affair with your uncle," Annabel said.

Sebastian went utterly still. "If you're trying to completely kill my ardor, there is no image more guaranteed to do it."

"I knew my uncles Thomas and Arthur were not my grandfather's, but Percy . . ." Annabel shook her head, still not quite able to believe the events of the evening. "I had no idea." She started to sigh into him, letting her back mold against his front, but then she straightened like a bolt.

"What is it?"

"My mother. I have no idea . . ."

"She was a Vickers," Seb said with quiet firmness. "You have your grandfather's eyes."

"I do?"

"Not the color, but the shape." He turned her around, putting his hands on her shoulders and gently rotating her until they were facing. "Right here," he said softly, touching his finger against the outer corner of her eye. "The same curve."

He tilted his head to the side, regarding her face with tender concentration. "The cheekbones, too," he murmured.

"I do look a great deal like my mother," she said, unable to take her eyes off him.

"You're a Vickers," he concluded with a benign smile.

She tried to suppress a smile of her own. "For what that's worth."

"Quite a lot, I think," he said, leaning down to kiss the corner of her mouth. "Do you think she's asleep yet?"

She shook her head.

He kissed the other side of her mouth. "What about now?"

She shook her head again.

He pulled back, and she could only laugh as he silently counted from one to ten, mouthing each number while his eyes flicked up toward the ceiling.

She watched him with amusement, laughter bubbling up inside of her but not quite coming out. When he was done, he looked back down at her, his eyes aglow like that of a young boy waiting for Christmas. "What about now?"

Her lips parted, and she meant to scold, to tell him to be patient, but it just wasn't in her. She was so in love with him, and she was going to marry him, and so many things had happened that day to make her realize that life was to be lived and people were to be cherished, and if she had a chance at happiness, she was going to grab it with both hands and never let go.

"Yes," she said, reaching up to entwine her arms around his neck. "I think she's asleep now."

Chapter Twenty-six

*I*f he were writing the story, Sebastian thought, as he swept Annabel into his arms, this would be the end of the chapter. No, the chapter would have ended at least three pages earlier, with no hint of intimacy or seduction and certainly nothing about the mind-shattering lust that surged through him the moment Annabel put her hands at the back of his neck and tilted her face up toward his.

One wasn't allowed to put such things to paper, after all.

But he wasn't writing the story, he was living it, and as he lifted her into his arms and carried her to the bed, he decided this was a very good thing, indeed.

"I love you," he whispered, laying her down. Her hair was loose, a dark wavy mass of delight. He wanted to trace every curl, to let each one wrap itself around his fingers. He wanted to feel them against his skin, tickling his shoulders, sweeping across his chest. He wanted to feel all of her, against all of him, and he wanted that every day for the rest of his life.

He settled down on the bed, a little bit next to her, a little bit on top, forcing himself to take a moment just to savor, and enjoy, and give thanks. She was looking up at him with all the love in the world in her eyes, and it humbled him, left him without words, without anything but this amazing sense of reverence and responsibility.

He belonged with someone now. He belonged *to* someone. His actions . . . they were no longer his alone. What he did, what he said . . . they meant something to someone else now. If he hurt her, if he disappointed her . . .

"You look so serious," she whispered, lifting her hand to touch his cheek. Her hand was cold, and he turned into it, kissing the palm.

"I always have cold hands," she said.

He felt himself smile. "You say it like it's a deep, dark secret."

"My feet get cold, too."

He dropped one soft, serious kiss on her nose. "I vow to spend the rest of my life keeping your hands and feet warm."

She smiled, that big, gorgeous, magnificent smile of hers, the kind that so often turned into her big, gorgeous, magnificent laugh. "I vow to . . ."

"To love me even if I lose my hair?" he suggested.

"Done."

"To play darts with me even though I will always win?"

"I'm not so sure about that . . ."

"To . . ." He paused for a moment. "That's all, actually."

"Really? Nothing about eternal devotion?"

"Included in the one about my hair."

"Lifelong friendship?"

"Right there with the darts."

She laughed. "You are an easy man to love, Sebastian Grey."

He gave her a modest smile. "I try my best."

"I have a secret, though."

"Really?" He licked his lips. "I love secrets."

"Bend down," she instructed.

He did.

"Closer." And then: "Closer."

He brought his ear very close to her lips. "I obey you in all ways."

"I'm *very* good at darts."

He started to laugh. Quietly—a big, shaking thing that moved from his belly to his toes and back. Then he brought his mouth even closer to her ear. Close enough to touch, to let the heat of his breath wash over her. And he whispered, "I'm better."

She reached up and took his head between her hands, shifting it so that *her* mouth was at *his* ear.

"You *are* bossy," he said before she could get a word in.

"Winslow Most Likely to Win at Darts," was all she said.

"Ah, but by next month you'll be a Grey."

She sighed, a happy, wonderful sound. He wanted to spend his whole life listening to sounds like those. "Wait!" he said suddenly, edging himself away. He'd almost forgotten. He had come to her room that night with a purpose.

"I want to do it again," he said.

She tilted her head to the side, her eyes showing her confusion.

"When I asked you to marry me," he told her, "I did not do it properly."

She opened her mouth to protest, but he put a finger to her lips. "Shush," he scolded. "I know it goes against your every natural impulse, oldest child that you are, but you are going to be quiet and listen."

She nodded dutifully, her eyes bright and glistening.

"I have to ask you again," he said. "I'm only doing it once, well, several times, but only to one woman, and I've got to get it right."

And then he realized he didn't really know what to say. He was fairly sure he'd rehearsed something in his head, but now, watching her face, watching the way her eyes searched his and her lips moved ever so slightly, even in her silence . . .

All those words were gone.

He was a man of language. He wrote novels, he conversed with effortless ease, and now, when it mattered most, his words were gone.

There weren't words, he realized. There weren't words good enough for what he wanted to tell her. Anything he might say would just be a pale facsimile of what was in his heart. A line drawing instead of a lush canvas with swirls of oils and color. And Annabel—*his* Annabel—was nothing if not a lush swirl of color.

But he was going to try. He had never been in love before, and he didn't plan to ever do it again, and right now, while he had her in the candle-light and in his arms, he was going to do it right.

"I am asking you to marry me," he said, "because I love you. I don't know how it happened so quickly, but I know that it is true. When I look at you . . ."

He had to stop. His voice had grown husky, and then choked, and he had to swallow, to give himself a moment to get past the aching lump of emotion that had formed in his throat. "When I look at you," he whispered, "I just *know*."

And he realized that sometimes the simplest words were all it took. He loved her, and he knew, and that was all there was to it.

"I love you," he said. "I love you." He kissed her softly. "I love you, and I would be honored if you would allow me the privilege of spending the rest of my life making you happy."

She nodded, tears slipping from her eyes. "Only if you will let me do the same," she whispered.

He kissed her again, this time more deeply. "It would be my pleasure."

The time for words was over. He moved to his knees, pulling his shirt from his trousers and sweeping it off with one fluid motion. Her eyes widened at the sight of his bare skin, and he shuddered with desire as he watched her reach slowly out to touch him.

And then when she did, when her hand found

his heartbeat, he groaned, unable to believe that one tiny touch could set him afire.

He wanted her. Dear God, he wanted her like nothing he'd ever known, nothing he'd ever imagined. "I love you," he said, because it was in him, and it had to come out. Again. And again. He said it as he slipped her nightgown from her body, and he said it as he shed the last of his own clothing. He said it when he finally held her against him, completely and utterly, with nothing between them, and he said it when he settled between her legs, preparing to make that final move, to enter her and join them forever.

She was so hot against him, so wet and welcoming, but he held back, forcing himself to stand firm against his raging desire.

"Annabel," he rasped. He was giving her this last chance to say no, that she wasn't ready, or she needed words in a church first. It would kill him, but he would stop. And he hoped to God that she understood all of this, because he didn't think he could manage another word, much less a complete sentence.

He looked down at her face, flush with passion. She was breathing hard, and he could feel every gasp in the rise and fall of her chest. He wanted to take both of her hands and hold them over her head, make her his captive, keep her here for an eternity.

And he wanted to kiss her, tenderly, everywhere.

He wanted to slam into her, showing her in the most primitive way imaginable that she was his, and his alone.

And he wanted to kneel before her, begging her to love him forever.

He wanted everything with her.

He wanted anything with her.

He wanted to hear her say—

"I love you."

She whispered it, the words coming from deep in her throat, far down to the very center of her being, and it was all that it took to set him free.

He pushed forward, moaning as he felt her grasping him, pulling him in. "You're so . . . so . . ." But he couldn't finish the thought. He could only feel, and sense, and allow his body to take over.

He had been made for this. For this moment. With her.

"Oh God," he moaned. "Oh, Annabel."

With each push, she gasped, arching her back, lifting her hips, drawing him closer. He was trying to go slowly, to give her time to adjust to him, but every time she moaned it was like a spark that fired his blood. And when she moved, it only brought them more deeply together.

He took one of her breasts in his hand, nearly losing himself then and there, just with that. She was perfect, overflowing his fingers, soft and round and glorious. "I want to taste you," he gasped, and he brought his mouth to her, flicking his tongue across the tender tip, feeling a moment of pure masculine triumph when she let out a tiny shriek, bucking off the bed.

Which of course only brought her more deeply to him.

He suckled her then, thinking she had to be

the most glorious, the most womanly creature ever made. He wanted to stay with her forever, buried inside, loving her.

Just loving her.

He wanted this to be good for her. No, he wanted it to be spectacular. But it was her first time, and he'd been told that the first time was rarely good for a woman. And he was so damned nervous that he was going to lose all control and take his own pleasure before he could help her reach hers. He couldn't remember the last time he'd been nervous making love to a woman. But then again, what he'd done before . . . that hadn't been making love. He hadn't realized it before now. There was a difference, and the difference was in his arms right now.

"Annabel," he whispered, barely recognizing his own voice. "Is it . . . ? Are you . . . ?" He swallowed, trying to form a coherent thought. "Does it hurt?"

She shook her head. "Only for a moment. Now it's . . ."

He held his breath.

"Strange," she finished. "Wonderful."

"It only gets better," he assured her. And it would. He began to move within her, not those first hesitant motions when he'd tried to set her at ease, but something real. He moved like a man who was coming home.

He slid a hand between them, reaching down to touch her, even as he thrust inside. Her hips nearly rose from the bed when he found her, and he stroked and teased, spurred on by the quickening of her breath. She grabbed his shoulders—

hard, with tight, tense fingers, and when she called out his name, it was an entreaty.

She wanted him.

She was begging for release.

And he swore he would give it to her.

He brought his head to her breast again, nipping and licking. If he could have he would have loved her everywhere, all at once, and maybe she felt like he did, because just when he thought he might not be able to hold off any longer, she bucked and tensed beneath him. Her fingers bit into his skin, and she tightened around him, squeezing, quivering. She was so tight, her muscles so powerful that she nearly pushed him out, but he surged forward, and before he knew it, he had spilled himself within her, reaching his climax at the very moment she started to come down from hers.

"I love you," he said, and he curled against her side. He pulled her against him, fitting like two spoons in a drawer, closed his eyes, and he slept.

Chapter Twenty-seven

The sun rose early this time of year, and when Annabel opened her eyes and checked the clock on the table beside her bed, it was barely half five. The room was still quite dim, so she slipped out of bed, put on a dressing gown, and walked to the window to open the curtains. Her grandmother may have given tacit permission for Sebastian to stay in her room the night before, but Annabel knew that he could not be there when the rest of the house woke up.

Her room faced east, and so she took a moment at the window to enjoy the sunrise. Most of the sky still held the purple tones of night, but along the horizon the sun was painting a brilliant stripe of orange and pink.

And yellow. Right there on the very bottom, yellow was beginning to creep into view.

The slanted light of dawn, Annabel thought. She still hadn't finished that Gorely book, but something about the first line had stayed with her. She liked it. She understood it. She wasn't a particularly visual person, but something about that description had resonated with her.

Behind her she heard Sebastian rustling in the bed, and she turned around. He appeared to be blinking himself awake.

"It's morning," she said, smiling.

He yawned. "Almost."

"Almost," she agreed, and turned back to the window.

She heard him yawn again, then make his way out of bed. He came up behind her, wrapping his arms around her and letting his chin settle on the top of her head. "It's a beautiful sunrise," he murmured.

"It's already changed so much, just in the few moments I've been watching it."

She felt him nod.

"I almost never see the sun rise this time of year," she said, feeling a yawn coming over her. "It's always so early."

"I thought you were an early riser."

"I am. But not usually this early." She turned in his arms, looking up to face him. "Are you? It does seem the sort of thing one should know about one's future husband."

"No," he said softly, "when I see the sun rise, it's because I've been awake too long."

She almost made a joke about staying out too late and attending too many parties, but she was stopped by the look of resignation in his eyes. "Because you can't sleep," she said.

He nodded.

"You slept last night," she said, remembering the slow, even sound of his breath. "You slept quite soundly."

He blinked, and his face took on an expression of surprise. And maybe a little wonder, too. "I did, didn't I?"

Impulsively, she stood on her tiptoes and kissed his cheek. "Perhaps this is a new dawn for you, too."

He looked at her for several moments, as if he wasn't quite sure what to say. "I love you," he finally said, and he kissed her back, softly, and filled with love, on her lips.

"Let's go outside," he said suddenly.

"What?"

He let go of her and went back toward the bed, to the pile of his clothing, lying rumpled on the floor. "Go on," he said. "Get dressed."

Annabel allowed herself a moment to admire his naked back, then managed to snap herself to attention. "Why do you want to go outside?" she asked, but she was already looking for something to wear.

"I can't be found here," he explained, "but I find myself loathe to leave your company. We shall tell everyone we met for an early-morning stroll."

"No one will believe us."

"Of course not, but they won't be able to prove we're lying." He flashed her a grin. His enthusiasm was infectious, and Annabel found herself practically racing to pull on all of her clothing. Before she could even throw on her coat, he grabbed her hand, and they took off running through the house, stifling laughter all the way. A few maids were up and about, transporting jugs of water to all of the guest rooms, but Annabel and Sebastian just scooted on by, tripping along until they reached the front door and the fresh air of morning.

Annabel took a deep breath. The air felt wonderful, crisp and clean, with just enough cool moisture to make her feel dewy and new.

"Shall we go down to the pond?" Sebastian asked. He leaned down and dropped a kiss on her ear. "I have marvelous memories of that pond."

Annabel's cheeks turned hot, even though she rather thought she ought to be beyond blushing by now.

"I'll teach you to skip stones," he said.

"Oh, I don't think you'll manage that. I tried for *years*. My brothers quite gave up on me."

He gave her a shrewd look. "Are you certain they were not, perhaps, employing a bit of sabotage?"

Annabel's mouth fell open.

"If I were your brother," he said, "and I believe we may both give thanks that I am not, I *might* find it amusing to give you false instruction."

"They wouldn't."

Sebastian shrugged. "Having never met them, I cannot say for sure, but having met *you*, I can say that *I* would."

She swatted him on the shoulder.

"Really," he went on, "Winslow Most Likely to Win at Darts, Winslow Most Likely to Outrun a Turkey—"

"I came in only third for that."

"—you're quite annoyingly capable," he finished.

"Annoyingly?"

"A man does like to feel that he is in charge," he murmured.

"Annoyingly?"

He kissed her nose. "Annoyingly adorable."

They had just about reached the shore of the pond, so Annabel yanked her hand free and marched down the small, sandy stretch. "I am finding a rock," she announced, "and if you don't teach me how to skip it by the end of the day, I shall . . ." She stopped. "Well, I don't know what I shall do, but it won't be pretty."

He chuckled and ambled over to her side. "First you must find the right sort of rock."

"I know that," she said promptly.

"It must be flat, not too heavy—"

"I know that, too."

"I am beginning to understand why your brothers did not wish to teach you."

She gave him a dirty look.

He only laughed. "Here," he said, reaching down to pick up a small stone. "This one is good. You need to hold it like this." He demonstrated, then put it in her palm, curving her fingers around it. "Your wrist should be bent just so, and . . ."

She looked up. "And what?" His words had trailed off, and he was gazing out over the pond.

"Nothing," he said with a little shake of his head. "Just the way the sun is hitting the water."

Annabel turned to the pond, and then turned back to him. The reflection of the sun on the water was beautiful, but she found she preferred watching him. He was looking at the pond so intently, so thoughtfully, as if he were memorizing every last ripple of light. She knew he had a reputation for careless charm. Everyone said he was so funny, so droll, but now, when he was so pensive . . .

She wondered if anyone—even his family— really knew him.

"The slanted light of dawn," she said.

He turned sharply. "What?"

"Well, I suppose it's a past dawn now, but not by much."

"Why did you say that?"

She blinked. He was behaving oddly. "I don't know." She looked back over the water. The sunlight was still rather flat, almost peachy, and the pond seemed almost magical, nestled in with the trees and gentle hills. "I just liked the image, I suppose. I thought it was a very good description. From *Miss Sainsbury*, you know."

"I know."

She shrugged. "I still haven't finished the book."

"Do you like it?"

She turned back to him. He sounded rather intense. Uncharacteristically so. "I suppose," she said, somewhat noncommittally.

He stared at her for a moment more. His eyes widened impatiently. "Either you like it or you don't."

"That's not true. There are some things I like quite a bit about it, and others I'm not so fond of. I really think I need to finish it before rendering judgment."

"How far along are you?"

"Why do you care so much?"

"I don't," he protested. But he looked exactly like her brother Frederick had when she had accused him of fancying Jenny Pitt, who lived in their village. Frederick had planted his hands on his hips and declared, "I don't," but *clearly* he did.

"I just like her books a great deal, that's all," he muttered.

"I like Yorkshire Pudding, but I don't take offense if others don't."

He had no response to that, so she just shrugged and turned back to the stone in her hand, trying to imitate the grip he'd shown her earlier.

"What don't you like?" he asked.

She looked up, blinking. She'd thought they were done with that conversation.

"Is it the plot?"

"No," she said, giving him a curious look, "I like the plot. It's a bit improbable, but that's what makes it fun."

"Then what is it?"

"Oh, I don't know." She frowned and sighed, trying to figure out the answer to his question. "The prose gets a bit unwieldy at times."

"Unwieldy," he stated.

"There are quite a lot of adjectives. But," she added brightly, "she does have a way with description. I do like the slanted light of dawn, after all."

"It would be difficult to write description without adjectives."

"True," she acceded.

"I could try, but—"

He shut his mouth. Very suddenly.

"What did you just say?" she demanded.

"Nothing."

But he had definitely not said nothing. "You said . . ." And then she gasped. "It's *you!*"

He didn't say anything, just crossed his arms and gave her an *I-don't-know-what-you're-talking-about* expression.

Her mind raced. How could she not have seen it? There had been so many clues. After his uncle had blackened his eye and he'd said that he never knew when he might need to describe something. The autographed books. And at the opera! He had said something about a hero not swooning on the first page. Not the first scene, the first page!

"You're Sarah Gorely!" she exclaimed. "You *are*. You even have the same initials."

"Really, Annabel, I—"

"Don't lie to me. I'm going to be your wife. You cannot lie to me. I know it's you. I even thought the book sounded a bit like you when I was reading it." She gave him a sheepish smile. "It was actually what I liked best about it."

"Really?" His eyes lit up and she wondered if he realized that he'd just admitted it.

She nodded. "How on earth have you kept it a secret for so long? I assume no one knows. Surely Lady Olivia would not have called the books dreadful if she knew—" She winced. "Oh, that's awful."

"Which is why she doesn't know," he told her. "She would feel dreadful."

"You are a very kindhearted man." She gasped. "And Sir Harry?"

"Also does not know," he confirmed.

"But he's translating you!" She paused. "Your books, I mean."

Sebastian just gave a shrug.

"Oh, he would feel *terrible*," Annabel said, trying to imagine it. She did not know Sir Harry very well, but still . . . they were cousins! "And they've never suspected?" she asked.

"I don't think so."

"Oh my." She sat down on the big flat rock. "Oh my."

He sat down beside her. "There are some," he said carefully, "who might think it a rather silly, undignified pursuit."

"Not me," she said immediately, shaking her head. Good gracious, Sebastian was Sarah Gorely. She was marrying Sarah Gorely.

She paused. Perhaps she ought not to think about it in quite those terms.

"I think it's marvelous," she declared, tipping her face up toward his.

"You do?" His eyes searched hers, and in that moment she realized just how very important her good opinion was to him. He was so confident, so comfortable and easy in his own skin. It was one of the first things she had noticed about him, before she'd even learned his name.

"I do," she said, wondering if she was awful for loving the vulnerable look in his eyes. She couldn't help it. She loved how much she meant to him. "It will be our secret." And then she laughed.

"What is it?"

"When I first met you, before I even knew your name, I remember thinking that you smiled as if you had a secret joke, and that I wanted to be a part of it."

"Always," he said solemnly.

"Perhaps I can be of help," she suggested, giving a sly smile. *"Miss Winslow and the Mysterious Author."*

It took him a moment to catch on, but then his eyes lit with the fun of it. "I can't use mysterious again. I've already had a mysterious colonel."

She let out a snort of mock irritation. "This writing business is so difficult."

"Miss Winslow and the Splendid Lover?" he suggested.

"Too lurid," she replied, batting him on the shoulder. "You'll lose your audience and then where will we be? We have future gray-eyed babies to feed, you know."

His own eyes flared with emotion, but still, he played along. *"Miss Winslow and the Precarious Heir."*

"Oh, I don't know. It's true you probably won't inherit, although thankfully I won't have anything to do with it, but still, 'precarious' sounds so . . ."

"Precarious?"

"Yes," she agreed, even though his sarcasm had not been disguised in the least. "What about Mrs. Grey?" she asked softly.

"Mrs. Grey," he repeated.

"I like the sound of it."

He nodded. *"Mrs. Grey and the Dutiful Husband."*

"*Mrs. Grey and the Beloved Husband.* No, no, *Mrs. Grey and Her Beloved Husband,*" she said, with an emphasis on "her."

"Will it be a story in progress?" he asked.

"Oh, I think so." She reached up to give him a kiss, then stayed there, their noses touching. "So long as you don't mind a new happy ending every day."

"It does sound like an awful lot of work . . ." he murmured.

She pulled back just far enough to give him a dry look. "But worth it."

He chuckled. "That didn't sound like a question."

"Plain speaking, Mr. Grey. Plain speaking."

"It's what I love about you, soon-to-be Mrs. Grey."

"Don't you think it should be Mrs. soon-to-be Grey?"

"Now you're *editing* me?"

"Sug*gest*ing."

"As it happens," he said, looking down his nose at her, "I was right. The 'soon-to-be' has to be placed before the 'Mrs.,' else it sounds like you were Mrs. Something Else."

She considered that.

He gave her an arch look.

"Very well," she gave in, "but about everything else, I am right."

"Everything?"

She smiled seductively. "I chose *you.*"

"*Mr. Grey and His Beloved Bride.*" He kissed her once, and then again. "I think I like it."

"I *love* it."

And she did.

Epilogue

Four years later

"The key to a successful marriage," Sebastian Grey pontificated from behind his desk, "is to marry a splendid wife."

As this was announced for no apparent reason, after an hour of companionable silence, Annabel Grey would normally have taken the statement with several grains of salt. Sebastian was not above beginning conversations with extravagant compliments when he wished to gain her approval, or at the very least agreement, about matters entirely unrelated to the aforementioned praise.

There were, however, ten things about his pronouncement that could not help but warm her heart.

One: Seb was looking particularly handsome when he said it, all warm-eyed and rumple-haired, and **Two**: the wife in question was *her*, which pertained to **Three**: she'd performed all sorts of lovely wifely duties that morning, which, given their history would probably lead to **Four**: another gray-eyed baby in nine months, to add to the three already pitter-pattering in the nursery.

Of minor but still happy significance was **Five**: none of the three Grey babies looked a thing like Lord Newbury, who must have been scared witless after his collapse in Annabel's bedchamber four years earlier, because he'd gone on a slimming regimen, married a widow of proven childbearing prowess, but **Six**: had not managed to sire another child, boy or girl.

Which meant that **Seven**: Sebastian was still the heir presumptive to the earldom, not that it mattered overmuch because **Eight**: he was selling scads of books, especially since the release of *Miss Spencer and the Wild Scotsman*, which **Nine**: the King himself had declared "delicious." This, combined with the fact that Sarah Gorely had become the most popular author in Russia, meant that **Ten**: all of Annabel's brothers and sisters were well settled in life, which in turn led to **Eleven**: Annabel never had to worry that her choice to pursue her own happiness had cost them theirs.

Eleven.

Annabel smiled. Some things were so wonderful they ran right past ten.

"What are you grinning about?"

She looked up at Sebastian, who was still seated at his desk, pretending he was working. "Oh, many things," she said blithely.

"How intriguing. I am also thinking of many things."

"Are you?"

"Ten, to be precise."

"I was thinking of eleven."

"You are so competitive."

"Grey Most Likely to Outrun a Turkey," she reminded him. "To say nothing of the skipping of stones."

She'd got up to six. It had been an *excellent* moment. Especially since no one had ever actually *seen* Sebastian do seven.

He raised a brow at that, gave his best imitation of condescension, and said, "Quality over quantity, that's what I always say. *I* was thinking of ten things I love about you."

Her breath caught.

"One," he announced, "your smile. Which is rivaled only by **Two**: your laugh. Which is in turn fueled by **Three**: the utter genuineness and generosity of your heart."

Annabel swallowed. Tears were forming in her eyes, and she knew they'd soon be pouring down her cheeks.

"Four," he continued, "you are excellent at keeping a secret, and **Five**: you have finally learned not to offer suggestions pertaining to my writing career."

"*No*," she protested, right through her tears, "*Miss Forsby and the Footman* would have been *marvelous*."

"It would have brought me down in a flaming pit of ruin."

"But—"

"You'll notice there is nothing on this list about how you never interrupt me." He cleared his throat. "**Six**: you have provided me with three remarkably brilliant children and **Seven**: you are an utterly marvelous mother. I, on the other hand, am utterly selfish, which is why **Eight** is all about the fact that you love me so splendidly well." He leaned forward and waggled his brows. "In every possible manner."

"Sebastian!"

"Actually, I think I'll make that **Nine**." He gave her a particularly warm smile. "I do think it's deserving of its own number."

She blushed. She couldn't believe it, that he could still make her blush after four years of marriage.

"**Ten**," he said softly, coming to his feet and walking toward her. He dropped to his knees and took her hands, kissing each in turn. "You are, quite simply, you. You are the most amazing, intelligent, kindhearted, ridiculously competitive woman I have ever met. And you can outrun a turkey."

She stared at him, not caring that she was crying, or that her eyes must be horribly bloodshot, or that—dear heavens—she badly needed a handkerchief. She loved him. That was all that could possibly matter. "I think that was more than ten," she whispered.

"Was it?" He kissed away her tears. "I've stopped counting."

Meet the Bridgertons . . .

BRIDGERTON
THE DUKE & I

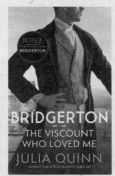

BRIDGERTON
THE VISCOUNT
WHO LOVED ME
JULIA QUINN

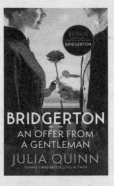

BRIDGERTON
AN OFFER FROM
A GENTLEMAN
JULIA QUINN

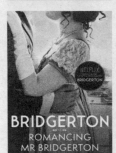

BRIDGERTON
ROMANCING
MR BRIDGERTON
JULIA QUINN

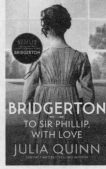

BRIDGERTON
TO SIR PHILLIP,
WITH LOVE
JULIA QUINN

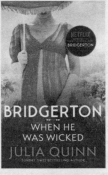

BRIDGERTON
WHEN HE
WAS WICKED
JULIA QUINN

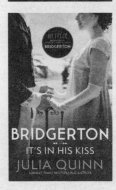

BRIDGERTON
IT'S IN HIS KISS
JULIA QUINN

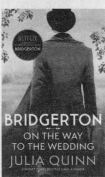

BRIDGERTON
ON THE WAY
TO THE WEDDING
JULIA QUINN

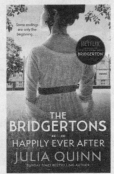

THE BRIDGERTONS
HAPPILY EVER AFTER
JULIA QUINN

Available from

PIATKUS